D1016195

Praise for Denise Mina

THE LONG DROP

One of the Best Crime Novels of the Year
*Washington Post, Boston Globe, The Guardian,
Financial Times, The Scotsman, The Telegraph*

"*The Long Drop* takes readers on a suspenseful tour into the past, through psyches and situations far grimmer than even those sooty Glasgow streets." —Maureen Corrigan, *Washington Post*

"Superb." —Mark Lawson, *The Guardian*

"A terrific exploration of crime and oppression." —*Kirkus Reviews*

"A lovingly detailed fictional retelling of the murders of a mother, a daughter, and the mother's sister that scandalized 1950s Glasgow, Mina's slim novel encompasses a harrowing picture of the social issues of the time—many of which still prevail—packing a truly powerful punch." —Daneet Steffens, *Boston Globe*

"Riveting…Mina is one of the finest practitioners of the modern criminous art—and is also a social commentator of perception and humanity." —Barry Forshaw, *Financial Times*

"Mina has always been a close observer of the brutality drunkards can inflict on their wives and children…this one feels painfully real." —Marilyn Stasio, *New York Times Book Review*

ALSO BY DENISE MINA

ALEX MORROW NOVELS

STILL MIDNIGHT

THE END OF THE WASP SEASON

GODS AND BEASTS

THE RED ROAD

BLOOD, SALT, WATER

PADDY MEEHAN NOVELS

FIELD OF BLOOD

THE DEAD HOUR

SLIP OF THE KNIFE

GARNETHILL TRILOGY

GARNETHILL

EXILE

RESOLUTION

OTHER NOVELS

DECEPTION

THE
LONG
DROP

A NOVEL

denise mina

BACK BAY BOOKS
LITTLE, BROWN AND COMPANY
New York Boston London

The characters and events in this book are fictitious. Any similarity to real persons, living or dead, is coincidental and not intended by the author.

Copyright © 2017 by Denise Mina

Hachette Book Group supports the right to free expression and the value of copyright. The purpose of copyright is to encourage writers and artists to produce the creative works that enrich our culture.

The scanning, uploading, and distribution of this book without permission is a theft of the author's intellectual property. If you would like permission to use material from the book (other than for review purposes), please contact permissions@hbgusa.com. Thank you for your support of the author's rights.

Back Bay Books / Little, Brown and Company
Hachette Book Group
1290 Avenue of the Americas, New York, NY 10104
littlebrown.com

Originally published in hardcover by Little, Brown and Company, May 2017
First Back Bay paperback edition, July 2018

Back Bay Books is an imprint of Little, Brown and Company, a division of Hachette Book Group, Inc. The Back Bay Books name and logo are trademarks of Hachette Book Group, Inc.

The publisher is not responsible for websites (or their content) that are not owned by the publisher.

The Hachette Speakers Bureau provides a wide range of authors for speaking events. To find out more, go to hachettespeakersbureau.com or call (866) 376-6591.

ISBN 978-0-316-38057-7 (hc) / 978-0-316-55244-8 (large print) /
978-0-316-38059-1 (pb)
LCCN 2016954169

10 9 8 7 6 5 4 3 2 1

LSC-C

Printed in the United States of America

THE
LONG
DROP

After the two Harrys killed him
a rumour started among the children
that Peter Manuel
could see in the dark.

I

Monday 2 December 1957

HE KNOWS TOO MUCH to be an honest man but says he wants to help. He says he can get the gun for them. William Watt is keen to meet him. Laurence Dowdall has already met Peter Manuel several times. He never wants to see him again.

Dowdall parks his beige Bentley on a dark city street and gets out. Watt is waiting on the pavement, next to his maroon Vauxhall Velox.

It is early evening in early December. Glasgow is wet and dark but still warm, the bitterness of winter has yet to bite.

Above the roofs every chimney belches black smoke. Rain drags smut down over the city like a mourning mantilla. Soon a Clean Air Act will outlaw coal-burning in town. Five square miles of the Victorian city will be ruled unfit for human habitation and torn down, redeveloped in concrete and glass and steel. The population will be moved to the periphery, thinned to a quarter of its current density. One hundred and thirty thousand homes will be demolished in the biggest urban redevelopment project in post-war Europe. Later, the black, bedraggled survivors of this architectural cull will be sandblasted, their hard skin scoured off to reveal glittering yellow and burgundy sandstone. The exposed stone is porous though, it sucks in rain and splits when it freezes in the winter.

But this story is before all of that. This story happens in the old boom city, crowded, wild west, chaotic. This city is commerce unfettered. It centres around the docks and the river, and it is all function. It dresses like the Irishwomen: head to toe in black, hair covered, eyes down.

In the street Dowdall falls into step with Watt, walking towards a doorway below by a red neon sign: *Whitehall's Restaurant/Lounge.*

Watt is tall and stout and bald, dressed in bourgeois yellow tweeds and a heavy wool overcoat. Dowdall is slim, dark, mustachioed. He's Watt's lawyer. He wears a sharp dark suit under an exquisitely cut camel hair.

They go through the door to Whitehall's and take a steep set of narrow stairs up. Watt can see the stitching on the back of Dowdall's shoes. Handmade, Watt thinks. Italian.

Watt wants a Bentley too, and Italian shoes, but he needs to put this Burnside Affair behind him first. This is why they are going to meet a man who was released from prison three days ago. They are going to find the gun and solve the crime.

Peter Manuel wrote to Dowdall saying he had information about the Burnside murders. A lot of prisoners did, but Manuel's letters were different. Most came from chancers who wanted money, some were from creeps who wanted details. Manuel didn't ask for anything except the chance to meet William Watt face-to-face. Odd.

Dowdall arranged this meeting before Manuel was released but vacillates. Sometimes he wants to cancel, sometimes he insists they should go. In negative mood he says it's pointless. Manuel is a professional criminal, a famous liar, you can't trust a word he says. Then he thinks they can outflank him, use Manuel to solve the mystery, he might give away a useful detail or two. Watt senses something other than a concern about the outcome: it feels as if Dowdall is afraid of Peter Manuel. Dowdall is

Glasgow's foremost criminal lawyer. He has seen a lot of life, met a lot of characters. It seems strange to Watt that Dowdall should be scared, but then, Watt hasn't met Manuel yet. He doesn't know what there is to be afraid of.

Dowdall stops three steps from the top, holding onto the handrails and leans back, whispering over his shoulder.

'If he asks you for money, William, refuse, point-blank.'

Watt grunts.

Dowdall already warned him about this back at the office. Any evidence they get from Manuel will be useless if money changes hands. But Watt is desperate and he's a businessman. He knows you don't get something for nothing.

'And don't offer him any information about yourself.'

Watt grunts again. He is irritated by these warnings. Dowdall is treating him like a child, as if he knows nothing about these people, this world. Watt knows more than Dowdall gives him credit for.

Dowdall walks up the remaining stairs, into a dim lobby that smells of pork fat and stale cigarette smoke. The walls are panelled with yellow burled walnut. The cloakroom window is a dark slit, it's Monday, hardly worth opening. Against the opposite wall a chaise longue is flanked by two onyx ashtrays on spindly brass legs. They are empty but still radiate the pungent odour of burnt offerings. Dowdall walks over to the facing wall hung with a velvet curtain. He uses his forearm to sweep it out of their path.

The restaurant is crammed with tables set with linen and cutlery but short of customers. Behind the bar a tinny wireless plays the Light Programme. It's the *Semprini Serenade*: overwrought symphonic reproductions of popular tunes.

Whitehall's Restaurant isn't a fancy joint. It's a second-best-suit, affair-with-your-secretary type of place. Near the door, a big blonde and a small man are hunched over grey pork chops. At another table a trio of tipsy dishevelled salesmen chat quietly.

The only customer who didn't look up when they came in is reading a newspaper in the lounge bar. He's the man who knows too much. He's alone.

Freshly shaven, Peter Manuel looks smart in his sports jacket, shirt and tie. His thick hair is combed back from his face. William Watt is surprised by how respectable he looks. He knows all about Manuel's record from Dowdall, the rapes, the prison terms, the incessant housebreaking. He understands now that meeting in Whitehall's was Manuel's idea, not Dowdall's. To Dowdall the place is downmarket. To Manuel a restaurant/lounge is aspirational. He aspires to be in places that are better than he is. Watt likes that about him.

On the table in front of Manuel sit an empty whisky glass and a half-pint with a finger of beer left in it. A half and half: the drouthy gent's refreshment. Watt is pleased when he sees that because he really, really wants a good drink, he wants it quickly and, in truth, he wants it all the time.

The maître d'-boy-of-all-works is polishing forks by the dumb waiter, his back to them. A tendril of fresh air has followed them in from the street and stirs the stagnant cigarette smoke hanging in the room, alerting him to their presence. He turns, nods an acknowledgement, abandons the cutlery and begins a tortuous, snaking journey towards them through tightly packed tables.

The blonde with the pork chops recognises Laurence Dowdall. Dowdall is a celebrity, often in the papers. She whispers to her companion and he turns for a gawp. The man mutters and they both smile down at their dinners. Dowdall's catchphrase.

For a decade, any Glaswegian caught red-handed has conjured Dowdall's name.

'Get me Dowdall!' shouts every drunk caught pissing up a close.

'Get me Dowdall!' says the apprentice boy, chinned for an unscheduled fag break.

'Get me Dowdall!' jokes the hostess who is running short of sherry.

Dowdall is a punchline, a softener in an awkward situation, but he's also a legal genius; he can get you out of anything. It might irritate him but the catchphrase is good for business and Laurence Dowdall is all business.

Watt knows that having Dowdall for a lawyer makes him look guilty but Dowdall Houdini'd him out of prison. He wouldn't have anyone else now.

The maître d' makes it over to them and Dowdall explains that they are here to see that gentleman. He points and Peter Manuel looks back at them.

Led by the maître d', the two men tack their way across the room. Manuel does not stand up to meet them but sits belligerently as they dock at his table. Dowdall effects the introductions. No one attempts to shake hands.

Watt and Manuel are in no way similar. They look as if they are in different stories altogether.

If this were a movie William Watt would be in an Ealing comedy. Watt is an inherently funny man. Six foot two in an age of small men, he is ungainly, rotund, especially in the middle where he wears his suit trousers belted. He is balding too, his thin hair smeared back on his big baby head. He has preposterously large hands. He is fifty and looks like an actor playing a bumbling authority figure in a gentle comedy of manners. In some ways he is. He was a police reservist during the war and his duties were essentially walking around while being taller than other people. It meant a lot to him, that time. Mr Watt likes power and being near powerful people. He likes respectability and being near respectable people. But most of all he likes being near powerful, respectable people.

Peter Manuel is in a very different film. His would be European, black and white, directed by Clouzot or Melville, printed on poor stock and shown in art-house cinemas to an adults-only audience. There wouldn't be violence or gore in the movie, this is not the era of squibs or guts-on-screen, but the implication of threat is always there. Short and solidly built, at five foot six Manuel has the rough-hewn good looks of Robert Mitchum. He is thirty. His eyebrows are heavy, his lips quite broad and sensual. He wears his black hair Brylcreemed back from his square face, combed into thick glistening strips like oily liquorice. He glowers through his heavy brows. His sudden smile is rare and always welcome, a reassuring signal, perhaps, that nothing bad will happen after all. The smartness of his dress is often remarked upon and he is confident of the impression he makes on women. He always insists they be allowed to serve on the juries at his trials.

They pull back chairs to sit down. To Watt's dismay, Dowdall takes his overcoat off. He means to stay, but Watt was clear back in Dowdall's office, he said he wants to talk to Manuel alone. He thought it was agreed but realises now that the answer Dowdall gave him wasn't definitive. Dowdall smiled. You may have been in prison, Bill, but you don't know these people, not really. Dowdall became almost tearful. Some of these people, he said, they're not even trying to be bad. They just are bad, everything they do is bad, and if it doesn't start bad with them, they'll turn it bad. Watt is a man of the world and said so but Dowdall smiled gently and told him, Bill, some of these men don't seem to be of this world. These people are stained, their very souls are tainted. Then he patted Watt's hand as if he regretted having to tell a child these dreadful things.

Dowdall is blatantly Roman Catholic. Most Catholics have the manners to disguise their leanings when they are in mixed company but Dowdall doesn't. He doesn't have a crucifix up in his office or ostentatiously name-drop priests or monsignors the way some aggressive Catholics do, but his everyday conversation makes oblique references to souls and stains and good and bad. Watt finds it rather outré. Unusually for the time, Watt is not a religious bigot but he doesn't know why a man as sophisticated as Dowdall would keep bringing up something so controversial all the time.

Standing by Manuel's table, Dowdall turns his expensive camel-hair overcoat inside out, showing off the shimmering orange silk lining. He folds it in half and lays it over the back of the fourth chair. He is trembling a little. It is unlike him. Watt doesn't need Dowdall to stay and look after him. Watt isn't the one who is trembling.

The maître d' takes their order. Dowdall orders a Johnnie Walker and soda. Watt orders a half and half for himself and another for Mr Manuel. He does it graciously. Manuel doesn't thank him but nods lightly, as if to say yes, that's something he will allow. His insouciance borders on insolence. This impresses Watt who has more money than almost everyone else he meets and knows how corrosive gratitude is to a person's dignity. He's impressed that Manuel has countered the gift with a gesture both regal and slightly belittling. He wonders how much money it will take to get the gun.

As Watt is thinking this he looks up. He finds Peter Manuel watching him, a cigarette dangling from his lips, eyes narrowed against the thin plume of smoke snaking across his face. Manuel draws on his cigarette and a smile creeps into his eyes. Watt wonders if they've met before but doesn't think so. He doesn't recognise the face but feels that he already knows him, somehow.

The salesmen are tittering, they've realised that the great Laurence Dowdall is here. But then they spot William Watt, recognise him from the papers too. Their grins fall sour. They whisper, serious things, sad things, nasty rumours about Watt and his daughter.

Watt needs a drink. He looks for the maître d' and spots him, behind the bar, looking away.

Dowdall and Manuel light cigarettes, one a Turkish hand-rolled from a wooden box, one a stubby Piccadilly from a crumpled paper packet. Dowdall smokes quickly, nervously. They avoid eye contact.

Watt sees this and wonders, fleetingly, if he is the mark, if they are working him together. But no. Dowdall would never jeopardise his reputation. Watt is Dowdall's latest calling card, the Burnside Affair is high-profile and Dowdall has come out of it well.

Watt draws a breath to speak but Dowdall stills him with a shake of his head. The maître d' is near enough to hear them talk and the restaurant is quiet, despite the hissing wireless.

So they all three sit and wait in silence for their drinks. The symphony soars and the couple whisper to each other. The salesmen laugh and snort at what seems to be an off-colour joke. The waiter takes his time, laying the tray with napkins and ashtrays.

Watt looks up and finds Manuel looking at him.

'D'ye take a smoke, Mr Watt?' His accent is Lanarkshire, his face unmoving. The question feels like a test.

Watt thinks before answering. He actually smokes a lot but doesn't want to say so. 'On occasion.'

Dowdall's eyes flick in his direction, pleased that Watt is lying.

Manuel pushes his scrawny packet of smokes across the table with his fingertips and Watt looks at it. They are cheap but not the cheapest and quite an unusual brand. He doesn't say yes or no but takes a cigarette from the packet of Piccadilly. Manuel offers him a light from a matchbook. It is red and yellow, a promotional matchbook from Jackson's Bar.

Jackson's Bar is a gangster pub in the Gorbals. It has a very specific clientele of suited men on the make. It is not for whorish women or clapped-out hard men. Fights happen outside, not in the glass-glinting bar. No one wants the cops in there, with jobs being arranged, deals getting done and connections being made.

Manuel sees Watt read the matchbook. Their eyes meet and they both understand. That part of the city is as small as a midgie's oxter. They probably know a lot of the same people. Watt is sure he can do good business with Manuel, if they could only get rid of Dowdall.

They both look at Dowdall, tapping his cigarette nervously on the edge of the ashtray. Watt sees Manuel's lip curling resentfully, wishing Dowdall away so they can speak to each other, unguarded. He sees that they have a common aim.

The waiter arrives with the tray of drinks. They all watch in silence as he puts them on the table and takes the money from Watt. He has charged Watt for the drinks Manuel had before they arrived. Manuel must have said he would pay. Manuel looks at Watt steadily. It's cheeky but Manuel doesn't seem embarrassed. He is so unembarrassed that Watt is confused. He searches his face for twitches of defiance but has the strange sensation that Manuel isn't feeling anything at all.

As the waiter saunters away, Dowdall concerns himself with his Scotch. Manuel widens his eyes at Watt. Watt frowns. Manuel juts his chin, telling Watt to begin but Watt doesn't know what to begin.

Manuel looks at the salesmen, the couple, the passing maître d' and then eyes Dowdall. He smirks at Watt. Dowdall is a public man. They all recognise him. He has a reputation to lose. Neither Watt nor Manuel have any reputation worth defending.

Watt understands what Manuel means. He nearly smiles but Manuel warns him not to with a little shake of his head, no, don't smile, just begin.

So Watt says loudly: 'MANUEL! If I find out that you had ANYTHING to do with the Burnside Affair, why, I will TEAR YOUR ARMS OFF, sir!'

The room holds its breath.

Manuel shouts back: 'NOBODY. DOES. THAT. TO MANUEL.'

Now no one in the restaurant is speaking. The couple stare at their plates, thrilled. The salesmen have drawn in tight around their table. The maître d' is watching, frightened, because it's down to him to break it up if they start throwing punches. And Dowdall, respectable, well-kent Dowdall, has suddenly got a very itchy arse. He's writhing in his chair but resists the urge to run.

Watt is delighted by how clever they have been, spotting this weakness in Dowdall's resolve. He leans across the table. Watt is massive. His giant hands are twice as big as Manuel's. His huge head, his wide face, his shoulders, they dwarf Manuel. By leaning forward an inch he has colonised the entire table.

'Manuel!' Watt's voice is sharp. 'See here! Before we begin, let me make myself abundantly clear on one issue, right from the off –'

'KNOW YE TALK TOO MUCH, PAL?' Manuel's tone is a prison-promise of a fight coming. He leans slowly in to meet Watt. Watt has to drop back or they'd be pressing their faces together like a couple of pansies.

Manuel exhales a stream of smoke from one side of his mouth and gives a bitter smile. Watt turns his whisky glass around and around on the spot. They smoke at each other.

Dowdall puts his hand on the table, calling an end to the round by tapping a finger on the tabletop. Tap tap tap. He asks Manuel if he has information for Mr Watt?

With an unblinking nod Manuel concedes that he does.

Dowdall asks, will he give Mr Watt the information?

A nod.

Does the information pertain to the murders at Burnside?

'Aye.' Manuel gives a careless shrug. 'Sure,' he says, as if it's nothing, as if it's not the murder of three members of Watt's family and the sex attack of his seventeen-year-old daughter.

Dowdall reaches for his coat, drawing it onto his knee. He's planning to escape the moment the information is imparted and he means to take William Watt with him. He nods for Manuel to begin but Manuel doesn't speak.

Watt raises his eyebrows, interested to see how Manuel will stop this happening.

Manuel has a stubby pencil in his hand. He scribbles something in the margin of his newspaper and pushes it across to Watt.

Newspapermen, it says, as one word.

Watt doesn't understand so Manuel nods at the table of salesmen who are now watching plates of gammon steak and potatoes being delivered by the waiter.

Manuel writes again, *Not here.*

Watt shakes his head. 'Why?'

Manuel sits back, staring at Watt, and slides his hand across the tabletop to the newspaper. His finger rests on the scribble in the margin: *Newspapermen*. He taps it.

It's bullshit, and bad bullshit at that. Those men are not journalists. Anyway, Manuel and Watt have been shouting at each other. Now they can't talk quietly for fear of it being in the newspapers? Dowdall draws a breath, his face sceptical, he's about to say it's nonsense but suddenly Manuel snarls a loud animal growl at Watt.

Dowdall is on his feet. His coat is over his arm, the Bentley key is in his hand. He empties his glass of whisky and soda in one smooth move, stepping away from the table with a little bow.

'Gentlemen,' he says, meaning quite the reverse. He squeezes Watt's shoulder as he passes. A warning: be careful.

The greasy velvet curtain drops behind him. His relief billows back at them in a draught.

They are alone.

Watt means to begin by sounding friendly, hoping the evening will remain collegiate in tone.

'Well, Chief,' he says. 'You handled that scenario very nicely. I must say, I am agreeably surprised to meet you.'

Manuel blows a thick stream of cigarette smoke at the tabletop and narrows his eyes, 'We've got a lot to talk about.'

Watt smiles pleasantly and toasts his new friend. 'We most certainly have.'

Their night together has begun.

2

Wednesday 14 May 1958

IT IS NEARLY SIX months later and Peter Manuel is on trial for eight murders. These include the three Watt women. Seven of the murders are 'in pursuit of theft': if he is found guilty of any one of them he will be hanged. The eighth, the murder of Anne Kneilands back in December 1956, is not in pursuit of theft. It's a lesser charge.

Laurence Dowdall is a prosecution witness. He is in the witness hall, waiting to be called. In the court, through the wall, every single seat is taken. People are lined along the walls.

A mob gathers outside the court every day, sometimes a hundred, sometimes a thousand. For the entire three-week trial they stand in the rain, swapping morsels of information. The city has been terrorised by the frenzy of murders, families have been murdered in their beds, blameless teenage girls bludgeoned to death in fields and left lying in the rain and the snow.

Inside, the bustling court smells of sour sweat, cigarettes and damp overcoats.

There are two tiers of people watching. On the ground floor are the press benches, print journalists and reporters for the wireless. Such is the public interest that some newspapers have sent five or six journalists to cover various aspects of the trial. Any leftover seats downstairs are reserved for witnesses who have already given evidence and those awarded priority by the court: legal personnel with an interest, nabobs and notaries. Dotted among the journalists today are councilmen, identifiable by a sprig of seasonal flowers on their lapels. Glasgow Corporation gives them out to attendees at its meetings.

Manuel is in the dock right in front of these seats, separated by a low wooden wall. Journalists and lawyers are trusted not to physically attack him but the public are kept away, upstairs on the balcony.

There are sixty balcony seats, all taken by women, watching a court staffed entirely by men.

The women queue overnight, every night for three weeks. They start at six in the evening, settling down on the pavement with thin blankets on their knees, chunks of bread in their pockets to stave off hunger. The queue runs halfway up the Saltmarket. A beat policeman passes every few hours, monitoring them, checking all is well. He counts the people in the queue and warns anyone over the sixtieth person that they probably won't get in. Might as well go home, dear. The papers print photographs of smiling gangs of chirpy gal-pals, toasting the reader with tea from flasks.

For the entire trial the viewing public have been almost exclusively women. No one knows why.

At first the newspapers speculate: are the women here for love? Manuel is handsome. Are they here for blood? The crimes are horrific. Is it because Manuel seems powerful to them? It is a proven scientific fact that women are attracted to power, to being dominated. It is 1958 and a husband has the legal right to rape and beat his wife. That's a private matter, a matter for the home.

The journalists ask the women why they're here. The women say they seek justice, they seek truth, they feel for the victims, hollow phrases that might well be lifted from the papers. But in the queue they don't seem very serious or justice-seeking. They're all excited and giggly.

As the brutal trial draws on the gendered pattern is so consistent and jarring that the newspapers stop struggling to make it chime with clichés about womanhood. The case says enough that is troubling.

At night, all night, another Glasgow is awake and breathing. This shadow city is full of dark, clever men climbing through suburban windows with guns in their hands, creeping around the homes of the law-abiding. They will hide in your attic for days. They will kill you and then make themselves a sandwich. They will drag young girls down railway embankments, chase them across dark fields, rip and rape them, leave them stuck on barbed wire, shoeless in snow, to bleed to death. They have guns and fancy social clubs in prestigious addresses. They drive an Avis Grey Lady, a car that costs the same as a modest house.

Whatever the queuing ladies are here for they are good-tempered. Friends have been made. Some have found celebrity.

Miss Helen McElroy is a regular in all of the newspapers. She is always first in the queue and is emphatic, if not eloquent, about her thirst for justice. Then, abruptly, on the eleventh night, she is missing. There is concern for her safety. She is elderly, wears thick glasses and lives in the Clyde Street Home, a model-lodging house in the Calton for homeless people. On the thirteenth evening she is back. Her absence is explained in a subheading –

MISS MCELROY TOLD . . .
'IF YOU CAN QUEUE
YOU CAN WORK.'

Miss McElroy is interviewed once again. She is quite indignant: 'Somehow,' she says, 'the Assistance have found out I was in the queue.' But her determination to attend is undimmed. They will not stop her.

Young people are not admitted. A sixteen-year-old boy sleeps out on the first night only to be turned away at the door. The officer warns that the nature of the crimes is too unsettling for impressionable minds. Photographs will be shown. Fifty-nine waiting women appeal on the boy's behalf but the officer has his orders and the boy is sent away. The women think it is a shame until they file into court and see all the evidence laid out on the productions table. Blood-sodden bedclothes, both of the guns, a mangled brassiere on a tray, the angle iron that was used to bludgeon the girl in East Kilbride. Then they're glad the boy isn't here to see this. After all the fun of a night on the pavement the reality of what they are about to witness stuns them dumb.

The court is crammed. The only empty seats are on the bench, next to Lord Cameron. As on the Elizabethan stage, there are VIP seats, looking out into the audience. These places are reserved for people so important that mingling in the general company would compromise their status. On the first day of the trial Myer Galpern, wearing his Chain of Office as Lord Provost of Glasgow, is seated next to Lord Cameron. He comes back for the first day of the defence case but leaves at lunchtime. He is not squeamish but, new in the post, is concerned about the seemliness of appearing either underemployed or too interested.

Dowdall is in the silent witness hall. Sturdy chairs line the walls. Water is provided for witnesses, as are cigarettes, matches and ashtrays. The court is just through the double doors but he can't hear any of the proceedings. This is by design. The room is soundproofed so that waiting witnesses can't hear one another's evidence before they give their own.

Dowdall is here to tell the court how Watt and Manuel came to meet. Telling stories is his job. He's a lawyer.

Good storytelling is all about what's left in, what's left out and the order in which the facts are presented. Dowdall knows how to shape a narrative, calling witnesses in the right order, emphasising the favourable through repeated questioning, skim-skim-skimming over the accused's habit of beating his widowed mother. Dowdall is a master storyteller, better than other lawyers. He has an innate sense of narrative and he is disciplined. Dowdall can find just the right trajectory to pin his tale to and he can stop before the end. It's the jury's job to write the ending. Dowdall will tell them about the penitent street fighter who has a good job waiting for him, an ailing, dependent mother and helpless young children. Dowdall knows how a jury will want this story to go. He knows a story has more power if they feel that they are choosing that ending themselves.

But today's story is complex. Dowdall is in this story and he has been tricked. By sleight of hand and word Manuel man-oeuvred Dowdall into breaking the law. Dowdall cannot excise himself from the story because none of the subsequent events make sense if he leaves his own misdemeanours out. He has been up half the night playing narrative chess.

Sitting alone in the witness hall, he worries about this. He feels instinctively that there is a loose thread in this Gordian narrative that he is failing to grasp. This is out of character. He usually can. He smokes and strokes his neat rectangular moustache, first one side, then the other, and wonders if he is becoming ill.

It's a shock when the doors open and the noise of the packed courtroom billows in at him. He leaps to his feet.

The Macer asks him to come, please, Mr Dowdall.

In court the public are taking the change of witness as an opportunity to move or cough or nip out for a smoke. Wood creaks, throats are cleared, doors shut and open, until the Macer has seen Dowdall into the warm room and closed the witness hall doors behind them. Then the Macer looks at the lower benches, at the public on the balcony above. A sudden silence falls. Dowdall knows that they will have been warned that they will be made to leave if they don't keep quiet.

On the balcony a woman is having a coughing fit. She sounds like a heavy smoker and struggles to shift the sticky mucus. Everyone is aware that she will be put out if she can't stop. As Dowdall takes a step into the court her staccato cough machine-guns over his head. He takes another step, glad of the covering fire.

He is halfway across the room when her smoker's cough snaps and she clears her throat. The room drops its shoulders.

He climbs the four steps up to the witness box, turns and gives Lord Cameron a small respectful bow, sans eye contact, because that would be inappropriately chummy in these circumstances. Cameron and Dowdall know each other socially. Dowdall knows every lawyer in this room, personally and professionally. They golf together, dine together at various clubs, they raise money for spastics, Dowdall's own favoured charity, but he oughtn't to bring those connections in here, where he is a prosecution witness.

He is sworn in. The whole truth and nothing but the truth. Dowdall is a storyteller. He knows how slippery truth is. The only part of the oath that Dowdall sincerely means is 'so help me God'. He really means that part.

The advocate-depute, Mr M.G. Gillies, stands up. He does a couple of theatrical postures to take control of the moment: touching his papers, standing tall, grasping the lapel of his gown. Somewhat stagy, thinks Dowdall. Dowdall is a solicitor, not an advocate, and doesn't have a right of audience before the court. He instructs advocates to represent his clients so he finds it hard to watch them work without giving a critical appraisal. He thinks M.G. Gillies' manoeuvres are a little grubby even if they are effective.

M.G. Gillies, projecting his clipped voice very nicely, asks Mr Dowdall if he can please tell the court how he came to meet Mr Manuel in connection with the murders at Burnside?

It is an ideal introduction to the story Dowdall wants to tell. And so he begins.

Dowdall began representing Mr William Watt while he was remanded in Barlinnie for the murders of his wife, his daughter and his sister-in-law, Mrs Margaret Brown. Mr Watt was – Dowdall hesitates over this word but uses it – *disconsolate*.

M.G. Gillies doesn't like that word. He doesn't think the jury will understand it. He asks Dowdall to clarify.

'Very upset,' says Dowdall. 'Mr Watt had been charged with appalling crimes. He had been in all of the newspapers, day after day, and now he found himself in prison. The police were convinced of his guilt.'

'Were you?'

All of the lawyers in the room shift uncomfortably at that question. It is not appropriate. Dowdall's opinion may shift the view of the court but hearsay and opinion could be cause for an appeal, for heaven's sake.

Oddly, Lord Cameron lets Dowdall answer. 'For me to express an opinion would, I think, be potentially misleading.'

Dowdall now feels gratitude radiating towards him from all the other lawyers in the room. He has nimbly saved them all. Then he adds, 'Of course, legally, I wouldn't be able to represent anyone as innocent if I knew they were guilty.'

He has pushed the point to the very edge of legal. Now the lawyers love him. Lord Cameron's heavy eyebrows twitch with understated admiration. Lawyers love the tiptoe across the landmine, the brilliant navigation of the grey area. Standing in the witness box Dowdall experiences the respect of his peers as a warm hand drawing a comforting circle on his back.

Half smiling, M.G. Gillies prompts a return to the story and Dowdall continues.

'Mr Watt knew that the police were not looking for anyone else. He knew that whoever killed his family was still out there and might strike again. So he began his own inquiries. He became a "detective", if you will.'

'How did he go about that?'

'He let it be known, through me, that he was investigating the Burnside Affair and would be receptive to anyone with information.'

'Did people come forward with information?'

'They did. Whatever information we gleaned we immediately took to the police. Mr Watt began to ask questions while in Barlinnie Prison and one name was a refrain in all of our inquiries: Peter Manuel.'

M.G. Gillies frowns, feigning confusion. 'A *"refrain"*?' Gillies really thinks the jury are stupid. He knows them better than Dowdall does. He might be right.

'Mr Manuel was mentioned by several people in connection with the incident.' Now, this is hearsay so Dowdall tempers it. 'But prisons are full of rumours. It wasn't until I received a letter from Mr Manuel that we took those rumours seriously . . .'

Dowdall must not mention that Manuel wrote to him from prison where he was serving a sentence for housebreaking. That would be prejudicial. Dowdall went to see Manuel because he was visiting Watt in Barlinnie anyway, so, what the hell.

'What did Mr Manuel's letter say?'

Dowdall has to step very carefully here. Manuel asked him to visit and act as his lawyer. Strictly speaking Dowdall is bound by client/lawyer confidentiality and shouldn't be telling anyone what was said.

'Mr Manuel sent me a letter concerning one matter but, in an addendum, stated that he had information concerning another client of mine, one who had been described in the press as "an all-round athlete"'

'And you took this to mean Mr Watt?'

This may sound unlikely to the jury because Watt is a big fat man, so Dowdall explains.

'Mr Watt had been a competitor in the Highland Games in his youth. He had been referred to in those terms by a newspaper just the week before so I deduced that it was about him.'

'Do you still have this letter?'

'I'm afraid it was not kept.' The letter is damning for Dowdall. It is clear Manuel is inviting him to visit in his capacity as his legal representative. He wanted Dowdall to put in a hopeless application for bail. Dowdall told him it was pointless but Manuel insisted they put it in anyway.

Dowdall knows what innocent looks like: he maintains eye contact with Gillies. He forces himself to take a breath and blink slowly.

'And so you went to see Mr Manuel?'

'I did.'

'And what did he say?'

'Our first meeting was brief. Mr Manuel told me that Mr Watt was innocent. He said he knew the man who had really committed the murders.'

The public benches gasp. The jury scribble in their notepads. Gillies strikes a pose and lets the statement sink in.

'And what did you say to Mr Manuel?'

'I urged him to go to the police and tell them.'

'And what did he say to that?'

'Well, Mr Manuel was reluctant to do that.'

'Why?'

'He indicated to me that he was not a very great fan of the police.'

'*How* did he indicate that?' Gillies is solemn. He is hoping Manuel threatened someone.

'Mr Manuel expressed his hostility to the police . . .' Dowdall hesitates over the wording, 'in an inelegant, three-word, copulative sentence.'

It takes a moment for the room to hear the three-word phrase. A sudden tidal wave of HAHAHA tension-breaking laughter sweeps through the court. Later, those present will relate this dialogue to others but no one else will find it just as funny. To them it is hilarious because they've heard 'fuck the police' in their heads in this formal setting, because of the bloody clothes and guns and the brassiere on the evidence table, because they've been on the edge of their seat.

The tide of laughter ebbs out, leaving everyone refreshed.

Dowdall continues. 'I told Mr Manuel that the lack of details made me conclude that his story was not credible. Then I left.'

'Did you see Mr Manuel again?'

'Yes. I received yet another letter from him. He said he had additional information.'

'What did this letter say?'

'It hinted that he was willing to give me details this time. So I went to see him for a second time. It was a more productive encounter.'

Dowdall remembers this meeting as he recounts the story of it. He doesn't have to be en guarde because he didn't go as Manuel's lawyer this time.

Peter Manuel sits at a table in a dark grey prison interview room that smells of Lysol and desperation. Hands clasped in front of him, smartly turned out even in his rough prison uniform, looking up at Dowdall through thick eyebrows.

They deal with the preliminaries. Then Manuel leans towards him and in a low growl says, 'I know who done it, the Watt murders, and it wasn't William Watt.'

Dowdall draws him out by affecting disinterest. 'Yes, you said that before. I've been hearing all sorts from all quarters.'

Manuel smirks. 'Is it details you want?'

Dowdall will never forget the look on Manuel's face as he murmurs the story. Eyes hooded, mouth loose, his cheeks pink in an almost girlish flush. He looks over Dowdall's shoulder as he speaks and his hands tell the story too.

'The man crept along the dark street to the house. He walked up the path to the front door. He's broke the glass panel at the left-hand side of the door. He's reached in –'

Manuel slides and curls his flat hand towards Dowdall as if he is in the dark street, breaking in right now.

'– He's reached in and unlocked the door. He's let hisself into the narrow hall with the chiffonier on the left and a picture of a yellow dog hanging above it. He's slid into the dark hallway, onto the red carpet. He's shut the door after himself. On the wall –'

He lifts his right hand, thumb and forefinger pinched.

'– A key rack. But he doesn't take any keys, there's no keys hanging there. He's walked on through the dark, into the still house, surprised that no one's come out or heard him. He pushes open the bedroom door and there's two beds, twin beds, and two women in them. He's took out his gun, and he's shot both the women in the head. Just there –'

He screws the tip of his forefinger into his temple.

'– And he stood looking at them for a bit. But then he's heard the girl.'

In the grey prison interview room Dowdall finds he has chewed his cheek so hard that he has broken the skin. He keeps chewing. He is hurting himself. Manuel's voice has dropped to a growl, a whisper, and Dowdall sees a spark of glee in his eyes. Not because of Dowdall's reaction. He doesn't seem to care about that, not much. He's reliving the story through the telling and he's enjoying it.

'But then he's heard the girl. She's in another room. So he's left the two women bleeding and gone down the hall to the girl's bedroom door. She's opened the door and his face is just there and – "Oh!" She's jumped back into the room. Must have been asleep. Her eyes are all puffy, like. Now – now, he is not a cruel man, this man I'm talking about. This man. He is not a cruel man. He doesn't want to hurt a young girl.'

As Dowdall listens to this he rubs the ripped inside of his cheek against his teeth again and again, feeling the dull throb of raw skin. Dowdall knows about Manuel's rape charges. The rapes stretch back to the age of fourteen. He broke out of Catholic approved school and attacked a staff member's wife in her home. Manuel has a thing about the women's heads. He goes for the head. Always for their head. He bludgeons, punches the head, threatens the head. *I will cut your fucking head off and bury it out here*, he told one victim, ten years into his career as a rapist, *Your kids will be walking out here, walking across your head on their way to school and they'll not even know.* She promised not to report him if he let her go but she went straight to the police. Manuel wasn't convicted of that rape. He defended himself in court and the jury found the case Not Proven. Manuel thinks he did a good job in court but, really, Dowdall knows it was just a jury of women. Glasgow juries, especially women jurors, don't believe that rape really happens. They think slutty girls get raped, claim rape, cry rape to cover their own sins. The lady he threatened to decapitate had taken the bus home from work and crossed a dark lane. He grabbed her hair and dragged her down a railway embankment, broke her dentures with a punch. The jury found the case Not Proven. They weren't told about Manuel's other conviction, a rape on the same embankment seven years before, a three-year-old boy left screaming on the path, watching his mother dragged away down the same slope into dark fields. Manuel got six years in Peterhead for that one. Dowdall is thinking about these women as Manuel continues the story of the man who is not him.

'He didn't want to hurt a young girl so he gives her a knock-out punch on the jaw. She fell on the floor. KO. Now he didn't know what to do, but he's hungry so he's went into the kitchen, a wee galley kitchen, yellow Formica worktops and cupboards along the wall and he fixed hisself a wee something to eat, just a wee sandwich with gammon. Good gammon too, off the bone, not in jelly from a tin. He's in a fix, see? Because the kid, she's seen his face. So, he's in the front room, eating his wee sandwich, when he hears a noise from the first bedroom, the one with the two women in it.'

Manuel's story speeds from a trot to a gallop. Faster and faster he tells it. 'The woman in the first bed wasn't dead. She was kinda gurgling, like a wet cough sort of a thing, so he shot her again. He'd no sooner done that and went back and nearly finished eating the sandwich when he heard the girl again. She's woke up. She's cried out. He went back in there and he shot her too and she fell in a corner. Then he stood there and smoked a couple of fags. He went into the front room and he took a swig of gin from the bottle on the dresser. Mascaró Dry Gin.'

Dowdall is damp with sweat and his cheek is swelling on the inside.

'One might wonder though,' says Dowdall quietly, 'if it was this other man, and not you, how it is that you know so many details?'

Manuel reaches across to him and it is all Dowdall can do not to slap his hand away.

'Oh, see, this man?' breezes Manuel. 'He's came to me, just after, the morning after and –'

Manuel stops. He stops for too long, staring at the tabletop. Neither happy nor sad. He just stares at the tabletop. And then he's back.

'– He's destroyed by what he's done. He's like this –'

Manuel trembles his hands at Dowdall.

'– In the horrors. "*Hide this gun for me*," he says. So I took it. And I hid it. And I can get it again.'

The gun has never been found. Manuel is offering a piece of concrete, physical evidence that could prove Mr Watt is innocent. Dowdall stands in the mouth of a trap. Manuel sees it.

Manuel sits back in his chair and slowly trails his hands along the tabletop, damp palms making a scumbled shriek that fills the room.

'Can you describe this gun?'

Manuel smirks. 'I'll go one better, I'll draw it.'

Dowdall gives him paper and a pencil and he does draw it. The trap springs tight around Dowdall. The teeth are so sharp he doesn't even feel them sinking in.

It is quite a good drawing of a Webley revolver. Manuel is proud of his drawing. Dowdall senses this and compliments him. 'You're a very able artist.'

Manuel shrugs. He already knows that.

'May I take this drawing?'

Manuel seems flattered. 'Sure, why not.'

Dowdall slips the drawing in among his papers. He can't legally take away any communications by a prisoner unless he is their lawyer.

'Thank you, Mr Manuel.'

Dowdall stands up to leave.

'Did you put in my bail application, then?' Manuel's eyes slide from the papers to Dowdall and a sly smile creeps across his face.

Dowdall freezes. He is not here about the hopeless bail application Manuel raised at their previous meeting. They both know Manuel isn't getting bail. The break-ins he is convicted of had his signature all over them: food half eaten and dropped, ground into rugs with his heel, liquor drunk from bottles. The bail application was pointless and Manuel is familiar enough with the law to know that. But if Dowdall answers Manuel's question this becomes a client/lawyer interview. Legally, Dowdall will not be able to repeat what Manuel has just told him. However, he will be able to take the drawing of the gun out of the prison perfectly legally.

Dowdall senses that Manuel fully understands the position he has put him in. The point of the bail application was never the bail itself but putting Dowdall in this quandary. Manuel has done this deliberately.

Thrown, for possibly the first time in his life, Dowdall picks up his papers. He means to say 'I am not here about that'. He thinks to say 'We will discuss this another time'. But his mouth disobeys him.

'Yes.'

Shocked at himself, he turns and walks out.

Dowdall doesn't tell this part in court. This part makes all of his testimony invalid. This part makes him a bad lawyer who betrays his clients and should not be allowed to practise. Instead, he tells the court that he left the meeting and immediately endeavoured to confirm the veracity of the information imparted by Mr Manuel at that second meeting.

'And is this the drawing of the gun Mr Manuel gave you at that interview?'

M.G. Gillies hands a sheet of paper labelled 'Crown Production 41' up to the witness dock.

Dowdall looks at it. 'Yes. That is the drawing of the Webley that Peter Manuel gave to me.'

'And is this the type of gun that was used to kill Mrs Watt, Vivienne Watt and Mrs Brown?'

They all know it is. The actual Webley is sitting right there, in front of them, on the evidence table.

'So I understand,' says Dowdall, adding, 'And it has a particularity. You will notice that the lanyard ring is missing in the sketch and on the actual gun.'

'The lanyard ring at the bottom of the handle?'

'Yes, the one customarily used to attach it to the belt.'

The Webley was favoured during the Great War. Officers and soldiers tied the revolver to their Sam Browne belts with cord so that they didn't lose them, even if they dropped them in the heat and horror of battle.

'Did you go to the police with this information, Mr Dowdall?'

'I did.'

I went straight to the police, Dowdall doesn't say. He doesn't tell the court that, reckless of his professional peril, he had to tell them because he left Manuel's company and got into his Bentley and drove to a quiet corner of a small field and found himself crying. Panicked and frightened and crying. Dowdall was furious that the filthy creeping man should know how to trick him with the law. The law was his defence against such men. Dowdall believed it was his weapon, not his weakness.

But all the court hears Dowdall say is 'I did'.

Those closer to Dowdall notice him blinking rapidly, see the rims of his eyes reddening. They know there is more to it than *I did* but no one asks him about it. Gillies moves swiftly on.

'And what did the police do with this information?'

'They went to the Manuel family home in Birkenshaw and they searched the garden.'

'Why?'

'They were looking for the gun he had drawn. Or the missing lanyard ring.'

Later Dowdall heard that Manuel boasted about it in prison. He told another client of Dowdall's that he could get the polis to dig his mother's garden for her while he lay on his bunk in Barlinnie. Ha ha. Be sure and tell Laurence, won't you? Manuel was telling Dowdall that he knows his confidentiality had been breached, that Dowdall had committed a crime. He's the only one who knows. From the corner of his eye Dowdall can see Manuel leaning forward in the dock to whisper to his lawyer. He is smirking and whispering. He could have used these facts to exclude Dowdall's testimony or the drawing. Dowdall doesn't understand why Manuel hasn't instructed his lawyers to do that. He set up this complicated play and then forgot, or neglected, to use it to his advantage. Or maybe he means to use it to ruin Dowdall, rather than save his own neck from the noose. Even with eight murder charges hanging over him, six of which are for the murder of women, one for a ten-year-old child, even with the nastiness of them known, Dowdall feels that he alone has any understanding of how profoundly malevolent Peter Manuel is.

Gillies interrupts his train of thought. 'So the police must have found his story quite credible then, if they searched for the gun?'

'They seemed to.'

Dowdall showed the police the drawing and they said yes, that could be the gun. Then Dowdall told them that Manuel had given him a lot of detailed information about the Watt house. Dowdall hasn't been there yet, might he go and have a look? They took Dowdall to the Watt house, still cordoned off, still guarded by a police officer, DS Mitchell.

Muncie, a senior officer from Lanarkshire, is waiting outside for Dowdall. He came because he heard Manuel mentioned in the request. Manuel lives on Muncie's patch. Muncie hates Manuel. He accosts Dowdall in the street outside the Watt bungalow. Peter Manuel's probably lying, Mr Dowdall. That filthy criminal is a serial confessor to high-profile cases. He plays games. He confessed to a big bank robbery in London and then produced an alibi. He claims he was a gangster in New York but the family moved back from New York when he was five and the Depression hit. He tells people his daddy died in the electric chair in America, but he lives with his daddy. His daddy works for the Gas Board. Manuel says he's an artist, he's a writer, he's a spy for the Yanks. Peter Manuel talks utter shite. He is known for lies. His lies are so crazy you sometimes wonder if he even knows he's lying. He's a sex fiend. A maniac.

The Watt house is in Fennsbank Avenue in Burnside on the Southside. It is a long road of sturdy detached villas with large gardens and driveways for cars. Dowdall walks up the path to the door and sees the broken glass on the window, sees Manuel's hand slide in through the broken glass, curl to the side and open the door, in the dark.

DS Mitchell opens the door for him. Dowdall steps in. Mitchell says not to touch anything and leaves, shutting the door behind him.

Dowdall is alone in the Watt bungalow. He sees a chiffonier on his left and a picture of a golden Labrador hanging on the wall. On his right hangs a key rack. It is empty. Surprised that no one has come out or heard him, he pushes open the bedroom door. Bloody splatter is fanned across the wall behind the headboards and the floor is smeared and stained with dried gore. The twin beds are stripped, mattresses and sheets and blankets gone, taken for evidence. Dowdall is glad he parked at the field because he couldn't cry if he tried now. He doesn't know if he will ever cry or eat again.

In the front room a bottle of Mascaró Dry Gin sits on the dresser. Balanced on the arm of the settee, on a linen antimacassar, the crust of a sandwich. The sliver of gammon between the bread is as dry and cracked as a dead cat's tongue. The police didn't know it was significant. They've just left it there.

In the galley kitchen, wall cupboards and yellow Formica.

In the dead girl's room the bed is stripped. Chalk marks are drawn around cigarette stubs found ground into the carpet.

Vivienne was left slumped in the corner, half covered over, lying on top of the bedding. It's a bloody mess. A seventeen-year-old girl, dead and bruised, her bosom exposed, badly bruised *down there*, interfered with. 'Before or after?' Dowdall had asked at the time. 'Both,' said the medical examiner frowning at his feet. 'Both before *and* after.'

M.G. Gillies asks, 'What happened then, Mr Dowdall?'

'Sorry?'

'What happened then?'

'Well, I had told the police, so . . .'

'Did you meet Mr Manuel again?'

Dowdall never wanted to see him again. But another letter, with more teasers. Whatever his feelings, Dowdall had to inform poor Mr Watt that Manuel was getting out of prison, having served ten months for housebreaking, and wanted to meet him.

'Manuel wrote that he was being released and he could get the gun back but he wanted to meet Mr Watt first.'

Lord Cameron asks, 'Is that letter available to the court, Mr Dowdall?'

No. I burned it so you would never see it. Manuel wanted money for the gun and if you, My Lord, knew that, you might rule this testimony inadmissible. So I burned that letter in the ashtray on my desk. And then I sat and looked at it for a while. I felt so uneasy that I called my secretary in and asked her to take the ashtray away. And actually, Miss McLaren, just throw that ashtray away, will you? Because it has a crack it in. Yes, it does. There. You can't see it? Well, I can see it, so just get it out of here. Miss McLaren shuts the door on her way out and Dowdall knows that she will wash the glass ashtray and take it home, probably give it to her father. And he's afraid for her.

'No, My Lord, I'm afraid that particular letter has been misplaced.'

The lawyers find this a wee bit odd. Lawyers like Dowdall don't misplace letters like that. But no one knows what to ask. They just blame a careless secretary and carry on with the questioning.

'So, yourself and Mr Watt went to meet Mr Manuel?'

'Yes. We met him at Whitehall's Restaurant in Renfield Street but I left after just ten minutes.'

'Why did you leave?'

Innocent question. Leading nowhere.

'I had somewhere to be.'

'But Watt and Manuel stayed there, together?'

'I believe they were together all night, until six o'clock the next morning.'

'What happened that night, Mr Dowdall?'

'I really don't know. We never discussed it.'

'Mr Watt never told you what happened?'

'No.'

'Did you ask him?'

'No.'

There is a pause. This seems implausible but Dowdall is obviously telling the truth. William Watt will be asked his version of events when he is on the stand tomorrow. M.G. Gillies flounders and says, 'Thank you, Mr Dowdall.'

And now Manuel's defence counsel stands up. William Grieve. Grieve indeed. His hair is very orange, his complexion unattractively rosy, and he looks half annoyed all the time. Grieve only took silk last year. Harald Leslie is the senior QC in Manuel's team and he should have cross-examined Dowdall. He is the more able by far. But this is a small world. Harald was representing William Watt when he was charged with these murders, Dowdall had instructed him, so there is a conflict of interest which requires him to step aside in favour of Grieve when Watt and Dowdall are giving evidence.

Dowdall watches Grieve lift his papers, cock his head at them and put them down. He pretends to be wondering. He's new to this and his act is not polished. Dowdall says a silent prayer of thanks, half to Harald Leslie and half to God, who has, after all, so-helped-him.

Grieve considers his first question. He purses and unpurses his lips and Dowdall notices that the jury already dislike him. He glances at Manuel, sitting in the dock with four policemen, two behind him and one on either side. He sees Manuel frown at the back of Grieve's head. Manuel has also noticed that the jury don't like Grieve. If Dowdall was defending this case he would think they had lost it already.

'Might I ask –' Grieve looks up, flashes a joyless smile – 'About this "other matter" on which you initially went to visit Mr Manuel?'

Manuel smirks. This is what he was whispering about.

'Of course.'

'What was this "other matter"?' Grieve's eyebrows rise slowly.

Dowdall has decided to argue this as a point of law, knowing that the jury will stop listening if he makes it sound complicated enough. He must not say that Manuel was in prison or mention any of his previous convictions and this gives him wriggle room.

'Mr Manuel had requested an interview with a view to a minor revision of the conditions of a legal application.'

He makes it sounds like a dog licence. Grieve nods five times. One nod too many for anyone to care what he means.

'He had, in short, sought your legal expertise?'

'Yes.'

'And it was in the course of that first interview, when you were in effect acting as his lawyer, that he sketched the gun for you?'

'No.'

Grieve looks up. 'No?'

'No. That was at the second meeting. At the first meeting he told me that William Watt was an innocent man and he knew the man who had actually committed the murders. He described the house in the second meeting. The events of the night. And drew the gun.'

Grieve consults his papers and sees that he is indeed wrong. Harald Leslie, sitting next to him, raises an eyebrow at his papers. It's a rudimentary mistake: Grieve hasn't done a time line.

'Ah, yes, I see, thank you for that correction, Mr Dowdall. But in the first interview you were acting as his lawyer?'

'No. I was giving him advice in the first half of that interview and in the second half of the *first* interview he was giving me information about a pre-existing client of mine.'

Manuel is crossing and uncrossing his legs, he is sitting forward and back. He wants certain things asked in certain ways and Grieve is busy getting dates wrong.

'I put it to you that this was quite improper, Mr Dowdall, you going to the police with confidential information passed by a client –'

'No.'

Grieve can't quite believe his gall.

'No, it was not improper. He was my client for the first half of the interview. In the second half of the first interview I was there in my capacity as Mr Watt's representative, as I was at all subsequent meetings. I accompanied Mr Watt to meet him. He was there when we arrived. Given the presence of both gentlemen, it was both *explicate* and *implicate* that Mr Watt was my client in that interview.'

'That is arguable,' says Grieve but he seems to have given up.

The small mistake of fact over the time line has thrown him. Very able defence lawyers will make unlikely mistakes time and again in this case, all of them to Manuel's detriment.

As a closer Grieve asks: 'Mr Dowdall, was any money exchanged between Mr Watt and Mr Manuel for this information?'

Dowdall has rehearsed this. 'I told Peter Manuel he would not get any money for the information.'

Grieve tries, valiant but half-hearted, because he knows what Dowdall is doing. 'But *did* any money change hands for this information?'

'Well, I left after ten minutes but I do know this: I told Mr Watt not to give Peter Manuel any money for the information.'

All it will take is one more move. *Did William Watt ever talk about giving Manuel money?* And Dowdall will have to say *Yes. He did. We discussed it.*

But Dowdall looks up and he sees relief shimmer across Grieve's face. He sees Manuel glare at the back of Grieve's head. And he sees a field through a windscreen and a veil of his own tears and a letter burning in an ashtray and he knows that, deep down, Grieve and Leslie, they loathe Peter Manuel too. They want him dead too.

'That will be all, Mr Dowdall. Thank you.'

'Thank you, Mr Grieve. Thank you.'

3

Monday 2 December 1957

'*I KILLED MY WIFE*,' William Watt is murmuring in Peter Manuel's ear. Then the door opens, he looks up and shouts, 'Scout O'BloodyNeil!'

They're in Jackson's Bar. They have been there for a while.

Watt is very drunk. His moods are shifting like a breeze over open water. Manuel has matched him drink for drink but he isn't very drunk. He thinks that either Watt was drinking before they met in Whitehall's or he is acting drunk to disarm him.

Manuel doesn't get drunk, not in the usual way. His body becomes uncoordinated, he may feel sleepy, but his basic mood doesn't change. He still has an eye for a weakness or a half-opened window or a chance. Maybe he will file it away for later, when he isn't as uncoordinated, but he still sees it and feels the same about it.

They are standing together in the prime spot in Jackson's, at the corner of the long bar. The corner calls the night in Jackson's.

Bar positioning in Jackson's is a complex language, a poem about power. The men who drink here are powerless. Some are fatherless sons, motherless sons, Barnardo's Boys gone bad. Some would have done better without the hapless parents fate has foisted on them. These are clever men though, some are brilliant, but none of them has the legitimate means to exploit it. They're prison fodder. If polis see these men coming out of somewhere nice they'll lift them on suspicion. Powerless, but within that powerlessness there are still grades to be measured and weighed. These men gather night after night, dressed in new duds, flashing wads of readies, determined to prove to other members of the underclass that they're not down yet.

From the corner of the bar Watt and Manuel can see the whole room and both doors. They see who comes in with hungry eyes, who is here on the scrounge, who swans in with a brand-new suit and a dame on each arm. Everyone coming through the doors sees them first and picks up on their mood.

Because of the power of the corner, it's a fight to keep it. Shows of weakness or impecunity, or a slight against you, witnessed but unavenged, will see you bumped around the corner. The least ambivalence and you'll be hustled off the spot.

Holding the corner is a first for Manuel. He has washed up here by accident a few times but has always been pushed off, not by one person but by the consensus of the crowd. Watt has had the corner before but he has never held it this long. It's because they are together and they don't belong together. It throws everyone.

The reckless threat that Manuel exudes adds to Watt's wealth and height. Eyes flick between them, confused by their conjoining and therefore disadvantaged. As with all unexpectedly powerful unions, they will eventually have to decide what to do with it, but for now they are just intoxicated by it, euphoric, drinking quickly, talking fast and loose. Watt is saying things to Manuel he wouldn't otherwise – *I killed my wife* – when they are interrupted by the sight of Scout O'Neil staggering in through the door.

Watt is trying to call him over to buy him a drink. Watt wouldn't have done that if he wasn't blootered because O'Neil shouldn't even be in here. He's a ridiculous mess tonight.

Scout stands at the door, two black eyes and the bridge of his nose swollen and split, his suit jacket ripped on the shoulder. He has partially wiped the blood from his chin with his sleeve. His cheeks are crusty with salt white. The broken nose must have made his eyes water. Even O'Neil knows he's not getting served tonight. He's just looking for someone, probably someone that owes him money from the Gordon Club.

Watt calls his name: 'Scout O'BloodyNeil!' Scout hears it and raises a hand while he scans the bar for the debtor's face. He shoots Watt a preoccupied smile. His front tooth is freshly missing.

Watt and Manuel both see this and laugh, though it must still be very sore. The gummy gap is ragged, his remaining teeth framed with bloody saliva. It's only funny because it's O'Neil.

Scout O'Neil is crazy. Wherever, whenever, Scout has always just had an adventure, usually involving money, a dame and a fist fight. At the end of most nights Scout will try to fight whoever is around, if he hasn't already had a fight. Everybody loves Scout O'Neil. He always has money and is honest about his proclivities – I love fighting, he says. When anyone says they don't like Scout it's just because they owe him money. They come around again when the debt is settled.

Scout O'Neil scans the bar but can't see who he's after. Walking backwards towards Watt, he catches the manager's eye.

Brady, a surly big bastard, is drying ashtrays at the gantry but has stopped still, staring at O'Neil.

'Sorry,' says Scout, raising a hand in surrender and ducking behind it as if to hide.

Brady watches him sidle to the corner, eyebrows rising slowly, asking if O'Neil's really going to make him put him out? Really? They both know Scout can't be in here with *that* face, in *that* suit, with blood on it. Scout brasses it out and sidesteps to Watt.

Brady moves towards Watt, 'Ho! O'Neil!'

'Couple o'minutes, Brady?'

Brady shakes his head and mutters a warning, the conditions of which are lost in the burble of the bar – ye better fucking fucking fucking, son. Something like that, not happy anyway, but O'Neil has two minutes' grace. He accepts the conditions with a nod.

'Hey, Watt, you seen Dandy the night?'

Scout is scanning the faces for his boss, Dandy McKay, so he doesn't see the reaction to his question. All he feels is the frost and stillness seeping back at him. He looks round to see if Watt has heard him. And then he sees Peter Manuel standing next to William Watt.

Scout is aghast. *'The fuck yees doing?'*

Smirking, Manuel shifts his weight so that he is obscured behind Watt's massive frame. Watt stands tall though. He's loyal because they have the corner and he's enjoying that. Scout runs his eye between them, sees that they are, indeed, together.

For a man who looked like he had been run over by a tram when he came in, O'Neil suddenly looks very much worse. He pales as he looks between them, from Watt up high and Manuel down low, to the dirty glasses in front of them that show they've been tanning it, matching each other for half and halfs, holding the prime position at the bar. He sees that Watt and Manuel are not just together, they're making a show of being together and they're doing it in Jackson's, of all fucking places.

'The fuck yees pulling?' O'Neil backs away. He shakes his head at Manuel. 'You better fucking run, boy. If I was you, I'd fucking run.'

Manuel bends back to call around the massive wall of Watt. 'Hey, Scout. Gonnae not say?'

William Watt is oblivious. He has picked up on none of this. 'A drink for O'Neil! Let us have drink!'

He doesn't clock Scout O'Neil's horror or hear his warning. He doesn't see Brady's annoyance. He doesn't sense the shift in O'Neil, from a man trying to get into Jackson's to look for Dandy, to a man who now wants to get out, get out, get out and away from whatever the fuck is unfolding between himself and Manuel.

'A whisky for Scout O'Neil!'

Scout holds both hands up again, higher this time, not in surrender this time. He's washing his hands of them.

The door flaps open to the night. Watt tries to blink away a sudden sting of cigarette smoke. The door flaps shut. Watt's eyes open and Scout O'Neil is gone.

Watt barely remembers that O'Neil was even there. All that remains is the shape of the name in his mouth, like a memory of a flavour. He goes back to what he was saying before.

'I killed my wife, they say. I suppose anyone might kill their wife, but *her sister*? Why would I? Who would? And my *daughter*?'

Watt frowns at his drink. Something has changed in the mood of the evening but he doesn't know what. He frowns. Maybe more drink will help. He drains his glass and hopes.

'Thing is,' he whispers in Manuel's ear, 'if I did that to my daughter, I would certainly have turned the gun on myself. But I didn't, you know, I was *fishing*.'

The 'sh' tickles Manuel's eardrum. He brings his shoulder up defensively and catches Brady's eye.

Brady has seen that there is something very wrong with them being together. They've been here for two hours, necking it on Watt's dime, but Brady doesn't want them there any more. They are about to lose the corner. Manuel draws on his cigarette, refusing to look back at Brady as Watt finishes what he is saying.

'*Fishing* is waiting. All waiting. And it's while you're waiting for the bite, you know, your mind just –' He can't think of the words for what he means so he shuts his eyes and waves vaguely. 'You know? *Things*. You know?'

He looks at Manuel to see if he understands.

Manuel nods impatiently, stubbing his cigarette out. Soon Dandy McKay will know that he is with William Watt.

'Let's get out of here.'

Watt is astonished. 'Why?'

'Just go somewhere else.' Manuel finishes his beer chaser.

Brady steps towards them, wiping the ashtray, about to put it down and tell them, fuck off yous two.

Watt can't believe what is being proposed. '*Why* go somewhere else? I like it here.'

'Come on.'

Manuel is at the door, yanking it open. Watt watches him, puzzled, because it isn't closing time. Watt still has money. They're winning! They have a corner to hold. But Manuel is leaving, quite definitely. Watt hurries out after him into the December night.

Back in Jackson's the power vacuum at the corner is filled by the man who was drinking next to them. He slides over to the space, puts his hands on the still warm bar. He is small, no one knows him and Brady has seen his money. It's all shrapnel. Brady glares and the man giggles as if he has just tried on his daddy's hat. 'Fuck off out of it,' says Brady and the man slides back to where he came from, uncomplaining.

Outside, Manuel is walking down Crown Street. He has drunk a lot and his legs are moving faster than he means them to. He is falling forwards, catching his weight with the next step, falling towards the river. He feels as if he is running but he isn't. His strides are long, is all.

Big tall Watt catches up effortlessly and asks him where's he going?

Manuel finds he can't speak. He says 'fooof' and staggers off down the pavement.

They are in the Gorbals, on a main road with churches and shops and ramshackle, crumbling tenements built around and above. A huge private school, Hutchesons', is set back from the road.

They slow and stop. They're both unbelievably tired all of a sudden. Manuel sees them both as if from far away. Two drunk men sagging in Crown Street. Quiet street, because it's not yet closing time. Sagging. Small drunk, big drunk. Wants money, has money. Knows something, wants to know.

'Give me money,' he blurts at Watt.

Watt considers his petition. He raises his hands and sighs, 'Haven't gotneny.'

Manuel points to the river, over the river, to away. 'Got somewhere?'

Watt shakes his big head and says nononono. But he has. They both know he has. 'Got the gun?'

'I've got. I'll *get*.'

Manuel shakes two cigarettes out of his packet and gives one to Watt. He lights a match and they take their time, no rush, trying to make contact with the flame. It takes a while.

They smoke in a considered manner.

It is frosty. Cold creeps through the bar-warmed soles of their shoes, up their shins. They pull their jackets tight around them.

Watt is looking at Hutchesons', a centuries-old public school. He smiles warmly at it and Manuel asks, 'Wha'? D'you go there?'

Watt says no but smiles and straightens his back, flattered. He looks at the wall next to him. It's a black tenement and the stone is crumbling. Sand and lumps of soft stone lie scattered on the pavement. It looks as if someone has been kicking bits out of it. Gang slogans and graffiti are scratched into the soft surface.

'This?' Watt turns and sweeps a panoramic hand over the street. 'Gone. All gone. *Big* money.'

Manuel nods. 'Knocking it down.'

'*Really big money.*' Watt makes a raspberry with his fat yellow tongue. 'Ptttthhhhhhh. Ten years. *All* gone.' He sees that Manuel isn't interested in land-development scams. Manuel should be. They'll cost him his life. When the city is flattened and being rebuilt with bathrooms and plumbing and kitchens, money will be scammed on the materials and the labour. But Watt is in on the meta-scam. This pleases him enormously. 'Big money.' He spins on his heel. 'Mon to the car.'

They stagger down to Watt's maroon Vauxhall, parked outside Jackson's.

Watt can't find the key. He finds the key. He can't fit it in the lock. He fits it in the lock. This though is seamless: door open, twist, fall into the driver's seat, breathe. Turn, lean deep back and lift his big legs in. Shut the door. Breathe. Reach over. Unlock the passenger door. Breathe.

Now they are both in the car. Now the doors are shut.

They take a short break. They are both looking out of the windscreen at Jackson's. Yellow light spills into black night.

The door to Jackson's opens and a man staggers out. He crab-walks away from them, along the pavement until he hits a lamp post. He clings to it, waiting until his legs agree to listen to orders. Confident he has reached an *entente cordiale* with his knees, he straightens up, watching his rebel legs to see if the truce holds. It does, but only for standing. The moment he attempts a step he is swept around the corner like a trawlerman thrown from a deck in a storm. Watt watches, glad he's not as drunk as him.

'I know who killed your wife and daughter.'

'I know you do. Will you tell me?'

Manuel sighs. It isn't a drunken sigh. It a different kind of a sigh. 'You know who did it.'

Watt nods and slumps, his forehead resting on the backs of his hands on the steering wheel.

Manuel mutters in the background, 'You need a joe. I've got one, a right good fit.'

Watt is confused for a moment. He doesn't need a joe. 'I just want the gun,' he says.

Manuel nods, as if that's what they were discussing anyway. 'And I'm the boy who knows where it is.'

Watt can finally see an end to this nightmare. It won't be easy but he is sure he was right to meet this terrible man. Fortune favours the brave.

'I know where it is,' slurs Manuel, 'but I'm gonnae need money.'

In the dark car Watt says, 'I have money. I can get money.'

Manuel nods. 'All right then. Let's go.'

4

Thursday 15 May 1958

GLASGOW HIGH COURT WAS finished the year Napoleon was defeated at Waterloo. The floor, the bench and the jury stall are oak, the walls bare lath and plaster. The acoustics in the room are acute.

William Watt's laboured breathing, and the grunts of the four policemen carrying him, fill the high, rapt room.

Watt is being carried into court on a stretcher. He arrived in an ambulance and his doctor is in attendance, standing at the side of the court, watching him carefully.

Watt crashed his car in the Gorbals last night. He drove straight into a wall. His knee is swollen and his neck hurts, but what really ails Mr Watt is self-pity. Mr Watt could cry even thinking about himself. He thinks that if only people knew how awful this is, they might be a bit nicer to him.

After the crash last night, when the doctor asked him how he felt, Watt tried to communicate this, but it is 1958 and men don't really have words for feelings. The doctor misunderstood. He thought Watt was in tremendous physical pain and now Watt is too embarrassed to admit the truth. He has to play along with the fiction that he is horribly injured but he's not a good actor.

The police have charged him with drunk-driving. This is not the first time. When the case comes to court he'll lose his licence. Dowdall told Watt to plead not guilty so that news of the incident will be *sub judice* until the Manuel trial is over and no one will hear about it. Dowdall strives to make Mr Watt sympathetic because what has happened to William Watt is horrific. He deserves a charitable hearing.

Watt and his phalanx of officers make it across to the witness stand. Watt is let down and hauls himself up the steps. A seat has been placed there for him. Lord Cameron asks him if he would like a rubber cushion for his knee? Watt accepts tearfully.

Flinching, he raises his hand to be sworn in and repeats the oath with ludicrous solemnity.

M.G. Gillies asks and this is the story Watt tells:

It was a Sunday night, the start of the second week of his annual fly-fishing holiday. His wife and daughter didn't want to come with him. Neither of them like to fish. His wife Marion is recovering from a heart operation. So he is alone, staying at the Cairnbaan Hotel, a ninety-mile drive from Glasgow.

He spends the Sunday night in the residents' lounge. Mr Watt, Mr and Mrs Leitch, who own the hotel, and a fishing chum, Mr Bruce, have 'quite a party'. Watt is serving behind the bar. There is some singing. It all sounds very jolly. They drink for five or six hours until 1 a.m. when Watt and Mr Leitch stand by the back door, smoking cigars and watching as Watt's black Labrador, Queenie, goes out. When she comes back in they both roll up to their beds.

Watt is next seen at 8 a.m. in the dining room for breakfast. The hotel's maid arrives for work at the same time and sees his car outside. The windscreen is covered in frost.

After breakfast Watt goes fishing. A while later a taxi arrives at the riverbank. The driver gets out and beckons him over. Puzzled, Watt wades to the bank. Whatever is going on? He is wanted at the hotel. Mrs Leitch, proprietress of the hotel, needs to see him urgently. Watt can't imagine why, but he knows it is very bad news.

A sobbing Mrs Leitch meets him at the door. She is incoherent, saying something confusing. At first Watt thinks Mrs Leitch's daughter has had a terrible accident. Finally she sits down and catches her breath and tells him: your brother John telephoned from Glasgow. Journalists came into the baker's shop asking strange questions about your wife, about you. John phoned the police to find out what was going on. They said:

Your wife is dead.

Your daughter is dead.

Your sister-in-law is dead.

Killed in your house.

Shot with a gun.

In their beds.

William keeps shaking his head. No, this is a mistake. My *wife* Marion? It is wrong. There weren't three people at my house last night. My sister-in-law wasn't at my house last night. I called home yesterday evening and Vivienne told me *specifically* that she would stay the night with Deanna Valente next door. This is all wrong.

Mrs Leitch telephones John Watt and puts William on the phone. John tells William that Marion is dead.

Vivienne is dead.

Margaret is dead.

Killed in your house.

Shot with a gun. Come home at once.

Mr Bruce arrives at the hotel and finds William very angry about this wicked mistake. He needs to go to Glasgow and sort this nonsense out.

Furious now, William gets into his car. Mr Bruce insists on coming with him because he thinks William is too upset to drive safely – Oh! What a silly fuss about a load of nonsense!

One harum-scarum mile down the road William pulls over and admits that he is not in a fit state to drive. They limp the

Vauxhall to the police station at Lochgilphead. A kindly police officer takes over, driving Watt and Mr Bruce in Watt's car to Alexandria, a town on the outskirts of Glasgow. And here Watt's troubles begin because here he meets DS Mitchell.

Watt is an odd man. He has always been odd, says the wrong thing, gets the mood wrong, but this has never been legally relevant before. Suddenly it is.

DS Mitchell finds him very strange. Watt smiles abruptly, keeps announcing that he is fine, wants to drive his own car and is angry at the Glasgow police for making a 'huge mistake'. Mitchell becomes suspicious of Watt and makes notes of some of the things he says in the car. He jots down these remarks:

'You won't see me shed a single tear.'

'You don't think I did it, do you?'

'I know this road like the back of my hand.'

For the defence, William Grieve asks Watt if he made these statements in the car because he had a guilty conscience?

Watt announces to the court: 'My conscience has never been guilty all of my life. I never did a wrong thing in all my life. Never once did I do a wrong thing in my life.'

The court pauses. The public shift in their seats and smirk to each other.

Even the lawyers find this level of bombast entertaining. They smile, raise eyebrows, make a note of it for their chest of war stories.

I never did a wrong thing in all my life.

Watt seems to sense that he has got something very wrong but isn't sure what: he tries blaming someone else.

'And anyway all of that is a lie. Quite like Mitchell to say that too. He's a liar.'

Standing up in court and calling a policeman a liar is utterly shocking in the 1950s. A police officer could stand in a witness dock and claim to be a tram, and the room would wonder if he was, in some sense, in many ways, actually telling the truth. Watt has good reason to be suspicious of policemen but, by speaking so boldly, he has lost the room.

M.G. Gillies tries several times to make him likeable again. He asks Watt if DS Mitchell gave him any warning of what he was about to be shown when they arrived at his house. Watt blinks back tears. No, he says in a choking voice. None.

They arrive in Fennsbank Avenue. DS Mitchell parks and pulls Watt out of the back of his own car in his own driveway. Journalists are crowding around the door. They take photographs of Watt being pulled out of the back of his own car in his own driveway.

FLASH. FLASH.

White lights. He wasn't ready. He was looking straight at them.

FLASH.

He's blinded. He reels and looks drunk in the photos. He blinks but white splashes of light are still going off in his eyes and he can't see properly. Mitchell pulls him by the elbow, up the driveway to his own front door.

FLASH.

In the doorway Watt blinks hard, his vision resolves for a moment and he sees that his house is full of angry strangers. Men. They have overcoats on, or uniforms on, and they all stare at him as he comes through his own front door.

Grabbed by the elbow, Watt is swung around to face into his own bedroom. Men in there and the beds all messy and scarlet blood spattered on the wall. Red. Marion's familiar ankle, blue thread-veined, is hanging over the side of her bed. A stranger's hands pull back the wet blood-sodden sheet.

LOOK AT HER.

He looks at his dead Marion.

IS THIS YOUR WIFE?

He looks at her.

Marion. Bloody. Her nightgown is pulled up. Undergarments, thighs, breasts on show. Angry scar all the way down her chest from her heart operation. Marion is modest. William has never seen her scar before now. Men in overcoats are looking at the scar. Men in uniforms in his house and his wife's bare thighs. He can't look but he must.

They are all staring at him. All the men in his house with overcoats and uniforms. The sheet on his own bed is yanked off.

IS THIS YOUR SISTER-IN-LAW?

One of Margaret's eyes is open. The other one is swollen shut.

IS THIS YOUR WIFE'S SISTER?

She has a hole in her temple. It's where the red has come from.

IS THIS MARGARET BROWN?

He looks at his dead sister-in-law. Her face is blue and swollen at the side.

Watt thinks he is in hell. He isn't. He's on the threshold.

Hands yank him down the corridor. His eyes still aren't working. White flashes are still blinding him but he is aware of DS Mitchell, sneering at his shoulder. They spin him around to face into the bedroom.

HER?

He recoils from his dead daughter. He clamps his eyes shut but his mind assembles a brutal picture from scraps.

Her breast.

A nipple.

Moon-white skin.

Hugely swollen jaw.

Slumped.

Dear, soft neck, stained with splashes of burgundy blood. Up the wall behind her, all up the wall.

Hot acid vomit jets from William Watt's mouth onto the wall in the hall. It shoots from his nose. It squeezes out of his tear ducts and blinds him further. It drips down the flock wallpaper Marion has only just put up. He blinks the digestive acid out of his eyes but the flash spots continue. He's glad of them now.

As he tells the court about identifying the bodies Watt relives it. He lifts the glass of water to sip but the memory of being sick is so vivid that he can't bring himself to put anything in his mouth. He remembers hot vomit burning his chin, dripping. He remembers the filthy, pungent smell. He's shaking as he puts the glass back down carefully.

If Watt was being devious he would fake a collapse here. It's the logical point to fall to pieces, have the attending doctor come up and take his pulse. But that happens later.

M.G. Gillies asks him if it is possible, as the defence have suggested, for Watt to drink for six hours in the residents' lounge and then drive ninety miles to Glasgow, kill his family, drive the ninety miles back in the same night without detection. Watt declares, 'Oh! You couldn't drive! *Never* could you drive!'

Everyone drives drunk. It's a self-deprecating joke to claim you were following the white lines in the middle of the road because you were so drunk. No one believes him.

The photos of Watt in his driveway, as he came into the house and then left afterwards, are printed in all of the papers. Watt looks stunned and frightened and half mad in them.

An anonymous tipster sees them and calls the police and says Mr Watt has a girlfriend.

In court, Watt is asked about extramarital dalliances and, shamefaced, admits to 'several lapses'. To take the bad look off him, Gillies asks about Marion's heart operation, as though a sick wife is, by necessity, a cuckolded wife. Men have needs. Marion's operation was very dangerous, Watt tells him. Experimental. He didn't want her to have it but she went ahead anyway.

Days after the pictures of Watt are published a mechanic comes forward. He works in Lochgilphead, near the Cairnbaan

Hotel. He thinks the police should know that Mr Watt had his car serviced that Sunday, in the morning. He had his petrol tank filled up. The Vauxhall's lights kept cutting out and the mechanic offered to fix them if Watt left the car overnight with him. Watt said he couldn't leave the car because he needed it for a journey.

But the police find the Vauxhall petrol tank is full, minus what it took to drive back to Glasgow with DS Mitchell in the morning. It should be missing three times that much petrol if he drove home, murdered everyone and got back to the Cairnbaan before breakfast. They visit everywhere en route but can't find anywhere Watt could have refilled.

The round trip is done and timed at five hours. But the test was done during the day. Watt would have done it in the dark, on unlit, potholed roads. The only route runs over a dangerous pass on a hill so steep that the summit is called 'The Rest and Be Thankful'. This is a time when cars overheat on any incline. A wise driver will always have one eye on the temperature gauge after taking a hill and will pull over to let the engine cool. It can take half an hour or so for the heat to lift. Watt would also have had to cross the River Clyde. The test drive was done when ferries are frequent but the Renfrew Ferry is erratic at night. Realistically, the drive would have taken much longer than five hours.

The police start to doubt that Watt could be responsible.

But then more witnesses come forward.

A week after the discovery of the bodies in Fennsbank Avenue, nine men stand in a line-up in Rutherglen Police Station. William Watt is one of them. The Renfrew ferryman walks along the line-up, peering into faces, looking men up and down. To pick a person out of the line-up the witness must touch them and say, 'This is the man.' This rule was introduced to stop the cops choosing the identified party themselves. The Renfrew ferryman reaches forward and touches William Watt's soft businessman's hand, scratching it with his ragged calloused fingers. *This is the man,* he hisses, *This is the man.*

In court Watt admits that he was picked out by the ferry-man as having been on the 3 a.m. Renfrew Ferry on the night in question. He says he doesn't understand how the man could have picked him out when he wasn't even there.

The ferryman also picked out the Vauxhall Velox in the Rutherglen Police Station car park. He identified Queenie from a pack of eight dogs. But he is a bad witness in court. He keeps calling the car 'the Wolseley', which is a very different-looking car from a Vauxhall. He comes over as an attention-seeker who obsessively contacts the police. He's never off the phone to the police about 'suspicious passengers'. He has a history of noting down the registration numbers of all the cars on the ferry but didn't do it that night because, he says, it wasn't his shift, he was covering for a friend.

The second witness swears he saw Watt parked on Loch Lomond side at a quarter past two on the morning of the murders. He was driving his wife when he saw a car hurtling towards him. The lights switched off suddenly, and the car pulled up. He passed it and saw a lone driver, smoking a cigarette. The witness admits in court that he didn't see the driver's face but picked Watt out of a line-up of thirty because the driver was smoking his cigarette in a particular way: his index finger was curled over the top, as one might smoke a pipe. In the identification parade he asked all thirty gentlemen to mime smoking a cigarette and picked Watt out on the basis of the gesture.

Watt tells the court about being arrested for the murders.

Because his photograph has been published in all of the papers witnesses have no trouble identifying him. Neither do the other prisoners in Barlinnie. As Watt is walked to his cell they gather on the landings and chant his name. Because Watt owns a string of bakery shops, one wit shouts 'One killer, one scone' and everyone laughs at him. The meaner men shout that he'll hang. The place smells of shit and piss left in buckets overnight.

Mr Watt is in Barlinnie for sixty-seven days until he changes lawyer. Dowdall gets him out. The evidence is thin, but the police never stop believing he is responsible. They follow him everywhere. They question all his business contacts. They park outside his residence and businesses. They continue to interview people about him. Watt finds out that they are not looking for anyone else.

Watt tells the court that he felt it was up to him to 'turn detective' and solve the case himself. He let it be known through Mr Dowdall and his own contacts in the underworld that he was seeking information about the Burnside Affair. He would be receptive to any and all information on the matter and was willing to travel or meet anyone who might help.

'Before this meeting with Mr Manuel you had accompanied Mr "Scout" O'Neil to the police station in Rutherglen?'

'Yes. I had occasion to meet with Mr O'Neil. He knew I was seeking information about this affair. He informed me that just a few days before the Burnside murders he had sold a Webley revolver to Mr Peter Manuel, the very man I had been hearing so much about.'

'What did you do when Mr O'Neil told you this?'

'I took Mr O'Neil to Rutherglen Police Station *at once* so that he might make a statement to that effect.'

'And what did this information lead the police to do?'

Mr Watt looks older suddenly. 'Nothing,' he says quietly.

Lord Cameron asks him to speak up.

Mr Watt raises his face to the court. 'The police did nothing with this information. Nor any subsequent information I brought them relating to the murders. It was after I took Mr O'Neil to the station, with this sensational information about which they did nothing at all, that I realised I had to crack the case myself.'

'You found the man who sold your suspected killer the gun, you took that man to the police, and they did *nothing*?'

'Nothing.'

M.G. Gillies asks kindly, 'You must have felt terribly discouraged?' It's a prompt for Watt to tell the court about his painful experiences.

'Certainly not!' declares Watt bumptiously. 'Never that!'

M.G. Gillies sags a little, fiddling with his notes. He tries again. 'Six months after Mr O'Neil went to the police with you, you finally met Mr Manuel face-to-face, in early December 1957, in Whitehall's?'

'Yes.'

'Though you were by now convinced that Manuel had killed your family, you were willing to spend an entire evening in his company?'

'What other option did I have? The police were certain I was responsible. Somebody *had* to do something. Find *something.*' Watt pauses for a breath. 'The police did nothing but follow me around all the time. Every time I had a business meeting they would turn up the next day and question everyone from the merest janitor to my business contemporaries. It was –' he fumbles for a word that isn't 'embarrassing' because it is bigger than that – '*awful.*'

And now he breaks down. Crying at the wrong time. A full-grown man, bubbling about foiled business opportunities when he could have cried for his murdered family and made them like him.

It's an uncomfortable moment. The lawyers look away. The public pass bags of sweeties, blow noses and rearrange the coats on their knees. The doctor steps forward and takes Watt's pulse.

Watt has obviously been coached in his evidence, as have many of the witnesses. Startling to a modern reader is the frequency with which witnesses ask lawyers if they should say this bit now, or interrupt their own evidence to point out that the prosecution has forgotten to prompt them into a bit of the story that they've practised together.

A good liar can be taught to spontaneously repeat statements ad nauseam. Honest witnesses often seem disingenuous after coaching.

The doctor nods to Lord Cameron, indicating that, in his professional opinion, Mr Watt is not dead or dying. Just to be certain, Lord Cameron commands that Watt be given a glass of water.

Mr Watt drinks it dutifully, like a child. He drinks all of it. He catches his breath and the doctor steps away.

M.G. Gillies continues. 'So, your investigations led you to arrange a meeting with Mr Manuel?'

'No,' Watt corrects him. '*He* arranged a meeting with *me*. He sought me out through Mr Dowdall. They arranged the meeting between them but I was very keen to meet him.'

'Why so?'

'From my investigations I had become convinced that Peter Manuel had killed my family.'

'And you were convinced of this at the time that you met him?'

'Utterly. I met him to ascertain what I could. Mr Dowdall informed me that Manuel knew where the gun was and I was trying to get that for the police. I thought if I could get him to give them the gun it would be something real, a physical *thing* that would prove it wasn't me.'

'And you spent the entire night with him?'

Watt nods adamantly. 'Until six in the morning. Until I dropped him off at his parents' house in Birkenshaw.'

Gillies says this very slowly: 'Mr Watt. With the benefit of hindsight, do you think you *should* have met and spent all this time with him?'

This is rehearsed and Watt picks up on the cue: he turns stiffly to the jury.

'I DIDN'T KNOW WHAT ELSE TO DO,' he says. Then turns and smiles at M.G. Gillies as if to say, See? I *can* take a prompt, sometimes. 'It made perfect sense at the time. I felt I had to meet him.'

Grieve gets up for the defence. He makes Watt go over the night with Manuel again and again. Grieve knows it is the oddest thing this very odd man has done. Chunks of the night are missing: they meet at Whitehall's, they go to Jackson's, they stop briefly in the Steps Bar, they meet Watt's brother, John, at the bakery in Bridgeton and wait in the Gleniffer Bar for John to finish work. Then they go to John's house in Dennistoun and eat bacon and eggs and drink for over an hour and a bit. Watt and Manuel leave there towards four in the morning and two hours later arrive in Birkenshaw, which is a ten-minute drive from John's house. No, Watt doesn't remember what happened during that time. It does seem like a long time for a short drive. Well, maybe they left later then, he doesn't know. It was a long night.

What did they talk about during the night? Well, Manuel said he had the gun and then told Watt that the people who committed the murders had made a mistake. They actually meant to kill and rob the Valentes next door. But Manuel knew practically every stick of furniture in the Fennsbank Avenue house, he knew where all the rooms were and what the bedspread felt like. He even knew what sort of gin they had in the house. Watt and Manuel were together for eleven hours. The reported conversation between them would have taken half an hour.

Abruptly, Grieve asks Watt if he has bad feet?

Yes, Watt admits that he does have rather bad feet.

'You suffer from corns?'

'Yes,' Watt says warily. He admits to having three corns, though he fails to see how this is relevant.

'Did you tell DS Mitchell that you had been cutting your corns in the hotel room in Cairnbaan before you came to Glasgow that day?'

'Yes, I did tell him that.'

'And this was to explain why you had blood on your hands, under your fingernails?'

'Yes.' Watt dabs his forehead. 'From cutting my corns.'

'But you had been fishing?'

'Yes.'

'Did you cut your corns before or after you had been fishing?'

'I don't recall.'

'Fish generally swim in water, do they not? One might assume your hands would have been washed clean of blood if you cut them *before*?'

'Well, it must have been after then.'

'You were brought back to the hotel on an urgent matter, you were told that your family had been all been shot dead and you must go immediately to Glasgow to identify their bodies yet then you went off to cut your corns? That's how you got blood all over your hands?'

'I don't recall!'

Grieve finishes Watt's torment with a final flick of the whip. 'Did you kill your family, Mr Watt?'

Watt waves a hand in the air and announces: 'What a profession! What a profession!'

Does he mean lawyering is an odd profession or that Grieve is wrong when he professes that Watt killed his family? No one knows but the statement is widely reported as an example of how odd Mr Watt sounded on the stand.

The last thing he says before getting down is an unprompted announcement. 'I would never hurt my girls,' he says. But the jury aren't making notes. They aren't listening. They have too much to take in already, about the blood and the witnesses and the apparent confessions to Mitchell. The press don't care because they already have a character for Watt and this doesn't fit.

As he is helped down from the witness box and climbs effortlessly onto the stretcher, Watt thinks his part in this case is over.

It isn't.

Peter Manuel will sack his lawyers and represent himself in the case. Arguing that important matters were not aired at this time, Manuel will recall William Watt as a witness. He will question him about their night together himself.

5

Monday 2 December 1957

WILLIAM WATT IS FAR too drunk to drive. Normally he wouldn't have more than eight or nine drinks before getting behind the wheel but tonight he has had a good deal more than that. So he is driving very slowly, for safety purposes. There's another reason he is going slowly: he hasn't quite worked out what to do yet. There are a number of possibilities but he's befuddled with the drink: he can't think them through to the final play. One wrong move could be catastrophic.

Watt has money. The bakery business is a cash business and Watt makes full use of that fact. He has cash stashed all over the place, in his house, in each of his five bakery shops. He has a five-pound note rolled up and tucked into his sock right now. He has money hidden in his girlfriend's flat. He can pay Manuel but Manuel is a career criminal. If he does give Manuel money he has to be careful. Watt doesn't want him to know where his money is.

He's not sure how to handle the gun. He can't simply get it from Manuel and take it to the police. They already suspect him so if he turns up with the gun they could use it against him. He needs to get Manuel to tell him where it is, needs a witness to him saying it, and then he needs to get the police to go and get it from there themselves. Unless Manuel has it on him now, in which case he mustn't touch it.

It's all too complicated for someone as drunk as he is, and he is trying to drive as well. Briefly, he considers getting money from his girlfriend, Phamie. He has two hundred pounds on top of a cupboard in her flat, but if he went there Manuel might go back later and attack her. Watt drives slowly and imagines Phamie being sex-attacked by Manuel. He knows Manuel's history, about the girls he has forced himself on. William Watt can't really conceive of rape. He imagines such an encounter as essentially consensual but perhaps more than gently insistent on the gentleman's behalf. He doesn't imagine a middle-aged woman, just off the bus, being hit in the face with a brick. He imagines Phamie, shocked and surprised as Manuel looms over her, being more than gently insistent. Watt wonders whether he finds this erotic but realises that no, he finds it very alarming. Phamie's shock makes Watt realise how much he cares for her. He wants to protect her from such surprises. He imagines dear, young Phamie's cheeks streaked with surprised tears and her face morphs into Vivienne's dead and bruised face, splattered with blood. Watt feels that like a punch in the colon. He needs to shit very suddenly.

Abruptly a horn blares and lights flash in his rear-view mirror. 'What in blazes!'

Manuel laughs at him. 'You've stopped the bloody car!'

Watt has stopped in the middle of the Albert Bridge. He hadn't noticed because he was driving so slowly in the first place. The engine has stalled.

'You're too drunk to drive.' Manuel waves the driver past.

Watt is proud of his ability to drive drunk. 'I'll have you know I'm a famously good driver.'

'Are ye now?'

Watt takes his foot off the brake and lets the car roll down the other side of the bridge. 'Better than Stirling Moss, any day of the week.'

At the other end of the bridge he restarts the engine. The High Court glides past on the left, a long, low blackened building with a columned portico.

Manuel's face follows it. 'Ever been in there?'

Watt knows the question is a prompt. Manuel wants Watt to bat the question back so he can roll out his stories. Watt decides not to, out of spite, because he is defensive about his driving,

'Why the hell would I have been in there?'

It's a throwaway line but neither of them says anything for a while so the spiky comment hangs uncomfortably in the car.

They're not getting on any more. They both start to think about what they want from each other.

Watt takes a left and plunges into the tunnel under St Enoch's railway lines. A train grinds slowly by overhead. The railway tunnels are dark, a piss-tang smell seeps in through the windows. The coal smog is heavy and damp here, it swirls at ankle height. This dank world is peopled with tramps and whores from Glasgow Green and clapped-out street fighters. A burning brazier lights men with fight-flattened noses slumped against a crumbling black wall.

The car makes it out the other side and they head up town, dodging rumbling trams and staggering drunks. Watt is sobering up. He feels his rational mind wake up. He felt terribly drunk just then because of the confusion of their leaving Jackson's Bar so suddenly, of their coming out from the warm into the cold, leaving the embrace of good regard for a cold street and a sore conversation, these things have thrown him off his stride, made him melancholy, but he's regaining equilibrium. He makes a decision: he will take Manuel to his brother John over in Bridgeton. John will be sober. John will witness Manuel telling William where the gun is. He glances at his watch. It's ten to ten. Too early. John will still be finishing the books. Watt needs to play for time.

They cross a busy junction and Watt realises why he is feeling so sad: he misses the power he felt in Jackson's. His mind rolls through ways to get that back and Ah! He realises where they are. The Chamber of Commerce is one street over, straight ahead is the Sheriff Court, the Merchants House, the City Chambers, the Trades Hall. This is the epicentre of Glaswegian prosperity and respectability.

A good, warm feeling washes over him. He drives slowly on, passing the Trades Hall, a perfectly symmetrical Robert Adam building. It is full of rich people and rich things, friezes, oak-panelled rooms with roll calls of officer bearers since 1605 etched on them. Power and prosperity and respectability. Watt wants to sit outside and warm his face in the glow of it.

But Peter Manuel is common and Watt cannot be seen with him and being this drunk is disgraceful. Still, even being near the Trades Hall would rekindle that lovely cosseted sensation. He draws over to the kerb and parks.

'Why d'you stop?'

Watt smiles graciously. He opens his mouth and shuts it and thinks – I want to be near powerful, upper-class people. It thrills and comforts me. I want to be near them, not you. You make me less. You are cheap.

He can't say that. He nods across the road. 'Swift one in the Steps Bar?'

It is a clerks' pub, full of office types, straights. Manuel smiles at the soft lights of it. He is aspirational, Watt forgot that. It'll be a treat for him to go in there for one and on the way back out Watt can look at the Trades Hall again, at the windows and the beautiful doors, at the historic stained glass. Since 1605 the Guilds of the Fleshers and the Hammermen, the Maltmen and the Gardeners and all the other trades have had their associations here or nearby. Some of the Baking families go back fifteen generations, almost to its foundation. Over the centuries the networks tighten and the money builds until a guild of grocers, worried about cheap apples from Ayr, have spawned slave armies, funded fleets and built an empire. The Trades Hall and the Merchants House work together. They are power and money and respectability. The Industrial Revolution saps their official power but by then they've amassed so much money it hardly makes a dent.

Watt sees himself as the coming man. He's a businessman, not a tradesman, his path will be through the Merchants House, but still, as he locks his car door, his eyes linger on the warm windows of their sister association, the Trades Hall. He thinks he will soon take his place in that line of dynamic men who made the world cleave to their will. This they did by having the mettle to do things others would find distasteful. They gain mastery by enslaving weaker men, by profiteering, doing that which must be done, by meeting Peter Manuel. It is a timely reminder of what he is doing this for. The lights warm the back of his fat neck as he crosses the road away from it.

The entrance to the Steps Bar is a few stairs up from the street. There are two doors. Red carpet creeping beneath one denotes the lounge area, red and white tiles under the other the public bar. They go through the door to the public bar, the cheap seats.

An oily smog of cigarette smoke hangs in the room. Four or five men sit alone at tables. They all look tired. They are suited in the old-fashioned way, double-breasted, wide-shouldered, conservative business fashion from ten years ago. The ashtrays are glass, not tin. It is a confident signal that the clientele are trusted not to hit each other and if you want that sort of evening then just move on, bub.

Watt and Manuel approach the bar. Watt orders half and halfs. The wiry, weathered barman has a grubby black apron and steel suspenders on his sleeves. Watt winks: Make the Scotch doubles. The barman salutes with two fingers to his temple, As you will, sir.

Watt looks at Manuel, expecting him to be pleased, but Manuel rolls his eyes. 'Watt, don't think you can get me drunk. I can pour this stuff down my neck all night.'

Watt is glad that Manuel has mistaken his need for drink for a cunning ploy. He is quite self-conscious about his drinking.

The drinks arrive. Watt drinks half of his beer and then drops his shot glass into it. It's a silly thing to do, childish, a way of making the drink more fun. He lifts the double glass to drink and sees Manuel disapprove.

That cuts him. He's warming himself at the thought of the Trades and the Merchants, sharing their money and power and status, and now a man who is just out of prison is sneering at him.

Watt drinks. Through the white froth smeared on the beer glass he sees Manuel's expression deepen. Uncomfortable, Watt keeps drinking because he doesn't want to put the glass down and have a conversation about his drinking. But there, it's finished and he has to. He puts the glass on the bar.

Manuel doesn't say anything about his drinking. He looks at Watt, neither kindly nor unkindly, and mouths one word. *Money.*

Watt looks at Manuel's drink, he flicks a finger, go on, drink that. Manuel leaves a pause, looking around the bar, making it clear that he isn't drinking because he's been told to by Watt. He could take it or leave it. He is choosing to drink. He picks up his beer and just before he takes a drink he glances at Watt's empty double-glass and says, 'Take a bucket, don't ye?'

Manuel has seen that he has a weakness for the drink. Watt feels uneasy now. He starts to sweat. His brain tells him to blurt something.

'There? Where we parked. Outside? 'S the Trades Hall.'

Manuel is still drinking but Watt has finished his drink. He looks forlornly at the glass. He desperately wants to order another but Manuel will judge him. He wishes he was drinking alone. He gibbers on.

'Trade guilds of Glasgow. Trade unions of the Middle Ages. Ancient. Beautiful. A *lot* of money.'

Manuel is listening. His beer is two-thirds full. His hand rests on his glass and Watt sees him look at his fingernails. They are broken and dirty. Hard physical work. Manuel curls the face of his nails in to face the glass.

Quite suddenly Watt understands. Manuel isn't judging Watt's drinking. Manuel is snarling because he is intimidated by the bar and the suited people in it. He is intimidated by the Trades Hall, or doesn't know anything about it. Because, of course, Peter Manuel is a workingman and a Catholic, they're not welcome. He won't even have heard of such things. The Trades Hall, the Merchants' Guild, they keep their heads down.

'You ever heard of the Merchants' Guild?'

Manuel shrugs vaguely and drinks to cover his face. Watt leans down to keep his voice low. 'They own Glasgow. Have seats on the Corporation. Between them they own all of the land Glasgow's built on. *Power.*'

Manuel is determined not to be impressed by anything Watt says.

'They own George Square, Hutchesontown, Tradeston, all of the banks of the Kelvin River. They take in *two million sterling* in feu duties every year.'

'Much?'

'Two million. Every year.'

Now he has Manuel's attention. Watt sees his eyes widen and narrow. Two. Million. Sterling. He sees Manuel smile, imagining sacks of cash. Sacks of money he can rob and take away. But it all goes through the books in cheques and bank drafts, paid through lawyers and suchlike. You can't rob that sort of money. It would take an elaborate swindle and Manuel doesn't have that in him.

Still, Manuel is so distracted by the thought Watt feels he can order a drink now. He looks up but, disappointingly, the barman is muttering into the telephone, a hand over his mouth.

Manuel turns to Watt with a stiff neck. 'Who did you say gets this money?'

Watt smiles, sees that Manuel's weakness is money, robbing it, getting it, knowing where it is. The barman has hung up. Watt catches his eye and nods for another round.

Manuel looks at Watt, his eyes widened with avarice. He thinks maybe Watt has seen the bags of cash. It makes Watt chuckle.

'Do they keep it across the road?' Manuel sounds casual. 'How do you know that?'

'Their accounts are made public at the end of every tax year.'

'You a member in it, then?'

The barman brings the salving drink just in time because Watt isn't a member of the Merchants' Guild and it's a bit of a sore point.

'Not yet. But I will be. One day.' He lifts his Scotch and drinks. He looks at Manuel, whose fingernails are chipped, who didn't even know the Merchants' Guild or the Trades Hall existed until Watt told him a minute ago. Watt suddenly realises how much better he is than Manuel. This buoys him. 'I'll be *President* of the Merchants' Guild one day, you mark my words. Know what that means?'

Manuel shakes his head, still smiling about the money.

'The President is the "Second Citizen of Glasgow". After the Provost. And that'll be me. Third Citizen is the Deacon Convener of the Trades Hall.'

'So, how come you're not a member now? Is it too dear?'

Watt laughs joylessly. '"*Too dear*"? No. Well, it is expensive, but I can easily –' He rolls his fat hands away before remembering that he shouldn't make a big thing of having money. He stops. 'Hm. No. Technical . . . To be a member you have to be nominated by other members and so on and so forth.'

'Ha! They won't have you.'

They are standing close.

'Yes. They will. They *will*.' Watt taps his nose. 'Ways and means.'

They drink thoughtfully.

'I'm a writer.'

Watt almost looks around to see who said that. Manuel is looking into his beer. He looks worried.

'I write stories. Haven't had any published yet but ...'

Watt is blown away. *'Really?'*

A little coy, Manuel nods. 'Aye.'

Watt blinks hard. 'Have you written many stories?'

Manuel shrugs. 'Nine.'

'Nine!'

Manuel is pleased by this reaction, 'Yeah. Nine full stories. Sent them off. I'm starting a novel soon.' Manuel lies all the time but he's telling the truth about this. He has never told anyone before, apart from his sister.

'Good Lord! An *author*? That's absolutely amazing!' Watt is impressed. He can't imagine sitting down to do that, or wanting to. 'I had no idea!'

'Well, I haven't had anything published yet.'

'I believe persistence is a virtue in that game, isn't it?' Watt knows nothing at all about this. 'I'm quite sure you will be published. *Quite* sure.'

Manuel drinks and feels kindly towards Watt. They're both excluded from things they shouldn't be. It bonds them. Standing so close in an empty public bar makes them feel that they are together, that they are close. Watt furnishes each of them with cigarettes.

A draught from the street hits Watt and Manuel at the same time. The barman startles and slides behind the gantry. They turn to look at the door.

Shifty Thomson skulks into the lounge.

Shifty's wide-leg grey slacks hang precariously from his bony hips. His jacket is a loud blue check, his shoes brown and beige. Shifty always looks as if he stole the clothes he is wearing. Nothing fits or suits him.

He's looking back at the windows to the street but heads straight for Watt and Manuel. He doesn't need to look for them. He knows exactly where they're standing. Shifty works for Dandy McKay and Watt suddenly realises that the barman called the Gordon Club to say they were in here. Watt looks at the barman who is hiding behind the gantry and watching. This is strange. Watt rarely drinks in here. Either the barman got lucky or Dandy has the whole city looking for them. The barman doesn't seem like a man who ever gets lucky.

Shifty Thomson is now standing in the tight huddle of them. He looks away and rubs his nose.

'Dandy's saying yees've get tae t'club.'

Shifty never looks you in the eye when he speaks. His diction is poor, as if his teeth are all smashed up or his jaw is wrong, but it isn't. He chooses words that jangle, inelegant rhythms that grate, so that his next word can never be anticipated by someone earwigging nearby. People usually have to ask him to repeat what he has just said but Watt and Manuel have both heard him. They don't know who he is talking to though.

'Might one enquire, Shifty: of the two of us, whom are you addressing?'

Shifty sucks his cheeks in. 'M'nel.' He looks at the ceiling. 'Dandy's at Gordon. You've tae up there. Pronto.'

Shifty reels away abruptly, falling back from the tight trio like a side peeling off an upright banana. Three big strides and he's at the door. And then he's gone.

Manuel sucks violently on his cigarette, empties his whisky into his mouth, swallows and only then breathes out a long stream of smoke through his nostrils. As he exhales Watt sees his eyes dart this way, that way, looking for the angles, for a way out.

'You going?'

Manuel shakes his head but they both know he has to go. Dandy McKay ordered it. The Gordon Club is just a few blocks away.

Watt looks at the barman who flinches.

'Did you call the Gordon?'

The barman shrugs and whispers, 'We wiz told we had to.'

'Who told you?'

'Word went out. Everb'dy's been told.'

Watt can't quite believe it. '*Everybody?*'

The barman shrugs helplessly.

Watt knows how powerful Dandy McKay is. He knows the weaselly barman had no choice, but still, Watt is frightened, and he takes it out on him.

'It stinks in here,' he announces to the room. 'Let's go.'

He throws money onto the bar. A shilling rolls off, dropping noisily onto the metal trap into the cellar. It makes the stoolie barman jump. They walk out, banging the door as they go.

In the street, struck by the cold once again, they stop and Manuel lifts his jacket collar. He is in a lot of trouble. Watt looks down at him. He knows Manuel is no innocent, but he also knows that trouble is a bad thing to be in a lot of.

He glances across the road and sees the Trades Hall door open. A gold-braided doorman hails a taxi for a prosperous couple. The man helps his mink stole'd wife into the cab before getting in himself, palming a tip to the doorman. The doorman watches the taxi drive away, adjusts his white gloves. The lights from inside the Hall are warm and clean and Protestant. They go back fifteen generations.

Watt prides himself on knowing all the different grades of society in Glasgow. He moves among them seamlessly. They all mistake him for their own, except the Merchants' Guild. They know he is not one of them. Especially now, since the Burnside Affair and the publicity. But Watt is convinced he can make up the ground. He can do it because he is certain that the way in is not respectability or staying out of the papers. The way in is money. You might be washed in the blood of the lamb, but the real cleanser of souls is money, and he's going to have a lot of money soon. If he can just sort this out.

'What's it going to take for me to get the gun?'

'I've got a joe. Take him, then I'll give you the gun.'

'But the police won't look at anyone but me.'

'Buzzies'll want him for it,' says Manuel. 'Bastard called Charles Tallis. Record as long as your arm.'

Manuel's eyes narrow, his mouth curls down. Watt has never heard of anyone called Tallis but he can see Manuel hates the man, wants bad things to happen to him. Manuel doesn't want to go down for it, Watt can see that, but he's struggling to find the connection between the gun and money and doing harm to a man called Tallis with a record as long as your arm. William Watt is good at long-term planning. Even where he can't see clear connections, he can usually imagine what they might be like. He can't here and grunts, shaking his head. It's not believable, not even to someone who wants to believe it.

Manuel sneers at the pavement. 'Tallis told me the whole thing was a mistake. He was after the Valentes next door.'

Watt is instantly sober. For a moment he forgets to breathe. The story could work. It may be more believable than the truth and really what difference does it make if it's Manuel or someone else? Watt isn't looking for justice but an ending to this story. He's a conversation away from the whole bloody mess being over. But Dandy McKay is after Manuel, seriously after him, this vessel of the potential solution. Watt needs to get this story resolved before Dandy gets him.

'Let's go and see my brother John.'

6

Monday 6 January 1958

THE THREE BOYS ARE all eight years old or thereabouts. They should be in school but aren't. They have been kicking around for an hour this morning looking for trouble and now they've found it.

A car, an Austin A35. It is parked in Florence Street in the Gorbals. A long, wide street of black-scalded four-storey tenements. Cars are rarely parked here and never left unattended. But this car is empty. It has dew on it so it has been here for a while. It is small and as cute as a button. It looks like a cartoon. Every edge is rounded, every contrasting line exaggerated. The grate is chrome, long and pinched, a prissy kiss of a grate.

The boys cross the road and sidle up to it. They try the driver's door and it opens. They can't believe their luck. They giggle, look around, waiting for a mother at a window to shout them away or a driver to run at them, but nobody does. Omniscient Gorbals mothers are watching from windows and doorways, but they don't care. It doesn't seem to belong to anyone. The boys get into an actual car.

They pretend to drive, take turns sitting in the driver's seat, waving their hands around the steering wheel like actors driving in the movies. One of them makes the passable sound of an engine by burring his lips and the others compliment him on it.

They search the car. In the glovebox they find a tin of travel sweets. The lid lifts off with a white puff of magician's smoke. Inside, translucent pink boiled sweeties are sunk into a nest of icing sugar. These are posh sweets.

Reverently, the boys take one each. They savour the flavour and this moment, when they are in a car, eating sweets, with friends. In the future, when they are grown, they will all own cars because ordinary people will own cars in the future but this seems fantastical to them now. In the future they will think they remember this moment because of what happened next, how significant it was that they found Mr Smart's car, but that's not what will stay with them. A door has been opened in their experience, the sensation of being in a car with friends, the special nature of being in a car; a distinct space, the possibility of travel, with sweets. Because of this moment one of them will forever experience a boyish lift to his mood when he is in a car with his pals. Another will go on to rebuild classic cars as a hobby. The third boy will spend the rest of his life fraudulently claiming he stole his first car when he was eight, and was somehow implicated in the Smart family murders. He will die young, of the drink, believing that to be true.

The boys are in the car for quite some time.

'GET THE FUCK OUT OF THERE, YA WEE SHITES.'

A polis has yanked the door open and his meaty hands are coming for them. The boys scramble out of the far door, spilling the sweets and the icing sugar all over the red leather seats and themselves.

They bomb it across the road, trailing sugary smoke. On the far pavement they run towards the river, their steps punctuated with excited leaps and squeals. They skip sideways past giant prams parked outside a shop. To the cries and burbles of the baby parliament, the boys belt up a close to a backcourt and run around a midden to hide. They crouch, panting and laughing, thinking they are miles and miles from the policeman when they're really just a few hundred yards away. He could find them if he wanted to.

Out in the street the policeman knows this is wrong. The car is new, clean and unlocked. It has been left unlocked in Florence Street where cars and policemen don't belong. He keeps his eye on it as he backs away to call it in from the police box around the corner.

The registration says it is a Mr Peter Smart's car. The police call the man's registered place of work. The work says Mr Smart is missing. He is the manager there but hasn't returned to work this morning after the five-day Hogmanay holiday. He hasn't been seen for nearly week.

A different policeman from Hamilton Police Station sets off to visit the family home in Sheepburn Road, Uddingston. Uddingston is a nice town, far enough away from Glasgow to stay nice. The poor people, mostly Catholics, are corralled into an estate nearby called Birkenshaw. Uddingston is an agricultural area, it is set in a landscape of soft hills, marred by mine works abandoned since nationalisation. Many of the mines were unsafe and inefficient, had dreadful working conditions.

He reaches Mr Smart's address in Sheepburn Road. It is a bungalow. Mr Smart is an engineer and built the house a few years ago with his own two hands. It looks a bit home-knitted, hasn't the detailing or finesse of a professional build. There is no ornamentation and the windows are smaller than the facade could support.

Tucked behind the house is a small garage, just big enough for a diminutive Austin A35. The officer walks up to it and finds it unlocked but empty. He feels sure he has the right house.

Though it is daytime both sets of curtains are drawn in the front windows. The policeman knocks. No answer. He tries the door and finds it locked. He walks around to the back of the house.

The kitchen door has a net-curtained window. He peers in. The kitchen is very tidy except for an empty tin discarded on the table. He squints and reads the label. Canadian Salmon in Oil. The lid has been dropped carelessly, odd in such an ordered room. The lid sits over the edge of the table, placed the wrong way down. If he moves his head, he can see light catch where the fish oil has soaked into the wood. They'll never get that smell out.

He sees a movement. A ginger tail curls lazily through the slightly open door into the back hall. It's a cat, which makes sense of the tin. The tail flicks and disappears.

He bends his knees and now he can see underneath the salmon tin lid on the edge of the table. A drip of oil has gathered, it catches the light. It is hanging there, threatening to fall onto the floor. Just hanging and waiting for a breeze or a knock, or two more molecules of oil to travel along the underside and join the build-up. Then the fishy oil will drop onto the floor and need cleaning up.

He goes back to the station. He hears that Mr Smart may have gone to visit his parents in Jedburgh on the 31st of December. It is now the 6th of January. The parents do not have a telephone. Mr Smart may have stayed on in Jedburgh, his parents are frail, but this does not assuage the officer's concern. Mr Smart would have taken his car, surely? The officer is uneasy. Mostly, it's the ginger tail and the tin on the table that bother him. He's very troubled by that and he doesn't know why.

He's eating his lunch pieces when he realises: if the Smarts had gone away visiting they would have put the cat out. If they forgot to do that then the cat would be trapped with no field mice or kind neighbours to feed it. It should be frantically hungry by now. The tin lid with the oil drip is still on the edge of the table. A hungry cat would have jumped up, knocked off the lid coated in delicious-smelling oil and licked it clean. But the cat hasn't. Someone is in the house.

With a sudden sense of alarm the policeman abandons his sandwich and hurries back to Sheepburn Road.

A neighbour rushes out to meet him, pulling her coat on over her pinny.

Officer! She runs across the road to him and explains that there is something odd going on in that house. She's already worried because of that Isabelle Cooke girl disappearing nearby. The lady telephoned the police herself about the Smarts' house, yesterday. Their car is gone but the curtains keep changing, closing and opening. She becomes more incoherent as she goes on: Doris Smart sets the curtains nicely, do you see? But the curtains are pulled roughly: they cross at the bottom but are open at the top. Doris is very house-proud –

The housewife stops. She touches her rollers and remembers that she is in the street. That is low class for this area. Suddenly aware that she is being seen, or very likely to be seen, she pulls the rollers out without removing her Kirby grips first, yanking at her hair angrily, making her eyes water. The officer feels for her. He thinks there is someone in there too but doesn't say.

He says he's going to force an entry to the house. Will she come and witness for him? She's glad to, even if she doesn't know what that means, not technically, she just wants someone to do something.

Together they go around the back of the house, walking up the twin tracks where the car has balded the grass.

She gibbers: Mr Smart built this house himself and she worries about gas and electricity and so on. How could he know about all of those things? And there's that business with the poor little Cooke girl. Well, it isn't a gas leak, he says, there's a cat in there.

There are twelve glass panels in the kitchen door. The officer uses his wooden truncheon on the lowest pane. It shatters easily, a tinkling shower of glass falls inside the still house.

The officer smiles reassuringly to the housewife. She tries to return the favour, but her smile is a cringe and her chin crumples. He reaches in through the empty frame, feeling for the snib. He twists it, turning the door handle on the outside and the door swings open.

The ginger cat is sitting very upright on the draining board next to the sink. It looks at him, shifts its front paws and waits to see what he will do.

He opens the door wide and calls soft hellos into the house. He steps in, his foot crunching on the glass, smelling for gas, listening.

It doesn't smell of gas. It smells of damp with a high tang of cat pee. Cold. So cold it dampens a strange smell which may be the earth foundations or something else. Or something else. He walks carefully across the kitchen to the back hall, listening. He can't hear anyone. In the hallway he skirts a sticky yellow puddle of cat's piss on the lino.

The door to the living room is open. Homemade paper chains are hung around the picture rail, newspaper text visible through watery red and green paint. It's the 6th of January and Christmas cards still line the mantelpiece. Doris Smart is very house-proud.

The officer doubles-back down the hall and finds a door slightly ajar. He pushes it with his elbow.

The soft creak of the door hinge gets louder and louder and louder until it is a scream, a shrill, eyeball-trembling scream, loud as Panzer tank fire, loud as a building collapsing on Belgian civilians, loud as the screams of a young soldier from Dundee with a pelvis mangled by a speeding truck carrying cabbages to Namur.

Don't come in! he screams at the housewife. She wasn't going to come in. His shouting only brings her to the door of the kitchen. She bends down and gives a Sunday smile through the pane of broken glass. Beg pardon?

Don't come in here. He speaks calmly, his panic harnessed. He didn't really mean 'don't come in'. What he really meant was he wished he had not come in.

He steps across the corridor to the opposite door. Pushes that one with his other elbow. Worse. Even worse in there.

The housewife smiles through the broken windowpane. Did you want me to come in?

In a loud sergeant major's voice he orders her to return to her home and telephone Hamilton Police Station. She will give this address and inform the senior officer that there have been murders here. His voice trills high because he is trying not to breathe in the smell.

The woman's eyebrows spring to her hairline, her face snaps away from the hole. He hears her walk, then run, around the side of the house, slippers flapping on the mud.

And he is alone in the damp cold.

Even without turning his head he can see, in the room on his right, a small boy's spectacles sitting on the night table. The boy is lying in the bed and the bed is red. The sheets are red, the blankets are red and the pillow is so profoundly red it has turned black. He can make out the curvature of the boy's small head on the pillow.

On his left, in the second room, a double bed. Worse in there. Daylight flickers through the curtains of the couple's bedroom, licking their covers. The bedclothes are red and dry and tucked up under their bloody chins. And there's a cat shit next to the bed. A small brown tube of cat shit.

The officer cannot move. His throat throbs. He cannot swallow. This officer fought through the Low Countries with the Scots Greys. He saw bits of people, bits of children, leftover bits, burnt bits. Back then he prayed to a God he still feared but no longer loved. He prayed never, ever to feel this again. But now he has.

7

Monday 2 December 1957

THE FACADE OF THE bakery in Bridgeton is pale yellow. 'Watt's Bakery and Dairy' is painted in blue above the window display. The paper blind behind the glass glows with a faint light. Watt opens the front door with his own fat set of keys and Manuel staggers in behind him. The shop is dark but for the light coming from the back office where John is counting up the takings.

'John! It's me! I have a —' he doesn't know what to call Manuel — '*pal* with me!'

There is a pause before John answers, though he must have heard them coming in.

'WAIT.' John's voice is flat and annoyed.

William knows he should not have brought anyone here at this time, when the money is being counted.

'John?'

'*WAIT.*'

So they wait.

Watt and Manuel stand in the dark shop looking at the empty glass shelves, swaying like a pair of lost idiot shoppers. Orange light from the street throbs in through the blind. Manuel takes his packet of cigarettes out. Watt says he can't smoke in here. Manuel turns to him, angry, but just then John comes out of the back office.

He is a slim version of William, the youngest of the three Watt brothers. He stands in the doorway and looks out at them.

In the company of someone sober, they both realise how very drunk they are.

Self-conscious, Watt raises a straight arm at his side. 'John! This is Peter Manuel who you have been hearing so much about. He is going to help me. He has a whole new slant on the Burnside Affair.'

Peter's chin is down. He looks up at John like a boxer on a poster. John is not the businessman William is, he can't see three moves ahead, but he makes up for it by doing the hard work. This is the end of his usual fifteen-hour shift and he's tired. He can't disguise his reaction to William arriving with a drunk chancer who claims to have stumbled on a conscience.

William attempts the sale again. 'This young man? *Splendid* fellow. An author, no less!'

Manuel sways with pleasure at the description, sneering and blinking slowly. John still doesn't seem to like the look of him.

Watt whispers in a hiss, spraying his sober, hygiene-conscious brother with spittle: '*He* knows who did the murders! He's going to *tell* us what happened and how we can get the gun.'

John sounds exhausted. 'Why are you here, Bill?'

'We need a witness. Peter has a story to tell about the Burnside Affair –'

'It's the TRUTH!' Manuel declares.

Watt hesitates. The statement undermines itself. He is suddenly not sure how well this is going to go or if he was wise to defy Dandy McKay by waylaying Manuel.

'And to get money,' adds Manuel.

'Yes,' says Watt, 'And to get money for Peter, here. For his trouble. He can tell us where the gun is, John.'

John watches Peter fumble a cigarette out of his packet and put it behind his ear for in-a-minute. Then John looks at William.

'You seem quite drunk, Bill.'

Watt is embarrassed by that and laughs. He can't think of anything to say. John says he has to finish up and why don't they go over to the Gleniffer Bar and he'll be over in half an hour.

William cringes. 'We're *slightly* hiding,' he says.

'Who from?'

William doesn't want to say Dandy McKay. That would make it seem very serious. John would make a big deal out of that.

'Disreputable fellows, a rough crowd.'

'Well, you'll be all right in the Gleniffer. It's just locals in there.'

'They found us in the Steps but we got away.'

John thinks he has misheard. 'They *met* you in the Steps?'

'No, they found us there.'

'They were looking for you and *found* you there?'

William nods. No one important ever goes into the Steps. It already sounds serious, 'We just need to hear his story.'

John doesn't know what William wants him to do. He glances to the back office, reminding William that the day's takings from all five of their shops are sitting on a table in there, being counted. He needs them to leave. John shrugs.

'You'll be all right for twenty minutes.'

There is nothing else to do. William nods at Manuel and they turn to the door. Watt opens it and holds it and Manuel bowls under his arm, out to the street.

William looks back at his sensible brother. John waves him out, rolling his eyes, but William nods, insisting: Go along with me, John, he is saying, this is a good plan. William is all plans. Most of them are good.

The door shuts behind them and the frosty night air envelops them. William can tell John is sceptical about the plan. William is too but less so. Manuel can get them the gun and he's an author. He'll tell them a good story, a credible story.

He looks down at his salvation. He sees Manuel through John's eyes for a moment: cheap shoes, threadbare jacket, baring his bad teeth. Manuel looks small and desperate and dishonest as he takes the cigarette from behind his ear and lights it. He glances down the road for the Gleniffer Bar.

Watt points across the road and they go over. He glances back at his shop. The window glows warm, the paintwork and glass are clean. It pleases him.

Watt has five shops now. The shops are very successful because their cakes are bigger than everyone else's. Rationing ended three years ago but women shoppers are trained to count every ounce. They know they are getting a good deal here, their eyes tell them that. They queue out of the door to buy in Watt's shops.

The shops are clean but the bakery house itself is in a vermin-infested shed in the backcourt. They have to put buckets out when it rains, which is nearly always. The war is over and new laws have just been passed to stop factories being run in unsanitary lean-tos. It is under this premise that William is buying land. Ostensibly to build factories on, he tells John and their company accountant. He has been helped to buy land. He buys bits of land other people don't even know are for sale, bits of Townhead and Cowcaddens that the council will be forced to buy to complete their Comprehensive Redevelopment Plan. Those strips of land will be priceless soon. It's all set: soon he will have a lot of money, but not respectability. He looks at Peter walking next to him. That depends on him.

They walk through the door and into the Gleniffer.

The floor is coated in swirled sawdust, put there to soak up spills. Ashtrays get emptied onto the floor because they'll sweep up at the end of the night anyway. There's a spittoon in the corner with a big sign warning patrons not to spit on the floor and spread diseases. The lights are bright and harsh. There's no toilet but the place still smells of piss. It is not a nice pub.

The woman serving has two scarves wrapped around her head like a gypsy. She's wearing several bangles and too much make-up for a woman in her thirties. Both Watt and Manuel avoid her eye.

They buy warm bottled beers and whisky that tastes a bit watery. Neither of them likes who they are in this pub. There are a few locals drinking together in moderation but mostly it's bitter lone drinkers swaying on their feet.

'So,' says Watt, trying to get them back to the point of the night when they were winners, 'will you write more?'

Peter smiles and looks around the bar. He stands taller in the compromising pub. He can comfortably be here now because Watt has asked that.

Peter Manuel is telling the truth about writing. He has written long-form fiction, ideas, short stories, precis of stories. He sends them off to well-known magazines. He has no success but he has fallen in love with the waiting. The waiting makes all of the indignities of his life tolerable because after that envelope slips his fingers into the postbox he feels reborn. In these glorious waiting times he imagines himself anew.

During these times Peter is going about, drinking in pubs, being barked at by dogs, sitting in the pictures, breaking into houses for meagre prizes, but simultaneously he is also being Peter Manuel Before-He-Was-A-Writer. The future crackles with possibility. Detached from the humdrum everyday, he begins to think of himself in the third person, to see himself through the prism of history.

There is the dog that barked at Peter Manuel.

Peter Manuel sat in this very seat at the pictures.

Peter Manuel drank just here, in this chair.

He loves this other Peter Manuel. This astonishing man, who moved among us, just as if he was nothing special.

He wants these pockets of wonder to go on forever. But they don't. Time ticks by and there is a gradual realisation that the magazine is not going to respond. The luminescent pride fades, as it dawns on him that weeks have passed and the Rolls-Royce hasn't arrived to whisk him off to magazine headquarters (he doesn't understand the economics of magazines).

The first time he posts a story it takes two months for the glow to dull. The second time it lasts for a month. The third time the hope dissipates after less than a fortnight, because he really tried that time, rewrote the story over and over, used his best handwriting.

Finally, one day, he holds an envelope on the lip of the post-box. He stares at the blackness inside. He can't drop the story in. He keeps it in his hand and walks to a field and sits on a hill and smokes a cigarette. Then he burns his story in the envelope. He tries to forget that feeling, the yearning for the man he might have been. But he can't forget it. It felt too good, this Other Possible Peter.

'You will help each other.'

The woman with the scarves and make-up is staring at them, her bangled hand dangling over the bar.

'Ah,' says Watt. 'Really?'

'He –' she points a lazy finger at Manuel then at Watt – 'Will help *you*. Your paths will cross again. He will pay the debt that hangs over him.'

Watt nods as Manuel seems to shrink by his side. Watt knows Moira is an idiot, he has met her before and she always does this. She thinks she's psychic, that's why she wears all the bangles and the headscarves. He turns to explain to Manuel. 'Moira, here, is a spiritualist. A seer.'

But Manuel is grey and frozen. He's staring at the floor, lost in the swirls of sawdust on the floor. He looks as if he might be sick.

The door opens. John is there. He nods to William but they still have drinks so William waves him over, trying to finish his while John makes his way across the room. John is not happy about any of this.

'We should go,' he says when he reaches them.

'*What did she mean?*' Manuel is asking Watt, as if John hasn't spoken.

William has been told many things by Moira. He comes in here often to wait for John to finish the books. She says vague things, good luck, bad luck, debts, sorrows. Never anything concrete, never anything that couldn't be sort of true.

'Moira, dear, might we have two bottles of Scotch to take away please?'

Moira smiles at Watt, delighted he is paying bar prices for a takeaway. She didn't see that coming.

Outside, John takes the truck and William and Manuel take the Vauxhall, and they all drive to John's house in Garthland Street in Dennistoun. They park behind each other, and go up the close to John's flat on the second floor. It is a nice close. All of the doors are painted to look like oak. The neighbours take their turn cleaning the stairs and doormats can be left outside without being stolen.

Nettie, John's wife, is in the warm kitchen. The table is set for two.

Nettie isn't at all pleased to see William with a drunk stranger in tow. She pinches her lips and says she only has enough stew for the two of them. John is making it clear that she is to welcome them though. Egg and bacon, he orders and she scuttles away and puts the frying pan on.

They sit around the kitchen table in the recess. She sits on the step stool at the table and gives the men the chairs.

Nettie and John are drinking tea with their dinner. Watt opens one of the two bottles of whisky he bought from the Gleniffer and pours himself and Peter generous mouthfuls. Peter Manuel eats his eggs by cramming them whole into his mouth.

When they have finished Nettie takes the dirty plates away and washes up. Then she leaves the kitchen.

The men stay at the table and Peter Manuel lights a cigarette. He looks at both of them. It feels like the start of a negotiation. John begins:

'What are you offering? I know you're an author but we need more than a good story at this point.'

Manuel blows a thick string of white smoke over John's head.

'I'm offering the gun. A named killer, the story and the gun.'

Watt waits for him to name a price, but Manuel doesn't. The money doesn't seem that important to him all of a sudden. John catches William's eye. John has spotted Manuel's mistake too. He's forgotten to charge them before giving them the information. John thinks it is a drunken mistake. William is seeing a pattern of chaotic behaviour, an inability to control impulses, a lack of long-term planning.

John leans in. 'How would we know it's not just any old gun?'

Manuel smokes and smirks. 'His name is Charles Tallis and he was after the Valentes.'

John and Watt look at each other. They speculated about the Valentes. The story sounds as if it might be plausible.

Manuel draws on his cigarette. He sits back and rests a knee on the side of the table. John and William sit forward, the better to hear.

'The whole thing was a mistake.'

Unseen in the hallway, Nettie leans against a wall and listens.

8

Thursday 15 May 1958

ISABELLE COOKE'S FATHER IS telling the court about the last night he ever saw his daughter. Mr Cooke knows he is a footnote in this story. His loss, his daughter, his life, is an aside. He is only here because Peter Manuel pled not guilty so the Crown needs his evidence. He would rather be anywhere else than here but he is dutiful.

Mr Cooke is a solid, decent man with an unblemished work record and a handsome wife. He describes his daughter in terms that are bland. Isabelle was a sweet girl. A good daughter. She always helped her mother around the house. She worked at the telephone exchange. She loved the dancing. He describes her like this because he doesn't want to talk about her openly, in front of other people, not the real Isabelle. They have looked at her underpants and fingered her underskirt. They dug her naked carcass up from the frozen January earth and saw her body, examined her private parts for signs of rape. Mr Cooke can't allow them any more of his real daughter, a giggler, unsure of the world and her place, feeling her way. The deep sleeper, funny, nasty sometimes too, loose in her prayers, with a fondness for fritters, tending to fat.

'For the benefit of the court, can you tell us about the last night you saw Isabelle?'

Mr Cooke clears his throat. He pauses.

'Isabelle was going to meet her boyfriend at a dance. It was a cold night. After tea she packed her dancing shoes into her handbag and put on her coat and her muffler. She was getting new dancing shoes for her birthday in January. She was excited about that. She said she was going to dance the soles off her old ones that night.'

Mr Cooke drops his chin to his chest. He feels unexpectedly emotional, overwhelmed by an image of her in the living-room doorway, pulling her coat on and smiling at him. He didn't pay attention to her because he was busy trying to starve the fire. The chimney needed cleaning, they'd been using damp coal, and the fire wasn't hot. He was holding a sheet of newspaper over the hearth, heating it up to burn the flue clean. Isabelle looked in on him but he only glanced back. His attention was on the fire, didn't want the middle of the newspaper to catch and burn.

'Don't be late.'

'Bye, Daddy.'

And then the door slammed behind her and she was gone and it was forever.

'But she didn't come home that night?'

'No, she didn't come home.'

'When did you realise she was missing?'

He draws a deep breath but the court is stuffy and it doesn't help. He tries again and this one works.

'We began to worry at eleven o'clock. She knows when she should be in and it was very unlike her to be late. I went out to look for her. I went to the bus stop and a bus came but Isabelle wasn't on it. Then I went home. By then it was a quarter to twelve. She still wasn't home. My wife telephoned the home of Isabelle's boyfriend and his mother put him on the phone. Isabelle had never arrived at the dance.'

Mr Cooke stops to take a drink of water. He cannot look at Peter Manuel in the dock. He is aware of him as a shadow in the corner of his eye, but he can't look at him. Mr Cooke keeps his eyes down and promises himself that soon it will be over and then he will feel better.

'She never got to the dance so we knew she was really missing. My wife telephoned the police and I went out to look for her on the road at first, in the train station, then in the fields.'

'The fields behind your house?'

'In the fields,' echoes Mr Cooke, 'the fields of Sandyhills and Burntbroom.'

His eyes drop to the wooden railing his hands are resting on, the fine oak grain lost to his fingertips. They are numb in the biting December cold. He feels it on his cheek, the tightness of his face closed against the robber wind. He feels wet ground squelch beneath his boots, sucking him into the earth. He looks for his Isabelle in the dark. He walks for four hours, up to Barrachnie, over to Foxley and up to Newlands Glen, returning to the house for tea he cannot taste, for another scarf, to talk to the police. He takes them and shows them where he has already looked. The fields are pitted with old mine shafts. It is dangerous in the dark if you don't know the area.

At first Mr Cooke is angry with Isabelle. He wants her to know what she is putting her mother through. When the anger lifts he wishes it back because then he is just terrified. He is so frightened he wants to hold his daughter tight and never let go. Then he just wants to hold her hand, then just to see her. Just to see her. The yearning is worse than the fear. The yearning is a sorrowing ache that burrows deep down into the core of him.

As the night wears on he gets less and less tired. Mr Cooke knows how men talk about girls. He knows what might have happened to his own Isabelle. Over the long hours in the dark, as all the hope he will ever feel is sucked out through his soles into the wet, treacherous earth, it comes to feel absolutely vital that he find the dancing shoes that she has worn thin with all her dancing.

In the hazy morning, when the careless sun bothers to come up, Mr Cooke sits in the living room by a fire that won't warm anyone, his outdoor clothes still on. He sits, listening to the re-assurances of policemen who are just doing a shift at their work.

She will be found. She has stayed the night with a friend who doesn't have a telephone. We are searching the hospitals, perhaps she has been run over.

But Mr Cooke knows what has happened to his daughter. It has happened before out there, in those fields. Girls and women attacked and no one caught. He thought, his wife thought, that women should not be out at that time. He thought and his wife said, they must be peculiar kinds of women to be out there at that time, in a field with a man. They didn't think these things because they were nasty people, or spiteful or uncaring. They thought these things so that they were not terrified all the time. Otherwise they would never have allowed their Isabelle out of the door.

As the hazy morning breaks Mr Cooke compromises his ambitions just once more: if he could just hold one of her shoes, her dancing shoes. Just one of them. He wants it so much he can feel the brush of soft worn leather, the curve of her heel against the pad of his work-hardened hand.

'We waited and she never came home,' he tells the court.

'And in the morning, what happened?'

'Her handbag was found in a burn about a mile and a half from the house. Her dancing shoes were missing.'

'Was the handbag found in the direction of the bus stop?'

'No. It was in the other direction. They found footprints. They think she had been chased over half a mile of fields. But they still couldn't find her.'

'And what happened then?'

'Nothing.'

Acres of nothing for year-long weeks. They found no more of her possessions. Mines were searched. They dredged the River Calder but found nothing. Until the 11th of January. Then they found her grave.

'How did you hear about that?'

Mr Cooke drinks again from the glass. He goes to put it down but he realises that he isn't ready to speak yet so he drains the glass and reminds himself that he is near the end of this and he is just a footnote and no one really cares but him.

'The police came to see us. They told us that a man had confessed, to that and other things. They said he took them to her grave in the middle of the night. "I'm standing on her." I remember them saying he said that. He showed them where her dancing shoes were. They were nearby. Under a pile of bricks.'

The shoes had been in the rain and the frost for almost a fortnight, under the dirt. Mr Cooke has yet to get them back but he knows they are not soft or shaped by her feet any more. They are ruined by exposure. They're just bits of ruined skin now.

The defence have no questions for Mr Cooke. He is allowed to stand down.

As he walks across the court Mr Cooke feels no better. He wonders where the sense of finality is. He is as bereft as he was before but now he feels his sorrow exposed for the entertainment of the public. His loss will be written about in the papers tomorrow, read about on buses by people who don't much care about Isabelle. People who don't really care are watching him now from the balcony seats. He wonders bitterly if they found his loss entertaining.

Angry, he looks up and catches the eye of a woman. She is ages with his wife. She is weeping openly, tears coursing down her cheeks, her hands clutched together as if she is holding his dead daughter's cold feet to warm them. A sob bursts from his mouth and Mr Cooke slaps a hand to his lips, ashamed, shocked at this sudden connection with a stranger. He jumps the stairs to the witness hall and clatters through the door.

In the privacy of the silent room his wife is waiting for him. She puts her arms around him and he sobs into her hair.

Mr Cooke thinks of the weeping woman in the gallery. His unique desolation was all he had left of his Isabelle. Now the crying woman has taken that as well. He has been robbed again.

Tuesday 3 December 1957

NETTIE WATT DOESN'T SAY anything, about any of it, ever. She is not called as a witness in the trial, she gives no interviews to the press. She is there though, throughout the night when Peter Manuel tells the story. She hears it sober, with the critical facility of a woman who has spent thirty-five years at the movies. She knows the difference between a good story and a bad one.

Nettie goes to the movies four or five times a week. She is ashamed of it. As regularly as Samuel Pepys swore off the theatre, Nettie swears off the movies. Just like Pepys, Nettie always back-slides. It's hard to go anywhere in Dennistoun without passing a cinema. There are two picture houses within a block of her house. Movies and newsreels run all day, every day. She moves between the Parade and the Picture House so that the staff don't notice how often she goes. If an usher comments – hello! you here again? – Nettie won't go back for a while. Sometimes, when she is in the town she will go to a bigger cinema where no one will see her. People don't go to the movies as much any more, since television came in, but Nettie is thirty-eight and she grew up at the movies, with movie stories.

She is listening to the men in the kitchen but they can't see her. She is leaning her back on the outside wall of the recess, her head to the side, the better to hear. The recess in the kitchen would have been used by the maid as a sleeping nook but people in two-bedroom flats don't have maids any more. Nettie and John use it as a dining area. It's a nice, draught-free part of the house. The men are talking quietly but the surrounding stone walls amplify their voices. She can hear everything, intakes of breath, glasses chinking against teeth, the 'pup' as a sucked cigarette is released from lips. It's like listening to a play on the wireless.

Manuel tells them that the whole thing was a mistake. The Watts were never the intended target. Tallis was after the Valentes, an Italian family who lived next door to William and Marion's house.

'Tallis went with an address for the Valentes but then the girl, Deanna, was at the window in your house so he thought they'd got it wrong.'

The story is compelling because Deanna *was* in the Watt house that night. She told the police that she went home at midnight, before the *Pop Parade* was finished, after Doris Day's 'Que Sera, Sera' was played at number 5. William points out to his brother: See? I told you he would clear this up. John grunts and Nettie can tell he's listening intently.

Charles Tallis thought the Valentes had money in the house. They have a successful confectioners business, a cash business, and they're Italian.

Italians are known for keeping cash and jewellery to hand in case they have to run. The war is not long past. As enemy aliens, Italians were rounded up and interned. Their houses and businesses were attacked. Now they're always ready to run. It's a safe guess that the Valentes would keep money in the house.

Charles Tallis, a man with a long history of housebreaking, went to Burnside with a widow-woman, Mary Bowes. Bowes is his girlfriend. They brought Martin Hart with them, he's a pair of thug hands Tallis takes housebreaking sometimes. Tallis really wanted Manuel, not Hart, what with all his experience and skills, but Manuel demurred because the plan was to break in and kill them all, except the girl, Deanna. They were going to make her tell them where the money was hidden and then kill her too. Manuel wouldn't go on the job because he doesn't want to hurt a young girl, that's not his way. So they took Hart as a substitute.

Then Tallis came to see Manuel the day before he went on the job. He asked to borrow Manuel's Webley revolver to kill the family with. Then he was going to give him the gun back. Sure, said Manuel, no problem.

Nettie straightens up. That's wrong. That is a narrative misstep. If Manuel's story was in a movie the audience would be jeering now. They would be shouting at the screen and throwing orange peel. Rubbish! They would shout. Go on wi' ye! You don't lend a murderer your gun. It can be traced back to you. No one would do that. And you certainly don't ask for it back afterwards unless you're pulling the old double cross. It occurs to her that maybe Manuel is pulling some sort of double cross. Nettie keeps one eyebrow raised though, as she settles back against the wall and waits to see if that's his game.

Manuel's tone is conspiratorial: so he loans Tallis the Webley. Next night Tallis goes to Burnside with Mary Bowes and Martin Hart.

In Fennsbank Avenue, they look for a place to watch the Valentes' house from. Lucky for them they find an empty house facing what they think is the Valentes' bungalow. Nettie nods. She knows this is true. The police found number 18 broken into that night as well. It's right across from the Valentes'. They break in and as they watch they see Deanna Valente at the window of number 5: William Watt's house. They think they had the address wrong.

In the vigil house Tallis, Hart and Bowes sit and smoke and wait and watch out of the window for the lights to go off. Tallis and the widow Bowes go to the bedroom for – you know – the men in the kitchen 'ho-ho'. Nettie's mouth tightens with disgust. The house belongs to two spinster women. It's not nice.

'WIFE.' John shouts for her. 'WIFE! ASHTRAY.'

Nettie startles. She doesn't want them to know she is just around the corner listening. She waits for a moment and then tiptoes silently into the kitchen. They pause while she gets a clean ashtray from the cupboard and puts it on the table, taking the dirty one away to empty into the grate. They stay silent until she is out in the hall so she knows they don't want her listening. She takes the ashtray into the living room and empties the ash and stubs in the unlit fire. Then she scurries back to her listening wall.

The murmur continues: Tallis, Bowes and Hart go over to the Watt bungalow.

Tallis breaks the glass on the side window, opens the front door and they all creep into the quiet house. They shut the door behind them. In the house, everyone is asleep.

Nettie sees them in William's hallway. Backlit through the glass on the door, their faces in black shadow, feathers in their hair, tomahawks silhouetted at their sides.

Everyone is asleep.

They can hear the breathing in the house, the in-out of breathing, as they stand in the silent hallway, on the red hall carpet, next to the chiffonier with the picture of the yellow dog above it and the empty key rack on the other wall.

'*Empty?*' asks John, puzzled.

'There's no keys on the key rack,' says Manuel 'All the wee hooks is empty.'

'*Hooks?*'

'Five wee hooks. For keys. Nothing on it.'

John says, 'Wha'?' He sounds confused.

From the kitchen, Nettie hears either John or William sit back, a faint creak of a wooden chair. She feels their puzzlement at him knowing that about a house he's never been in.

Manuel tells them: Tallis opens the door to the first bedroom, the one on the right-hand side. There are twin beds and a table in between, two women sleeping in those beds. Tallis goes in and stands between the two beds and he looks down at the soft-sleeping women. He draws the gun and shoots the woman nearest the door, shoots her in the temple, then he shoots the woman furthest away. One bullet in each.

'Pop,' he says. '*Pop*.'

Out in the hall Hart and Bowes get a fright and scramble for the front door, run out into the street and go back to hide in number 18. They leave Tallis alone in number 5.

William's voice: 'Why did they run? Tallis had told them his intentions, hadn't he?'

Manuel snorts. 'Ever heard a revolver go off in a small bedroom? Pretty goddamned loud ...'

No one in the kitchen says anything for a moment but Nettie stands tall: Manuel did it. He's describing what he did. Nettie knows that for sure now.

Does John know? Has William realised? William is very drunk, he can't know. If he had realised that he is sitting with the very man who murdered his wife and his daughter and Margaret Brown then William would be beating him, slapping him, hitting him and chasing that man from John and Nettie's home.

Nettie feels that she alone knows a murderer is among them. A man who shot three people in their own home. Nettie and John and William are three people. This is their home.

Stiff with terror, she tiptoes silently to the front door and slips out into the close. She stands at the top of the stairs, panting.

Good Lord, what is she doing? She can't leave John in there. But she can't call the police, either. If they find William with the actual murderer they'll just arrest William again, they hate him so. She looks at the front door across the landing: she could wake the neighbours but what use is that? He'd just murder them too.

She looks back at her front door. She has to warn John but she doesn't know how. She slips into the toilet on the landing to think.

This outside toilet has an open window cut high up on the wall, a godsend in summer but freezing now in the December air. Wind blows in, swaying the strip of flypaper uncurling from the light bulb, threatening to shower her with frozen dead flies. She only has her slippers on and the floor feels tacky, as if a child has missed the pan. It's cold and horrible but Nettie would stay here for a year to be out of the house.

She wants to run. She has some money of her own scurried away, change saved from groceries. She keeps it wrapped in paper and tucked into the toe of her Sunday shoes. She would have to go back in, but then she could hide in the train station until morning and get on the first train to Aberdeen where her sister lives. But she can't run. There is a murderer in her house and her John is in there. She can't run or call the police or a neighbour. There is no one to call for help.

The combination of biting cold and terror make her need a tinkle. Exposing as little flesh as possible to the frosty air, she pulls her underskirt up and her underpants down, hovers on the pan and does her dirty business. She positions herself so that her wee hits the side of the bowl noiselessly. Outside toilets are very public, everyone has their own technique. Nettie's mind is on the money wrapped in a paper in her Sunday shoes as she reaches for the newspaper, cut into strips and hung on the nail, to wipe herself. She freezes. That's it! The newspapers!

Hurriedly cleaning herself, she pulls her clothes down, up and unlocks the door. She slips back into the house, trembling. Silently she shuts the door and, for as long as a shiver, she stands listening.

Manuel is still talking in a low tone, as if he is describing a dream.

John's voice cuts through the dreamlike murmur: 'What did he see in there?'

Manuel's rhythm is thrown off by the question. 'Um, in the room?'

'Yes, did he describe the girl's room?'

'Well, just a bedroom. A bed. A torch on the bedside table. She had a radiogram in there. An old-fashioned one, a big, like, wooden cabinet. And a pink chenille bedspread, fluffy.'

'Fluffy?' John asks as if he's misheard the word.

'Aye.' Manuel is confused by why this is being discussed. 'Kind of puffy, fluffy, you know, like you could run your hand over the top of it? Fluffy.'

There is a pause. Nettie feels sure that John knows now.

'Kind of chenille,' says Manuel. Then he moves straight on to tell them that the girl sees his face there, at the door, and jumps back into the room. Tallis follows her in. There's a struggle. He wants her to get onto the bed and she won't do it. It annoys him, Tallis. He gets . . . he gets annoyed with her. Tallis socks her one and she goes down. Then he's hungry so he goes and makes a sandwich. Gammon. And he drinks from the bottle of Mascaró Dry Gin.

'The bottle in the front room?' From the high pitch of William's voice, Nettie can hear that he knows too.

'The one on the drinks cabinet, next to the Whyte & Mackay. But he doesn't get to finish his sandwich because the girl wakes up and screams.' There is a pause. It sounds as if he is drinking.

John shouts: 'WIFE? WIFE!'

Nettie hurries in. John looks up at her imploringly. He knows. He can see that Nettie does too. In a strained voice he says, 'Might we have some tea, Nettie?'

Nettie fills the kettle and puts it on the range. Would the other two like a cup of tea? Her own voice sounds strange to her. Breathy. Last-words-y.

William would like a cup of tea, thank you, dear. Peter Manuel doesn't answer but announces that he is off to use the cludgie.

He goes out to the close, leaving the front door ajar. He bangs the toilet door loud enough to wake the whole close. They hear him urinating.

Nettie keeps an eye on the door and she whispers: 'Get him out of here or, so help me, I will call the papers.'

It's an awful threat. They'll be here faster than the police and they'll make a month's worth of stories out of it. They love this story and Watt.

John is livid but nods, his eyes are brimming. He turns to his brother. 'Get that b. out of my home.'

William is not shocked by any of this. He is drunk and not the best liar anyway. Nettie can see that he knew all along. She has never entertained this thought before but now she wonders if the police are right and William did have a hand in killing his family.

The lavatory flushes and Manuel opens the toilet door before it is finished. The sound of sucking reverberates around the stone walls of the close.

He comes in, slams the front door behind him and sits back down. John confronts him: 'How do you know all these details about the house?'

'Well . . . people tell me things. What details?'

'The key rack? The feel of the bedspread? How do you know that if it wasn't you?'

Manuel isn't thrown. He says, 'Listen, the next morning Tallis, he came to me – going mad, he was, he tells me everything, in detail like. He says hide this gun.'

William jumps in. 'Did you? Where?'

'In the Clyde at a special bit, a bit only I know. I can get it back.'

Nettie delivers the tea. William nods at John. But John won't look at him. Nettie pours two teas, carefully cupping the strainer with her shaking hand. William keeps talking, as if he has forgotten that the man is a murderer.

'Listen: this story is no use to me,' slurs William. 'Even if you have the gun and take it to the police, it fails to clear me of anything, much less in the public imagination. My business is still affected.'

Hot tea drips into Nettie's palm as she carries the strainer back to the sink. Manuel's voice is a low murmur behind her. 'Prove something if Charles Tallis was found shot dead, holding the gun used to kill your family, though, wouldn't it? Clear everything up nicely, that would.'

Nettie freezes.

John gathers a breath to shout but he is cut off by William scraping his chair back and standing up. 'Let's go, Chief!'

Manuel stays in his seat. He's confused by the change in atmosphere. 'What?'

Nettie stands at the sink with the burning tea dripping into her palm.

'Come on, Chief! Time to go!'

'But nothing's open ... we've still got drink here. Nah, let's stay here.'

Watt sidles clumsily out of the recess, muttering, 'Well, maybe, we can just ... there's a club, a wee club, the cellar under the Cot Bar.'

Manuel suddenly stands up. Nettie hears him pull his jacket off the back of the chair, the chair leg clunks on the floor. Then he stops. 'Oh,' he says, 'but what about Dandy?'

William's voice is smiling. 'The Cot cellar is famously discreet. He won't find us in there.'

John whispers, '*Dandy McKay?*'

Nettie watches their reflections in the window above the sink. Manuel and William are pulling their coats on. John stands too, hands out, eyes wide with panic. '*Dandy McKay* is looking for you? And you're hiding from *McKay*? William, are you bloody mad?'

William doesn't answer, he is smiling awkwardly as he backs away from John. Manuel is at the front door already.

John shoves the full whisky bottle at his brother. 'Take it.'

'John, this is for you,' says William, by habit high-handed. 'You keep it.'

'*I don't want this in my house.*'

The door closes behind them. Their steps recede on the stone stairs. Nettie turns to see John slump into his seat. She is still holding the burning drips of tea in the cup of her hand.

'Husband,' she hisses, 'I don't want that *filthy* man in my house ever again.'

'I know,' says John, 'I know.'

Neither of them is talking about Peter Manuel.

10

Tuesday 3 December 1957

WATT AND MANUEL DRIVE away from John and Nettie's house and into the night city. It is three thirty in the morning and the streets are empty. They pass the high hedges of a bowling green and head uphill, through tall tenements with dark windows. Frozen mist clings to the pavement and the chimneys are all dead.

It is a time of night Manuel is familiar with. Watt isn't and he doesn't like it. He is sick with tiredness and drink and finds the empty, misty streets creepy. It feels as if everyone in the city has died. This is when Manuel loves Glasgow, when it's defenceless and the people are still.

But they are both excited by the prospect of the Cot Bar cellar. The cellar under the Cot Bar is a place of legend. Naked women serve you drink? Women in their underwear serve you drink? Women dance naked or become naked? Men who will never go to the cellar have heard rumours about it from other men who will never go there. It is a small dark room and costs a pound a head just to get in.

Manuel remembers what just happened and sounds annoyed when he says, 'You wanted me out of that house sharpish.'

William is contemplative. 'They know, I think.'

Manuel is surprised. 'Did they say?'

'No, I'm guessing.'

'How could you guess that?'

'Just . . . from the way they looked at you.'

Watt turns onto the Alexandra Parade, a long broad road running between huge Victorian factory buildings. It is a place of industry and is usually mobbed with workers as the vast tobacco factories change shifts. Lights shine in the windows but the streets are deserted. Newspapers and litter tumble softly along the pavement, following the stream of wind down from Townhead.

Manuel clears his throat. He seems troubled. 'D'you tell them? When I was in the lavvy?'

'No. They just knew, they guessed.' Watt can feel the alcohol ebb in his veins. He needs a top-up. He pulls the car over to the kerb, takes the Gleniffer whisky bottle out of the footwell and uncorks the lid. A lorry rumbles past them.

Watt takes a glug. He offers it to Manuel but Manuel says no. Watt pushes it at him again. Manuel shakes his head, irritated by how much Watt thinks about drink. He mutters, 'Fucking hell.' He seems upset by something. He looks away, out of the window, at the tobacco factory. He gets his cigarettes out and lights up. Watt takes the opportunity to have another sneaky drink.

Manuel's voice cracks as he whispers: 'It's a fuck of a lot to just *guess*, is what I'm saying.'

Watt shrugs, feeling better. 'They won't know the details, Peter, just the general . . . you know.'

'Is that what they said?'

Watt feels the whisky dull his nerves, salve the sense of bristling panic that worsens when the drink wears off. 'They never said anything, Peter. I'm just supposing from the way they looked at you.'

Manuel smokes and shakes his head. Watt drinks again. Liquid confidence. He feels normal now. He looks at Manuel. 'You don't see it, do you?'

Manuel looks at him with the blank expression he saw in Whitehall's when the bill came: he doesn't know what William is talking about.

'You don't see what other people think. You can't tell. You can't see.'

Manuel tuts, 'Shut your fat fucking gub, Watt.'

Watt shrugs. He wants to add – and that's why you can't make a plan and stick to it, you can't anticipate what other people will be thinking about or expecting. He has noticed over the course of the night that Manuel's plan of action changes constantly: I'll give you the gun, I'll give you a suspect, I'll give you a story. In the business world sticking to a course of action is the key to winning. Even if Manuel's ideas are brilliant, which they are sometimes, he hasn't got the self-control to see them through. As soon as a new thing occurs to him he goes off and does that. This fellow is all over the shop. So much the better for Watt. He starts the car again and pulls out but then realises the whisky bottle is open.

He pulls over again and struggles to fit the cork into the bottle held upright between his thighs. It won't seem to go in. Manuel watches him. Watt tries again and misses badly and giggles and a bit of spit shoots from his mouth, landing on his suited leg.

Manuel laughs at him. He laughs so much he bangs his foot on the floor of the car for emphasis.

Watt laughs along with him. Laughing makes him shift his chubby legs and the bottle nearly falls and he grabs it and laughs more and more.

They look up at the empty street, laughing, remembering the spit and the falling bottle and the cork that won't go in. Watt laughs loud and hands the cork and the bottle to Manuel but Manuel drops the cork onto the floor of the car.

'Jesus H. Christ,' laughs Manuel, 'we are fucking ruined.'

And Watt laughs more.

Finally, Manuel manages to get the cork in the bottle. He looks at Watt and says, 'You want a –?' He offers him the bottle.

Then they laugh at that one too. Watt gets out his own cigarettes and they both smoke and calm down.

Watt exhales as Manuel says, 'Really, how do *you* know *they* know?'

'I don't know really . . . from their faces? The faces they made.'

'Oh.' Manuel titters, remembering. He looks at his cigarette. 'You think I read the faces wrong?'

Watt doesn't really want to have a conversation about what is wrong with Peter Manuel. He shrugs.

'Oh!' Manuel pulls a crumpled piece of paper out of his pocket. He is staring at Watt. 'Did you put that in there?'

'What?'

'This. A pound note. In my pocket. Did you put that in there?'

Watt doesn't get it immediately. 'No.'

'Huh.' Manuel smiles on one side of his face. 'It wasn't there before I went to the cludgie. Maybe you put it in there when I was out the room?'

It dawns on Watt: this is a threat. I'll say you gave me money. I'll renege on everything. So he says a mean thing back:

'You're so obviously guilty, Peter. Anyone could tell it was you.'

'Fuck you,' says Manuel dismissively.

'You can't tell a story,' says Watt, not knowing that this is cutting Manuel to the bone.

Manuel is so hurt that he can't speak for a minute. He looks out of the window and covers his face with his hand, as if he is tired.

'You going to take the joe?'

'Tallis?'

'Aye, Charles Tallis.'

'Not if it's a phoney-baloney suicide scenario.'

'Just take him. I'll get the gun and put it on him. Cops'll want him for it.'

Watt breathes and sits up slowly. He looks out of the side window, away from Manuel. He doesn't think Manuel knows what the cops want or anyone wants. He thinks meeting Peter was a mistake after all. Now John and Nettie are suspicious, Dowdall is annoyed, Dandy McKay will be angry with him and he is no further forward. But still, the night needn't be a complete washout.

'Let's go to the Cot cellar and see what we can see.'

11

Friday 16 May 1958

EVERYONE IS LYING.

Day five of the trial is a whistle-stop tour of Glasgow's underbelly. There are two handguns on the productions table in the middle of the court: the Webley used to kill the Watts and the Beretta used to murder the Smart family. Sworn witnesses tell the court that these guns have tumbled from hand to hand, unbidden. They have dropped themselves into paper bags, hidden themselves away on the top shelves in cupboards. No one ever buys them, no one ever sells them, though, it is admitted, unrelated fivers have passed from hand to hand, always in the opposite direction from the guns, during approximately the same time frame. Buying guns is illegal and has a steep sentencing tariff. This deception is understandable.

Other deceptions are just as obvious but incomprehensible. Three of the independent witnesses to Manuel buying the guns work together at the Gordon Club. Shifty Thomson, Scout O'Neil and Dandy McKay. Another deception is this happenstance: Peter Manuel obtained both of these revolvers from completely unrelated apartments in the same street in the Gorbals, Florence Street. Florence Street is where Dandy McKay lives. It is where Mr Smart's car was found abandoned and where Mr Watt will have his car accident the night before he gives evidence. The street is famously unpoliceable because of the clear sight lines and the belligerence of its inhabitants.

Some underworld witnesses saw only damning evidence against Manuel. Some saw nothing significant, though they were looking directly at significant things as they occurred and were the only other person present at the time.

In among the smog of lies and cheap theatre, ever-present on the table, sit the two black handguns. The Webley is a cowboy revolver with a barrel for the bullets and a long round shaft. It has a wooden handle. The Beretta is an Italian pistol. It is sleek and ergonomic. It has a square barrel and is an automatic, the bullets are held in the handle. The Webley is older but more reliable. The Beretta jams all the time.

Each of these guns has been on a journey to get here.

This is the Webley's story.

A fat, pockmarked guy called Henry Campbell tells the court that he was doing his national service in the RAF. He stole the Webley from an officers' barracks and went AWOL in Glasgow where he gave it to a man he'd just met in a pub. That man was called Dick Hamilton. He made this gift to Hamilton because they stood next to each other and Hamilton mentioned that he was in a bit of trouble. Yes, Hamilton did give Campbell money afterwards. He wasn't *selling* the gun to him though. He just gave it to him. He doesn't know why, he just did.

Campbell is shown the Webley that was used to murder three women in the Watt house. It is the same gun, Campbell says, apart from the fact that the lanyard ring at the bottom is now missing and it wasn't when he gave it to Dick Hamilton, as a gift, like, because he seemed kinda worried.

Dick Hamilton gets up. He has a shock of black hair so thick his pomade can barely tame it. He takes the oath solemnly, then he smiles and waves up to the public gallery as if he has been pulled out of the audience at a variety show. Hamilton does this every single time he is in court, to make it look as if he has never been in a court before. None of the lawyers are fooled, they know he always does this, but the public and the jury are in the palm of his hand.

The bones of Hamilton's story are these: he got the gun from Henry Campbell and took it home. He left it on a shelf in his house. Then, eight days before the Watt murders, on a Saturday, 8 September 1956, at around 5 p.m., he popped into Meldrum's Bar for a quick one. There he found Peter Manuel and Scout O'Neil drinking together. Oh, they were very, very drunk. He says this as if he has never witnessed public drunkenness before and was saddened by the sight. Anyone fooled by the waving to the crowd might now be slightly sceptical. If Hamilton is upset by the sight of drunkenness then he's living in the wrong city. Between lunch-time closing and the pubs reopening for the evening Glasgow is carpeted with drunk men. They loll on pavements, piss themselves at bus stops, fight invisible foes in the streets. Hamilton doesn't notice that he has lost his audience and carries on: Oh! They were so drunk he didn't want anything to do with them, but he stayed drinking with them for two hours. At some point Manuel mentioned he needed a gun for a hold-up job in Liverpool. Hamilton said he had a Webley and Manuel could have that.

So, by arrangement the next day, a Sunday, Hamilton met Manuel and Scout O'Neil outside the Gordon Club. O'Neil had a loan of a car and drove them to Florence Street in the Gorbals, where Hamilton happened to be living. The street is only ten minutes' walk from the Gordon Club so Scout O'Neil has no reason to be in this story at all. But he is and he's an important corroborating witness. Anyway, they got out of the car and Hamilton took Manuel up the close to his flat. There, on a high shelf in the lobby, was the gun in a paper bag with seven or eight bullets in a matchbox. He gave the gun to Manuel for no consideration and then Mr Manuel spontaneously gave him a fiver. They left the close together but Hamilton went off to get a shave and Scout O'Neil drove Manuel off in the car.

Hamilton is shown the gun from the productions table but he isn't sure if it is the same gun. That one looks bigger than the one he had. M.G. Gillies points out that Webley revolvers really only come in the one size. Well, Hamilton really doesn't know, he can't say for sure.

He can't even identify Manuel. Hamilton touches his heart and says that he couldn't, in all good conscience, say which person in this court is Manuel. Now no one believes him. M.G. Gillies feels honour-bound to point out that they all know he is lying:

'You drank with him for two hours, met him again the next day and gave him a gun but you can't recognise him in court?'

'Well, he was sitting in the back seat of the car, Your Worship, and I've an awful bad memory for faces.'

By contrast with Hamilton, Scout O'Neil is a beautiful liar. His balletic style is a privilege to witness. Sometimes he engages the court in astonishing feats of slippery logic, at other times he is simply charm incarnate.

M.G. Gillies wants the jury to know that O'Neil keeps changing his version of events and can't be trusted. He can't introduce all the conflicting versions into evidence without creating a distracting trial-within-a-trial, so instead he asks, 'Mr O'Neil, this story you are telling the court, is this the story you have *always* told about this incident?'

Scout shrugs innocently. 'Well,' he says, 'it's certainly the story I am telling here today.'

Scout looks clean and tidy on the stand. He doesn't have any blood on his face or sleeve, but still, you wouldn't let your sister leave a dance with him. He has an air of cheeky mischief, speaks in the colloquial and has a way of talking and smiling that hide his teeth, which are very bad.

Asked by Harald Leslie if he is in the habit of getting guns for people like Mr Manuel, Scout says, 'I don't *think* so,' as if he has just met himself and isn't quite sure.

The public snicker at that, showing Scout that they are in on the joke. This annoys Harald Leslie and he snaps, 'Mr O'Neil! Will you please just answer with "yes" or "no".'

Scout thinks about it for a moment then says '*No*', compliant and defiant all at once. The public and jury laugh again and Scout smiles, showing off a set of teeth as craggy as an eight-year-old's.

Scout O'Neil is a likeable man. As a child he realised that being charming made hitting stop. He made his mother laugh like none of the other children. He made his daddy smile, drunk or sober, angry or angry. Scout was never leathered like the others. Mrs O'Neil's other children are good-living and God-fearing. Scout O'Neil is not now, nor has he ever been, either.

People like to think Scout says something about Glasgow, that Glasgow is like him or he is like Glasgow. Gallus and roguish. Lovable but rough. But they're flattering the city because Scout is like Scout and that's all.

O'Neil tells a vivid story about the Webley, so damning and detailed that everyone knows it can only be half true, but it's a great story, well told and told by Scout O'Neil.

Scout met Manuel and Hamilton outside the Gordon Club on the Sunday and drove them to Florence Street. Scout stayed in the car. When Manuel and Hamilton came back out of the close they stood in the street for a minute, Hamilton saying he was going for a shave, kind of rubbing his chin and that, and Manuel holding a paper bag. Then Manuel looks back at O'Neil sitting in the car, and he grins and he makes a kind of a gun shape with his hand, like a kid, know?

To illustrate this Scout makes a gun with his hand. And he sort of puffs his lips out, like as if he was firing a gun, like this:

p-tyaw! O'Neil shoots Lord Cameron with his fingers. When the public galleries laugh, Scout grins and shoots M.G. Gillies as well, *p-tyaw!* Then he blows the smoke from the end of the finger-barrel and slips the gun into an imaginary holster.

M.G. Gillies says wryly, yes, he thinks they know what Mr O'Neil means.

Scout continues with his story.

As if all of this weren't damning enough, Manuel then got back into the car and shut the door. He opened the paper bag and showed the contents to O'Neil for no reason at all: there was a Webley revolver in the bag. Plus a matchbox with six or seven bullets in it. Yes, it *was* that gun, yes. Manuel had it. Seven days before the Watt murders, yes. He had that gun. Yes, I can see him in court today. That is Peter Manuel over there.

Scout points over at Manuel. Then he smiles and Manuel smiles back. As a reflex, O'Neil gives Manuel a cheery wee wave with his accusing hand. It's all Manuel can do not to wave back.

William Grieve asks how Scout came to tell the police about Manuel getting the gun?

'William Watt's asked us to go and tell the police about what happened.'

Grieve addresses the jury but finds they are all looking at Scout. 'Mr Watt approached you and took you to the police to tell this story?'

'Yup.'

Grieve raises an arm to the side, trying hard to draw the jury's eye to him, to get them to stop listening to these blatant lies. 'But *why* did you do what he asked, Mr O'Neil?'

Still none of the jury are looking at him. They're watching Scout and they are all grinning.

'Well,' Scout says solemnly, 'it's the right thing to do, isn't it?'

Everyone in this room knows that Scout O'Neil is not a man invariably compelled to do the right thing. As if he can hear their doubts, Scout grins and holds beseeching hands up out to the public galleries,

'Isn't it, though? The right thing?' Then he gives a deep rumbling belly laugh and everyone in the courtroom laughs too.

Grieve recognises that O'Neil has the room, and he has no control of him. There is a distinct danger of Scout bursting into song so he says, 'Mr O'Neil, you may get down.'

The court watches Scout walk down the stairs, sorry to see him leave.

When he was arrested Manuel gave the police a detailed account of how he bought the Webley: he got it from a stranger in the Mercat Bar at Glasgow Cross, paid a fiver, left immediately.

It is lunchtime and they haven't started tracing the provenance of the Beretta.

Manuel is taken down to the cells where his lunch is waiting. Bread and cheese are provided for all the prisoners on trial. Manuel has chosen to pay extra and get the salmon salad provided by the court for the QCs.

12

Tuesday 3 December 1957

SITE OF BIRTHS, DEATHS and marriages, Townhead is the high-
est point in the old city. The Royal Infirmary looms across the
road, black as the devil and ten storeys high. Squatting behind
it is the medieval cathedral and then the sharp high hills of the
Necropolis.

The Cot Bar is on a sharp corner at Townhead. It is a filthy
place. By an unhappy accident of aerodynamics, litter and dust
and ash are swept downhill, around corners, over streets, and
deposited against the side wall. Gang slogans are scratched into
the dirt. This is Cody gang territory so the tags are mostly theirs
(*CODY = Come On, Die Young*).

The early-morning streets are dusted with a thin frost that
melts underfoot, leaving black smears on the pavement. The re-
sidual heat of the city, held in the ground, defies the season.

Watt and Manuel park and get out of the car. They walk
round the back, exchanging excited glances. Their eyes are wide,
they nod to each other over and over, exaggerating their sexual
engagement to the brink of pantomime. Peter Manuel is impo-
tent. He can ejaculate when a woman is frightened enough
but he can't have normal relations. When the police examine
his clothes they will find all of his trousers have ejaculatory
stains inside. It has been like this since he was in Hollesley Bay

Borstal. Brendan Behan was in Hollesley Bay around the same time. He said of it that inmates engaged in sexual practices 'the lowest ruffian in Ireland could be born, live and die and never even guess at'. Manuel was sent there when he was twelve. William Watt doesn't like sexy shows or stripping, he wouldn't go on his own. But they are prisoners of this macho convention and there is no room for either of them to express anything but increasingly intense interest. Still, both quite like the idea of being in a room where their satisfaction is the main focus. They suspect, as do many people, that there is some sexual practice that they don't yet know about, something new that will pique their interest.

The cellar is round the back, by the bins and behind a high wall. It was once a coal cellar so the stairs down are narrow and plain, sliced out of the yard floor. When a man is standing on the bottom step he looks as if he has sunk into the ground up to his waist.

Manuel and Watt step carefully down into the well. There is hardly enough room for both sets of feet. Watt knocks on the steel door.

The eye slot slides opens and a puffy-eyed man looks at them critically. They try to see past him but his face blocks the view.

'Wait,' he says, and shuts it.

They wait, their annoyance tempered by sexual interest.

The slot opens again and the bouncer examines them as if he is looking for something. Watt holds up a five-pound note and smiles pleasantly.

'We're no buzzies!' Manuel says, but the slit scrapes shut.

There is nothing to do but wait.

'Did you give me a pound?' asks Manuel, a smirk on his face.

'You've sung that song already, Chief,' says Watt, but he's smiling too.

A huge engine rumbles in the street beyond the wall, wheels crunch on the cobbles. The engine cuts. Doors slam. The stairwell is too narrow for them to turn around. They hear feet tramp towards them.

'Right, boys?'

Twisting awkwardly around they find Scout and Shifty Thomson looking down at them.

Scout has a plaster on the bridge of his burst nose and has changed his jacket. His eyes are purple-puffed. He half smiles. 'Mon, fellas. Time to go.'

They are trapped. They both know the jig is up.

Shifty and Scout escort them to the car, an Alvis Grey Lady, two-tone, in burgundy and black. The bonnet is longer than the cabin. The wheel hoods are fat and round and the chrome trim perfectly polished.

Watt is too drunk to put his case eloquently but he doesn't think he should really be here. They want Manuel. They don't want him. He's not the problem.

They are put in the back of the car with Scout sitting in the middle.

Before they set off Scout warns them with a grin, 'Anybody tries anything funny and they'll be getting their fucking lights put out. Clear?'

Manuel and Watt agree that Scout has made himself clear. Shifty pulls out onto the road and Watt thinks 'I need a drink'. He doesn't. He has drunk so much tonight that he is having mini blackouts. He suddenly comes to in odd situations: listening in John's kitchen, walking down the close, ordering drinks in the Gleniffer, changing up to fifth gear. The one thing he doesn't need is more drink.

Shifty is driving. The Grey Lady is a thing of beauty. The seats are soft grey leather. The dashboard is a solid slab of high-varnished walnut with a matching steering wheel. Both front seats are pushed back as far as they can go, which is not so much of a problem for

Manuel at five foot six, but Watt is concertinaed, his knees against his chin.

Wheels purr against cobbles as Shifty turns down the sweep of Cathedral Street. It is still dark but the workers' dawn is breaking. Grey civilians walk purposefully, sandwiches and flasks in their hands, faces raw from sleep, making their way to their own small part of the great machine of Empire.

Manuel grabs the back of the front seat, yanking himself forward. This seems to count as 'anything funny' and Scout takes hold of Manuel's middle finger, levering it the way fingers don't want to go. Manuel raises a pissed-off eyebrow at Scout.

Shifty tells the windscreen, 'Yees wur telt.'

Watt and Manuel know that they have no defence. They wur telt.

They turn down Buchanan Street. Shifty swings gently around piles of horseshit. There are a lot of pubs down here and brewers still deliver with drays and carts. Halfway down Buchanan Street he takes the turn for Gordon Street and parks right outside number 25.

The door to the Gordon Club has a Georgian formality. It is glossy, black and ten foot tall, set into the building, four steps up from the mucky street. The Gordon Club is on the second floor, above the Girl Guides' headquarters.

Everyone is wary as they get out of the car. This is not going to be nice.

The Gordon Club is in the middle of everything. At the end of the block *Glasgow Herald* vans are lined up along the street, waiting to pick up the second edition. Within a half-mile radius of this place are the courts, the Corporation, the Trades Hall and the Merchants' Guild, three national newspapers and the police headquarters.

Both Watt and Manuel have been to the club before. That's not surprising. Every man of interest in Glasgow has been in the Gordon Club at one time or another. This is a time of clubs. Men with common interests meet in closed rooms and make deals, lend money, decide outcomes before formal negotiations are even timetabled. Still, though, the Gordon is special. It is a social portal through which the bottom and the top can meet and drink and talk, in the absence of women and church and moralising judgement.

The Gordon Club is a thrumming valve in Glasgow's mercantile heart. But mostly it isn't about deals. Mostly it is about bonhomie and men acknowledging their common interests across the chasm of class distinction. But it's no place for the faint-hearted, it takes audacity to be part of this. It hazards disgrace.

Scout and Shifty flank the two men who wur telt to the door, up the steps to get out of a sudden bluster of sleet. Shifty has a key to the front door and uses it. This is quite impressive. Most people have to ring, wait and give the boy who comes to the door their membership number. Shifty opens the door and waves them up the stairwell.

On the second floor they come to black storm doors with a brass plaque announcing '*The Gordon*'. Shifty opens the doors with another key, ushers them inside and locks it carefully behind them.

The hallway is red and pink, softly lit and filled with a smog of fresh cigar smoke and whisky smell. From a side room they can hear laughing and a high voice struggling to deliver a punchline through chortles.

The uniformed cloakroom boy stands to attention. His eyes are red.

'Right, son?' asks Shifty.

'Yes, *sir*, Mr Thomson.'

Everyone looks at Shifty, surprised that he can evoke respect from anyone.

Shifty leads them down the back corridor. They pass the open double doors to the main room and catch sight of two catatonically drunk men in leather armchairs. It's the tail end of a long night. One man is asleep, his chin collapsed onto his chest, drooling. The other is facing them and lifts a glass of whisky to his mouth but his eyes look panicked, as if the hand is holding him to drunken ransom. Pinned to his lapel is a sprig of mistletoe. He is a Glasgow Corporation councilman.

Shifty leads them down the dark corridor to the very furthest door. He knocks twice, listens and opens it.

Maurice Dickov is at his large desk. He is in his shirtsleeves, working on a set of books. Dandy McKay is standing next to him. Dandy wears a suit, double-breasted with a broad stripe in blue and pink. He looks like a settee. He has a red carnation in his buttonhole, wilted, denoting the hour. His tie is purple and green.

When the door shuts behind them, Watt, Manuel, O'Neil and Thomson line up against the far wall.

Dickov stands up. He slaps the accounts book shut. He looks at the men.

'Gentlemen,' he says softly, 'this is terribly awkward.'

13

Friday 16 May 1958

AFTER LUNCH THEY HEAR the history of the Beretta. It is similar but less classy. The original source of the gun was a soldier in a pub, again. No one paid for the gun or asked if they could buy it, again. And again unrelated money is exchanged during time frames contemporaneous with the gifting. The first person to be gifted the Beretta is Billy Fullerton, a famous hard case and leader of the Billy Boys of Brig'ton Razor Gang.

In a city that reveres angry men Billy Fullerton is a god. He walks across the stuffy courtroom in the late afternoon, trailing a reputation that sparkles with spite and absolutes. The stillness in the room is profound. Everyone watches him walk, in their heads rerunning whichever story they've heard about him.

Billy leading his boys into nearby Catholic neighbourhoods on their holy days of obligation.

The Billy Boys wielding razors, and knives and broken bottles, playing penny whistles and drums, calling out the Irish to meet them.

Catholic mothers flattened to the inside of front doors, begging their boys not to leave the house.

Catholic mothers putting knives in their hands and ordering them to go.

Billy Fullerton has been angry all of his life. When young, he joined the British Union of Fascists. He got a medal for strike-breaking during the General Strike. As he grew older, disillusioned by the liberalism he encountered among the Fascists, he established one of the first chapters of the Ku Klux Klan on British soil. Retired from street fighting now, he beats his wife every night. His children's backs stiffen at the sound of his first footfall in the close. He has served time for wife-beating which, in the 1950s, means he nearly killed her. She doesn't leave the house without his permission and her face is as scarred as her husband's.

Fullerton mounts the witness stand heavily. He is flat-footed and can't help this, but it sounds as if he is trying to smash his foot through each step.

When he turns to face the court the lawyers avert their eyes. His face is scarred, a map of vicious encounters with other angry men.

Billy takes in the room. He sees the lawyers in their funny costumes, posh boys. He sees the women on the balcony, all sitting back, heads tipped, looking down on him. He lifts his chin to challenge them. They've annoyed him just by being there.

M.G. Gillies, gentleman, stands up reluctantly and clears his throat. Fullerton nods permission to speak.

Gillies lifts production 72, the Beretta gun used to kill the Smart family, and asks him to identify it. Fullerton says he owned that gun briefly.

'Mr Fullerton, would you mind telling the court where you first encountered this Beretta?'

So, Fullerton explains: a man called John Totten approached him a couple of years ago and asked Billy to find a gun for him.

'To what purpose?'

The question is phrased in a way that makes its meaning obscure. Fullerton hesitates before answering. He is annoyed by this enforced pause. He thinks it makes him look stupid. Blood rises to his neck and he struggles to stay calm.

'Totten has ran a pitch-and-toss school out at Glasgow Green. It was a big school, two hundred, three hundred men sometimes. Totten said he'd been hearing a rival gang were meaning to take it over.'

'A "pitch-and-toss" school?'

'A gambling school. On the Green. Totten was after a gun for to protect hissel'.'

'And did you furnish him with a gun?'

'I did, aye. I got offered a Beretta from a soldier in a pub.'

The whole of Britain is awash with guns bought from a-soldier-in-a-pub. At the end of the First War soldiers were allowed to take their Webley service revolvers home, as a memento. The Second War is thirteen years ago and mandatory national service means that everyone is near guns or has guns or can steal a gun. A soldier in a pub with a gun doesn't elicit any further questioning.

'How much did Totten pay you for it?'

'Five quid.'

'How much did you pay for it?'

'Nothing. I loaned the soldier a fiver though and Totten paid us the fiver back and gaed us another quid for a finder's fee.'

'Why would Mr Totten ask you to get him a gun, Mr Fullerton?'

Fullerton swells. His scarred face crumples into an approximation of a grin. 'A few year ago I was a wee bit famous for fighting.'

'With guns?' asks Gillies innocently.

Fullerton is insulted. Fighting with guns is not manly. It is cowardly, a thing done by jilted women and Frenchmen. His lips tighten. His blood pressure rises. His cheeks turn a deep furious red but the scar tissue, capillary-less, remains white, vivid against his mottled red face.

Fullerton lifts his tight fists to the court. They are swollen and scarred.

'*Never* wi' guns,' he growls. 'Wi' ma hands!'

As he says this he jabs at the gallery of women.

Fullerton is thanked and asked if he wouldn't mind getting down now.

John Totten is called. Totten has matinee-idol good looks, a coiffed pompadour and is dressed in a shimmering blue Italian-cut silk suit. He wears a Celtic FC tie, a green kerchief tucked nattily into his breast pocket and a Celtic FC tiepin. After he has taken his oath he turns to the court with a shoulder sway and a Frankie Vaughan smile. You just know the guy can dance.

Totten is a surprise to the court. Billy Fullerton is so fervently anti-Irish Republican that he is the subject of a sectarian song that celebrates him being up to his 'knees in Fenian blood'. The song will live on long after Fullerton. Come the digital age, football directors will lose jobs because they were filmed singing this song. The song is so incendiary that men will be hounded out of public office when other people sing it in their company. It will be forbidden, rewritten, bowdlerised. Fullerton's anger will live on in legend because of that song. But Fullerton the man is not above finding frightened Catholics guns it seems, so maybe he wasn't who they said he was at all. Maybe he was just an angry man with nothing to be but his reputation.

'Yes,' Totten admits, 'I did used to run a pitch-and-toss school.'

And yes, it did run to two or three hundred participants at one time. It was out on the Green. He points through the wall because Glasgow Green is just out there and across the road.

Two or three hundred is vast for a gambling school. The room is wondering why the police allowed an open-air gathering of that size for the purposes of gambling, how much they got as a bung to allow that and how much Totten got as his cut. The profits must have been huge.

Did Mr Totten ever use the gun?

Yes, he did, but not on anyone. He just kept it in a shed nearby and took it out sometimes, firing it into the ground at the start of a game. It was a way of fending off trouble. The rival gang he was worried about never materialised and Totten had, unfortunately, to give up the school because he got a four-year stretch for a 'wee bit of fighting'. Then the gun was left in a cupboard in his house, along with a Luger he had as well. It worried him, guns in the house. While he was in Barlinnie a guy called Tony Lowe was asking for a gun and Totten was happy to oblige, to get rid, basically. Totten is excused and leaves the stand, smiling up to the balcony as if he is sorry to leave without doing an encore, but has another engagement.

Tony Lowe has been brought from Wandsworth Prison to give his evidence. Tony is as grey as fag ash. He is dressed in badly laundered clothes that are too big. No one wants to look at him because he is depressing after the colour of the other witnesses. Lowe mumbles that he asked Totten for a gun because he was 'in a bit of trouble' at that time. Even this threat to his life sounds dreary and down at heel. Totten said he had a gun and Lowe was welcome to go and get it from Totten's home as soon as he was released. Lowe would be out well before Totten. The problem was Mrs Totten, who wouldn't allow any of Mr Totten's disreputable friends near the family home. Because of this, Lowe had to contact Dandy McKay, co-owner of the Gordon Club, to come with him to Mrs Totten's house. Mr McKay duly escorted Lowe to the house and they got the guns from Mrs Totten who was glad to give them away. Then, for safe keeping, they took the guns to Shifty Thomson's house, which happened to be in Florence Street.

Shifty Thomson is sweating even before he turns to face the court from the dock. He covers his mouth with his hand, he mumbles, he obfuscates. No one can hear him and everyone is annoyed. Thomson is such a poor liar that everyone listening feels insulted but Shifty doesn't give a stuff. He serves other masters.

Shifty Thomson says he was given the gun by Lowe and Mr McKay to hold. He had the gun in his house for about a year. Then Mr McKay came with Peter Manuel to pick up the Beretta. Shifty always says 'Mr McKay', never 'Dandy McKay'. Mr McKay this, Mr McKay that. Mr McKay took the gun down. Mr McKay said it was all right. Mr McKay left and that's about all he knows about that.

Thomson describes the activities of the Gordon Club as, 'you know, bit a' horse racing and that'. He describes his own role at the club as a bookmaker's clerk. Do you have an office? Not as such. Yes or no? I suppose, not really. Do you conduct your accounts in the street, Mr Thomson? Maybe, sometimes, I dunno. You're a bookie's runner, aren't you? Not really, always.

Of all the liars in court that day Lord Cameron finds Shifty Thomson the least convincing. He interjects forcefully during Shifty's evidence.

'Mr Thomson. You are here to do two things: speak clearly and tell the truth. You are not doing the first one and I have *severe* reservations about whether or not you are doing the second.'

This doesn't incline Shifty to either honesty or clarity, it just makes him more nervous.

He is asked, 'If you weren't selling the gun why did you take the five pounds Mr Manuel offered you?'

Shifty shrugs and mumbles, 'Dunno. He's just only gave it to me. Would you no ha' took it?'

'Do you see Mr Manuel in court today, Mr Thomson?'

He looks at Lord Cameron and the jury for a good long while. Then he looks around. Finally he takes a stab at it: is that him? No, Mr Thomson, that's not him, that's the stenographer.

Maurice Dickov takes the stand. Dickov is an underworld gentleman of the old-fashioned kind. He doesn't want to be in a golf club or have a semi in the suburbs or a bigger car than his neighbour. What Dickov wants is for everyone to be comfortable and have a pleasant evening and give him their money. He knows everyone worth knowing, their foibles and what they're good for. In court he openly admits to co-owning the Gordon Club with Dandy McKay.

'And what sort of private members' club is it?'

'Well, it's a bridge club,' Dickov says. 'Gentlemen can play cards and relax there among like-minded chaps.'

He smiles. It does sound nice, the way he says it.

'A social club?'

'Yes, a private members' club. Pleasant surroundings, well-stocked bar and good company. Splendid fellows. A way for gentlemen from all over to meet each other. Mingling.'

'Do they all play bridge?'

The public gallery laugh a little, not because it was a funny joke or because they're being facetious, really just to tell Dickov that they know he is lying.

But Dickov frowns at them. He isn't lying. That is what he thinks his business is. 'Yes, for men who like congenial company and playing cards.'

'Do most of the members play bridge?'

He shrugs and drops his voice. 'Well, it's not an essential condition of membership but certainly some of them do.'

'What proportion of the members might be playing bridge on any given night?'

'It's hard to say really.'

'Is it hard to say because none of them are playing bridge, Mr Dickov?'

'No.'

'I suppose some of the gentlemen like to make their card games more interesting? Perhaps they wager on the outcome of certain games?'

'I don't know, I don't watch them playing bridge.'

'Please answer with either yes or no: the Gordon Club is a place where men can bet with each other on the outcome of card games.'

Dickov doesn't answer. They have missed the point of the club entirely. Just yes or no please, Mr Dickov. After prompting he says perhaps, maybe, sometimes.

Mr Dickov was brought up by his grandparents, refugees from Bulgaria. Mr Dickov is Glaswegian but has retained some of their accent and conversational conventions. He calls children 'darling', pronouncing it 'darlink'. Once he has made his fortune, which will be very soon, he will move to Florida and talk about how much he loves Scotland for the rest of his life. He will never come back. Maurice has inherited his grandparents' habit of being from somewhere else.

Maurice is dismissed from the dock. In ten days' time the police will raid the Gordon Club and find roulette wheels and blackjack tables. They'll find eight thousand pounds in the safe, all in small bills, quite a lot of jewellery, stolen chequebooks and a number of blank passports. They'll also find stag films and a projector in a box, under a folded bed sheet which had been pinned up to act as a screen. They will shut the club down for good, confiscate the money and passports and gambling equipment. The stag films will remain in the possession of a series of unmarried police officers until the films shred or melt from age. They've missed the point of the Gordon. Those senior police officers who were secretly members will know that. They could not confiscate the net of friendships and contacts made there. Dickov will be sad at the demise of the Gordon Club in some ways, but in others not. It has run its course, he feels, served its purpose. He is a pragmatist and he's moving on.

When Dandy McKay, Dickov's co-owner, comes into the court everyone cranes to see what he is wearing.

Dandy is small and chubby, clean-shaven, with a neat Tony Curtis haircut and very small eyes. His suit is a herringbone check in black and white, double-breasted, the old style. His shirt is a strange shimmery orangey-red colour. He sports a puce handkerchief in his pocket and has a small green carnation in his buttonhole. But the main event is the tie. The tie is a swirl of what to Dandy appears to be muted shades of blue and yellow. It is actually red and blue with flecks of green. Dandy is colour-blind but no one has ever dared to tell him. Dandy McKay runs Glasgow and he can wear whatever the fuck he likes. And this is what he likes. Hence the nickname.

Dandy turns in the witness box and sees the look he always sees on the faces of strangers: surprised and then averted eyes. The only people who ever ask him why he is dressed like that are children. Poor children, because that's the only kind he ever meets, and what do they know about style? Dandy tells them he dresses like that because he is rich. Should they chance a supple-mentary question Dandy slaps them hard and tells them to fuck off back to their whore o' a mother.

He is sworn in. He admits that he is the co-owner of the Gordon Club but if, as Grieve suggests, it is a gambling club, this is certainly news to him. He doesn't take a lot do with the floor. He's in the office mostly.

Dandy admits driving Lowe to Totten's house. They picked the guns up from Mrs Totten and took them to Shifty Thomson's house in Florence Street. They left them there for safe keeping. In what way was that safe? Well, says McKay, Mrs Totten has eleven children. You can't very well leave guns in a two-apartment with eleven children. The men in the court think well of him for this. It's very responsible and they're not even his children. The women in the public gallery are too distracted by the thought of eleven children in a two-apartment to be impressed by Dandy's civic-mindedness. They're wondering how much Totten's silk

138 • denise mina

suit cost and where the pitch-and-toss money went. The statement distracts everyone so that the narrative disconnect between grey-faced Tony Lowe getting a gun to protect himself and then leaving it with Shifty Thomson is left unexplored.

McKay says that about a year or so later he drove Manuel to Thomson's to pick up the Beretta. Manuel said he needed it for personal protection. No, Dandy never asked Manuel from whom or for why. He had a car and Manuel needed a lift so he took him there and back. Dandy doesn't seem like a man who drives underlings around to be nice and M.G. Gillies delves for a motive. No, no money exchanged hands. Not even a fiver? asks Gillies, tired of being lied to about the money. McKay smiles and says he drove Manuel there in his Alvis Grey Lady. This is a huge luxury car, brand new. It is clear that McKay doesn't need to chase grubby fivers for stolen guns. McKay's inexplicable kindness is left unexplored.

Did McKay see Mr Manuel after that occasion? Yes he did. Manuel came to see him on the 10th of January this year at the club. The date is a few days after the Smarts were found dead in Uddingston, the day before Manuel was arrested.

'Why did Mr Manuel come to see you on the 10th of January?'

'He came to ask me for one hundred and fifty pounds. He said he wanted to leave the country.'

'Did you oblige?'

'No, I did not oblige. I saw Mr Manuel down the stairs of the club and he did not return.'

No one asks why Peter Manuel thought Dandy might give him one hundred and fifty pounds to leave the country the day before he was arrested.

No one asks about the identification parade the next morning either, which was held at Hamilton Police Station, when Peter Manuel picked Dandy out of a line-up and Dandy set about him – Not the face, Mr McKay, please! Not the face!

Dandy is the man who owns the club where all the witnesses worked. He is the man who lives in Florence Street in the Gorbals, where the guns were got and Mr Watt crashed his car and Manuel left Mr Smart's Austin 35.

But no one asks these things, though everyone knows about them. They never come up.

While Dandy gives his evidence he looks straight at Manuel. Manuel is glad that no one can see his face from the press or public galleries. He keeps his eyes trained on McKay's chin, hoping that distance makes it look as if he is meeting his eye. During a lull in the questioning, when Grieve and Leslie are discussing something or other in low whispers, McKay gives Manuel a twitch of a smile. Manuel feels sick when he sees it. If Dandy McKay wishes you ill, then ill will surely come to you. When Dandy holds his eye and blinks slowly Manuel knows he will die soon, one way or another, because Dandy has ordained it. And Manuel remembers the night in December, when Shifty and Scout took him and Watt to the Gordon. Manuel remembers that there is worse that Dandy McKay can do to him.

When he was arrested Manuel said he bought the Beretta from 'a man' inside the Gordon Club.

Dandy is thanked for his cooperation. He gets down from the stand. Unlike the other witnesses, he doesn't scuttle guiltily through the witness-hall door. Dandy has decided to stay. He wants to watch from the witness seats but they are all full. Three different men half stand to offer him their chairs. Dandy takes the best one and orders the man next to him to leave as well. Dandy likes to spread out.

14

Tuesday 3 December 1957

MAURICE DICKOV SIGHS HEAVILY and asks William Watt, 'What do you think you are doing?'

'I'm trying to speed things up,' Watt says sheepishly.

'DON'T.'

Watt shakes his head and speaks softly, 'Maurice, when I paid for my wife, I didn't expect –'

'Did you think I would go there myself?' Dickov bares his teeth in a smile. 'Did you?'

Watt doesn't answer. Scout seems to be giggling and trying to hide it. Shifty is ablank. It's as if he isn't there.

Maurice comes around the desk to Watt, who cowers.

'William, we are both businessmen. We have all chosen the wrong men to work for us at one time or other. It is not easy to find a man for a task like that. What can I say? I chose the wrong man for the job.'

It sounds so reasonable, Watt doesn't know what to say.

Maurice continues, his hands out, 'I have asked you before: let me fix this. You said yes. Now you're interfering with our plans. You have been recompensed with the land deal, a big deal, and now –' Dickov opens his embrace towards Manuel and looks disappointed – '*this.*'

Watt tries to explain. 'Maurice, it's been over a year . . . it's too long.'

Dickov glowers at the rug. He is actually furious now.

Dandy reads how angry Maurice is and it makes him nervous. Everyone is afraid of Dandy but Maurice Dickov is the problem. Dandy steps in to take over before something terrible happens. He comes around the desk and stands between them and Maurice's wrath.

'We've been chasing you two bastards a' night.'

William Watt means to step forward to address his accusers but he is extraordinarily drunk and staggers about in a strange offbeat dance. The circle of men watch until he is still. Now he has blacked out again and forgets why he is dancing in front of men in a dark office.

Dickov raises his voice. 'THIS IS DECIDED.' This is rare. Everyone is scared now, except Watt because he's blacked out and wouldn't know trouble if it bit him on the arse.

Watt shrugs and steps back to Manuel's side. That is a big mistake. It suggests an alliance.

Dandy watches Dickov carefully as Dickov tilts his head, a smile localised to one corner of his mouth.

Watt begins his defence. 'The night fell away from us,' he says. 'But, Maurice, you must understand. I've been disgraced, my business –'

'NA'B'DY GAES A FUCK, WILLIAM.' Dickov's accent is no longer affected émigré. It's pure Shettleston. 'You want people to think you're a good guy. *You* want to think you're a good guy. You think you can pay us to kill your wife and still you're not responsible? You're a fucking *VUSHKA*.'

Dickov has shocked himself by using a word of his baba's. It is low Bulgarian for parasite. He stops. He breathes and says calmly, 'The whole deal has been a mess, I admit. In part because you don't even know who is in your house at night-time. But we are fixing this –'

Watt whines, 'It's taking so *long*.'

'WE'RE CLEARING THIS UP AND YOU'RE PISSING ALL OVER IT. You've been with Scout to the cops. *It's decided*.'

No one says anything for a moment. It is in the pause that Manuel steps forward and speaks to Maurice Dickov. His life has been a catalogue of impulsive errors but this is the biggest mistake he will ever make.

'I'm going to hang?' he slurs. 'Just me, myself? Why wouldn't I just tell them yous have give me the job?'

Maurice seems calm. He smiles pleasantly. He crosses his arms. 'You let yourself go in that house, Peter, didn't you? You did what ever little fancy came to mind. Now you pay. You hang. We will take your mother. We will rape and kill your mother.'

Manuel's mouth falls open. He looks as if he might cry.

'We will rape and stab her tits,' says Maurice. 'We will dump her fucked bleeding naked corpse in the front garden of your pitiful home. Your father will be found guilty of it.' Manuel is afraid to breathe. Maurice hasn't made the threat conditional yet and he makes Manuel wait. Then he leans in. '*If* you tell.'

Manuel knows Dickov means this. Dickov will find a man for the job, a man with a history of doing things like that, and he will pay him to indulge the worst of himself on Manuel's mother, just as Manuel did his worst on Watt's family.

Dandy McKay is watching this and listening as his world collapses. Dandy has done dark things, bad things. He justifies them through a complex, fragile theology. All of this is shattered by Maurice threatening to have someone's mother raped and killed. Suddenly, unexpectedly, he sees that the Gordon Club will end soon. Dandy will lose a lot of money and status because of Peter Fucking Manuel.

Abruptly, Dandy punches Manuel hard on the side of his head. Manuel loses his footing. It wasn't a very hard hit but he was off balance. He stumbles three steps and the circle of Scout and Shifty close in around him. Watt is left outside, looking away, confused and needing the toilet.

Manuel has his fists up but only to block. He knows he can't hit back. He looks from Scout to Dickov to Shifty to Dandy. Only Scout, grinning and showing his raggedy teeth, meets his eye. Scout's eyes say, Sorry, pal, but I'm at work.

Dandy punches Manuel again and again until he hits Manuel's cheekbone at an awkward angle and splits the skin on his knuckle. Dandy shakes his hand and huffs. He's angry about it.

Scout waves Dandy back, offering to take over, which is good of him because he's got two shiners and a broken nose already.

Graciously, Dandy lets him.

Scout tips his head to ask if Manuel is ready?

Manuel is ready and drops his hands. Scout throws a punch in a wide arc, looking as if he will hit his face but actually aiming for his stomach. As the fist hits it winds Manuel and Scout laughs at his own joke. Manuel wasn't ready for it. It knocks the breath from him, makes him stagger.

Scout giggles and, smack, hits Manuel on the side of the head, then on his ear. He short-jabs Manuel's mouth and cuts the inside of his lip; blood bubbles up between Manuel's teeth.

Scout maintains eye contact with Manuel while he hits him. They're having a conversation – ready? Bam! Here comes another one. Crack. Over soon. Come on, pal. Here's another. Not too bad.

Manuel knows who he is among. He has taken beatings all of his life and knows when it is worth fighting back. He has taken much worse than this, knows Scout is being measured. He is hurting Manuel but it's really only symbolic.

'Yes, darlink, but do be careful,' Dickov admonishes gently. His eyes are on the carpet and the glass display cabinet. He doesn't want his office smashed up.

'Sure,' grins Scout, panting a little. He looks at Manuel again, punching him on the side of the neck this time.

Manuel chokes, coughing blood, wheezing. The circle tightens around the beating. William Watt is out of the circle. He looks up and sees himself in a mirror over Dickov's desk. A shadow is over his face, it hoods his eyes. He looks dead. He can hear the smack of knuckle on bone, the huff of breath from Manuel, feet shuffling on carpet.

Watt looks like death. If he was dead he would be with Marion, who knew him as no one else ever will. He didn't know what sort of man Dickov would send. He didn't know Vivienne was there, she'd said she was going to Deanna's house. He didn't know Margaret was there. He isn't responsible for what happened. He just got in with a bad, bad crowd.

Scout stops suddenly, and says, 'Oh no!'

He yanks his shoe off. He caught the heel on the side of Dickov's desk and pulled it loose. He examines it, mutters, 'For fuck's sake.' He has ripped the leather. He's annoyed about it. He likes these shoes.

Manuel holds his hot face, swallows blood and looks at the broken heel. It is only ripped along the seam, he says, any cobbler could fix that, easy.

'Really?' asks Scout.

'Aye,' says Manuel. 'They can stitch along there. Any good cobbler.'

Shifty leans in to look at the damage. "S cobbler. Good 'un. Skinny wee joint by Central.'

'Next to the sweeties place?' asks Scout.

'Nah,' says Shifty, 'down by the low-levels.'

146 • denise mina

The beating has reached its natural end. They look to Dickov for direction and he nods. 'So, that's enough. No more of this.' Dickov gives Manuel a linen handkerchief to wipe the blood from his chin. He pats his arm. 'This is how it has to be.'

Manuel nods.

Scout pats Manuel on the back. 'No harm done.' They all look at the damage Scout has done to Manuel's face. Manuel couldn't hit back so it feels kind of wrong, as if Scout was taking his black eyes out on Manuel. Scout wants to apologise, redress the balance of power between them, but Manuel is already down. An expression of sympathy would compound his disadvantage, so Scout leans in and whispers, 'Couldn't see your way to lend us five bob, could ye, pal?'

Manuel laughs, spluttering blood onto Dickov's lovely rug. Scout laughs with him. Even Dandy chuckles a bit.

'Right, that's enough.' Dickov claps his hands together and raises a gentlemanly hand towards the door.

Grinning, Scout reaches for the handle. His knuckles are bloody and ripped and swollen but Scout doesn't seem to have noticed.

Watt and Manuel head out and Dandy follows them. Scout calls 'Cheerio' and Manuel grins back through his rapidly swelling lips.

Dandy leads them to the stairs. They stand in the cold and quiet. No one knows what to say. 'I left my car at the Cot,' says Watt to no one in particular. Dandy looks down the stairs, feels the cold morning coming and this whole glorious period of his life coming to an end. He had money and power and celebrity but it is over. Dandy knows who is responsible. He goes for Manuel again, grabbing him by the hair, dragging him to the top step. He throws Peter down sideways.

The sound of a bag of meat being rolled down stone steps echoes through the stairwell. The falling stops. Manuel doesn't groan but Watt knows he isn't dead because he hears him panting. Then he hears him trying to get up, sliding down the wall, groaning. He's not dead.

Watt is frozen. He thinks Dandy will come back and get him if he moves. Dandy's shoulders are slumped. He seems very sad. Then, with the smallest gesture imaginable, Dandy nods Watt out.

William Watt scurries past him, keeping to the far side of the stairs. He jogs down the landing, takes Manuel by the elbow, lifts him to his feet and gets him out onto the street.

Manuel is winded and cannot speak. He tries to pull away but Watt holds his elbow tight with one hand and hails a taxi with the other.

'Mm fine,' growls Manuel, his teeth clenched, blood bubbling on his lips. His knee buckles but Watt holds him up.

A taxi draws up and Watt opens the door without letting go of Manuel.

'I'm taking you home, Peter. It's the least I can do.'

15

Monday 19 May 1958

THE MEDICAL EXAMINER, PROFESSOR Allison, is in his mid-seventies. He is bald and thin. He doesn't like the feel of dentures, not even for moments as formal as a High Court appearance. His mouth is clapped in. He looks like a cheerful crescent moon.

Despite his Gothic appearance and the horrific nature of his testimony, he has a twinkle in his eye and a cheery demeanour because he is talking about his work. The courtroom is spellbound, everyone cranes to listen. He smiles a gummy smile up at the balcony of women, wishing that his students would listen as carefully.

Manuel gave detailed confessions to all eight murders but he has pled not guilty in court. This is why the forensic details of each and every death have to be presented to the jury.

M.G. Gillies asks him to tell them about Isabelle Cooke first. Professor Allison tells the court that she was strangled. When her body was finally found her muffler was still tied around her mouth, which would have contributed to her asphyxiation in no small measure, but the real cause of her death was her brassiere. Her brassiere had been ripped off. He proves this by showing the broken clasp and the way the metal hook has been yanked straight. The brassiere was then wrapped firmly around her neck, crossed at the back and pulled tightly thus: he jerks his hands away from each other. It would be a threatening sight but Professor Allison is very old and frail and it doesn't look scary, just informative.

'Had Isabelle sustained any other injuries?'

'She had been beaten on the back and the neck. She had lost both shoes and cut her foot during the episode of running. And she had extensive bruising on her crutch.'

M.G. Gillies hesitates. Professor Allison has said 'crutch' instead of 'crotch'. Gillies doesn't want to linger on the poor child's crotch but he worries that it is unclear. He stares at Allison, hoping the professor will correct himself but he doesn't. Gillies doesn't know what to do so he just moves on.

'Were there signs of intercourse on Isabelle's body?'

'No. But she had been handled very roughly and her under-garments had been ripped off. Also, when she was buried, she was naked and posed so that she was exposed on the bosom and the "crutch" area.'

Professor Allison smiles a little and nods, letting M.G. Gillies know that he is saying 'crutch' deliberately, because of all the women listening. He expects the advocate-depute to be pleased at his delicacy but M.G. Gillies is of a different generation. Gillies was in the Royal Artillery. He was evacuated from France in 1940, went back with the Allied invasion of Italy and fought on for two more brutal years. He knows there are worse things in the world than directly referencing a woman's crotch, but he enjoys Professor Allison's conviction that there isn't. It is sweet and naive, so much of a gentler time that he envies it. Gillies moves on to ask about Anne Kneilands.

Anne Kneilands is an older case. A bludgeoning as opposed to asphyxiation, says Professor Allison. Her head was battered and 'human debris' was found as far as ten feet away. Yes, Allison smiles and nods, indeed, an *awful* lot of force would be required to break through the human skull and spread the contents so widely over the golf course. Really, an *awful* lot of force. This piece of angle iron was found at the scene and is a remarkably good fit to the wounds.

To illustrate, he is given Anne Kneilands' skull and the angle iron. The skull has an oblong hole smashed in the back. Professor Allison turns the iron lump in his hand, fits it into the matching hole in the skull and smiles triumphantly up at the court. His pragmatic face says, See? See what I did?

The angle iron is 'devoid of human debris' though because it was found in a burn.

Professor Allison is furnishing the court with the cold scientific facts but they have the narrative too. Manuel signed a detailed confession.

This is Manuel's story:

Anne is in East Kilbride, waiting for the bus home, when a man walks out of the dark. She calls out to him: Tommy? No, he says, I'm not Tommy. My name is Peter. He joins her at the bus stop. Has the number 70 has been yet? She says no and they fall to talking. She tells him she's just been stood up by a soldier she met at a dance last week. She's fed up.

Auch, never mind, he says, that happens to everyone.

Does it?

Aye, everyone gets dizzied sometimes. People miss buses, forget or run out of dough to get where they need to be.

Well, she feels like a fool.

Never mind, he says, don't take it so serious. What age are you?

Seventeen, she says.

You're young, he says. Don't take it so serious.

When her bus comes he gets on too, though it's going a different way than the 70. They don't sit together, he sits a few seats behind her, but four stops later he gets off when she does.

Oh, are you getting off here too?

Yes.

They're pals by then.

Well, I'm off this way, she says, and remembers her manners – Nice to meet you.

He looks over the golf course.

It's a bit dark for a girl alone, he says, I'll walk you over.

There's no need, says Anne, I go this way all the time, it's quite safe.

He flattens a hand to his chest, stands tall and formal, mocking himself a little. I couldn't possibly let you.

So he walks her across the fields towards her house. They climb a stile and walk onto the dark golf course. Anne screams and claws at his face, scratching three long welts in his left cheek. No, he doesn't know why she did that, it sort of came out of nowhere. Then she runs away from him. He runs after her, across mud, across grass, following her panicking shadow. She is swallowed by the earth.

He catches up to where she disappeared. She has fallen down the dyke, the one by the burn. It's very steep, about a seven-foot drop, and he can see the slide marks in the muddy banks where she went down. She's lost a kitten-heel shoe. The heel is stuck in the muddy bank. He looks down the dyke and sees her running along it. She gets out the other side and runs to a wooded area. He gets down the dyke and follows, climbs out and sees a copse of woods. She is gone but not gone. She is hiding. He knows she is. He slides behind a tree and stills. He waits, breathless, listening.

Two small animals hide in the dark. They wait for five minutes. It's a long time to stand still in the cold, alert to only one other person in the world, listening for a breath or a step or a shift of weight. It's intimate.

A branch moves somewhere nearby. He can hear her stand up. A step, a twig snapping, she creeps out of a bush. She looks around, shoulders hunched, scanning the open ground, looking for him.

He lets her take a few steps into the open. He lets her shoulders drop, lets her look to the lights of the road. He lets her hope. Then he runs out.

She is screaming quite loud and runs through the undergrowth and doesn't see the discarded barbed wire until she is stuck on it. She is pulling and he watches. She sees him watching and screams. He wants her to stop screaming but she doesn't. He picks up a bit of metal from the ground and hits her head with it. Yes, it was a few times. By the tree in the undergrowth. Quite a few times. He had to hit hard to stop the screaming.

She stops screaming. She is stuck on the rusty roll of barbed wire. He looks at her for a while. The metal thing is heavy in his hand, dragging his shoulder down, making his neck ache, but he doesn't let go. It gets too much for him and he drops it to the ground and it rolls down the bank and into the burn. He realises what he has done and where they are. He smokes some cigarettes.

He turns away and walks the mile across raw December fields to a Gas Board work shed. He knew it was there because he was working for the Gas Board then, up at East Kilbride. He changed his boots in the shed, they had blood all over them. Then he walked the eight miles home to Birkenshaw.

Manuel has made three different confessions, on the same night in Hamilton Police Station, just after Dandy McKay beat him up in front of eight officers. The confessions are typed by cops and then signed by Peter Manuel. The confessions are given to Detective Inspector Robert McNeill of Glasgow, and to Chief Inspector William Muncie, the South Lanarkshire cop who hates Manuel more than anyone else in the world. Muncie has been pursuing Manuel for twelve years, since he first arrested him for housebreaking and sexual assault. Muncie always gets his man. His career covers fifty-four murder inquiries. 'Incredibly, every one was solved,' it says in his own memoir. That is incredible.

Manuel's first confession is a promise to help with certain matters.

His second confession is a promise to help them solve the murders of Anne Kneilands, Isabelle Cooke, the Watts and the Smarts.

His third is many pages long. It is a detailed narrative account of the things he has done.

Isabelle Cooke: Just over the bridge at Burntbroom I met a girl walking. I dragged her into a field. I made her watch as I put stones in her handbag and threw it into a burn. I walked her into the dark. She started to scream. I tore off her clothes and tied something round her neck and choked her. I picked her up and took her to a field. I started to dig a hole but a man cycled past on the path and he stopped to see what I was doing. I waited until he was gone and then moved her over to a darker place and I buried her.

The description of the Watt murders tells how Manuel crept along the dark street and approached the house. How he smashed the window and slid his hand in to open the door. How quiet it was and about the picture of the dog and chiffonnier and the Mascaró Dry Gin and the sandwich. And the women: pop pop. Pop. Pop.

He tells them how he broke into the Smarts' house on New Year's morning and found the family in their beds, how he shot the boy first. He didn't know it was a child. He thought it was a small man.

How he took Mr Smart's car and drove it around for a few days, leaving it in a factory car park and going to get it again, leaving it in Florence Street, outside Dandy McKay's house. He confesses to returning to the Smarts' house and hanging around it for days. Hanging around in there, being peaceful, being in control of everything. He opened and shut the curtains in the front rooms to throw the neighbours off. He fed the cat a tin of salmon, because he's got the Kitekat out of the cupboard, but then he's looked at the tin of salmon and he's went, you know what, no one else is going to eat that, are they? Not now.

In the confession he tells them how he got the Webley and the Beretta and from who. He admits wrapping up both the Webley and the Beretta and dropping them in the Clyde by the suspension bridge. It takes a team of divers two weeks of raking through sludge in the freezing brown water to find them. Finally, when they bring them up, the guns are wrapped just as Manuel described: the Webley in a pair of his own sister's gloves, the Beretta in a scrap of cloth from the Smarts' house.

Manuel gave these confessions but now refutes them. He instructs his counsel to argue against their admission in court on the grounds of police fraud: they typed things he did not say and then signed on his behalf. As evidence for this he points out that each confession is signed by a different hand and the name varies. The first is signed 'Peter Manuel', the second 'Peter Anthony Manuel', the third one is signed 'P.T. Manuel'.

Harald Leslie refuses to present this argument in court because it is stupid. If they argue that the police signed the confessions then the Crown will simply call the police officers who witnessed Peter Manuel signing the confessions. Any cop who was attempting fraud would be careful to keep their signature consistent over three documents signed in a six-hour period.

Relations between Manuel and his counsel, already strained, get worse when they also refuse to plead 'intolerable pressure' to the confessions. 'Intolerable pressure' is a technical term for blameless children who have confessed to crimes without first being cautioned. Manuel was under caution and has been drawing convictions for rapes and robbery with violence since he was twelve. He is now a hardened criminal of thirty-one with a string of charges.

Harald Leslie does argue against them being admitted but only on the grounds that his client had no access to a solicitor for forty-eight hours after his arrest and hadn't slept for two days. His father was arrested when they came for Peter, a pair of gloves from a burglary were found in his dresser and he refused to say they came from his son. The arrest of Samuel was solely for the purpose of putting pressure on his son. When a writer suggested this to Muncie years later the old cop smirked and accused him of having a 'nasty mind'.

Lord Cameron hears Leslie's arguments, but rules that the confessions be admitted into evidence. They are shown to the jury.

The morning after the debate over the confessions the court reassembles. Peter Manuel waits until the jury are in, Lord Cameron is seated and the public are all there and settled. He likes an audience. Then he asks to confer with his counsel.

The discussions are intense but inaudible. Grieve is smiling excitedly, quite out of character. Leslie nods solemnly and seems to ask Manuel for confirmation again and again. Manuel gives it.

Harald Leslie asks permission to approach the bench and, in a whisper, informs Lord Cameron that Manuel has just sacked Mr Grieve and himself. Mr Leslie's final act as counsel is to inform the court that Mr Manuel wants to represent himself in the case from now on.

The stakes are raised. Representing himself on a capital charge is risky for everyone. Manuel risks messing up the evidence and being hung. It is Lord Cameron's first capital murder case, he doesn't want an appeal on the grounds of the wrong evidence being admitted. M.G. Gillies, prosecuting the case, has no idea where the defence case is going now. Nothing is predictable. The press are beside themselves with glee. They have bought interviews with just about everyone in the case, ready to run when the verdict comes in, but Manuel is who everyone wants to hear from and now they're going to get it for free.

As his first action, Manuel moves to recall several witnesses. Harald Leslie and William Grieve failed to question them according to Manuel's specific instructions. The first witness he wants to recall is William Watt. He also wants to call both of his parents to the stand.

In the next morning's editions Harald Leslie is pictured arriving home at his house in Edinburgh's Morningside after being sacked. His young son meets him at the gate and takes his daddy's hat and briefcase. Leslie looks younger and relaxed. He is smiling. Many years later Leslie is interviewed about the Manuel trial. All he will say is that it was a difficult case, principally because of the way his client's story had changed and kept changing.

16

Tuesday 3 December 1957

WATT AND MANUEL SIT in the Vauhall Velox, looking at the wall of black night at the end of the road. This spur of Fourth Street is a stubby dead end, leading straight out into country fields.

Birkenshaw housing scheme is based on geometric utilitarian principles: First Street, Second Street, Third Street. The houses are terraced up-and-down, with small windows to keep the heat in. Each roof has four chimneys, one to serve each of the principal rooms. The hour at which a house's chimney starts to belch is a signifier: decent houses rise early and prosperous houses have coal. The Manuels' chimney is awake. His mother is up already, warming the kitchen, making the breakfast, ready for the workers.

It is 6 a.m., December dark, and the inside of the car is so cold that condensation settles on the dashboard chrome. The wooden floor of the car feels soggy and soft under the carpet, damp radiates from the metal chassis. Yet Watt and Manuel linger. Neither wants the astounding night to be over. They are both nostalgic for it already, here on the threshold of the end.

Watt wipes condensation from the window glass with the side of his hand and looks at the Fourth Street house. The Manuels have the upstairs and downstairs, one window on each floor. The front door is around the side, facing the dark fields. A concrete bracket shields the door from view, supporting a flat portico. A man could come and go without being seen.

Manuel's chin is swollen. His eye is bruised. He has a cut on his lip, not deep but swollen, red and angry. The real damage is to his ribs, which are cracked. He keeps his arm tucked into his side and his breathing is shallow.

To waste time, Manuel takes his cigarettes out of his inside pocket and taps the packet on his knee, knocking a single cigarette up. It's a good trick. It impresses people. He saw it in a movie and practised and practised until he perfected it. He sees Watt watch the gravity-defying miracle from the corner of his eye and give a fond, drunken smile at the trick.

Manuel puts the cigarette between his lips and pulls the packet away, flicking his lighter and holding the flame to the tip. The paper crackles as it takes the flame. He inhales but doesn't reach for the door handle and now they both understand that he'll stay in the car until he has finished smoking it. They are both pleased at the reprieve.

Orange halogen street light catches thick cables of white smoke exhaled through his nostrils. The smoke flattens on his knees. Oily smoke rolls across his lap and lifts slowly into the air.

For no good reason Watt titters, remembering something of the night and Manuel echoes the sentiment, puffing a laughing sound out of his mouth. Watt nods and smiles and Manuel realises for the first time that Watt thinks they are the same. That makes Manuel laugh properly, and Watt laughs along with him. Watt is the only one laughing together. Manuel is just laughing. They're tired and drunk and they sit in the car laughing.

They hear the tramp of work boots behind them, coming up the quiet street. Manuel watches in the side mirror. An older man in a jacket and bunnet, a muffler and overalls, carrying his lunch tin under his arm.

The man reads the car, the not-work-jackets, the smoke curling in the cabin and knows the men have been out carousing all night. He tuts and sparking ash blows from the stubby Woodbine hanging from his lip. Manuel watches the sparks die in the wind. Manuel reads that the man makes a virtue of hard graft. He thinks he is a good man because he works hard for no money. He sees suddenly that Manuel is looking at him and drops his gaze, masking his judgement, passing the car. He speeds up and is swallowed by the blackness at the end of the road.

Manuel works out where that man lives. He is coming from the back of the estate, is about fifty and wearing clothes fit for heavy, dirty work. He has a piece tin with him, which means he isn't coming home for lunch. The jacket is pressed though, so he has a wife. He must work far away. He is walking over the fields, not down to the main road for the bus to either Hamilton or a works in Glasgow. He's going over to the Edinburgh bus stop. His gait suggests he has been walking for a block or more, he's into the stride of it. It's the father Connelly. Three daughters. The oldest daughter married two weeks ago. Manuel remembers seeing the scramble outside the house. His mother will know them from the chapel.

The bride's scramble is a tradition. As she leaves her parents' house for her wedding the bride casts handfuls of loose change into the street as a last gesture. Children scramble for the money. The bride throws money away because she won't need her own money any more, once she's married. It's a tradition that will die as cars become more common and the shortcomings of inviting small children to reach under moving vehicles becomes more obvious. Good scramblers can get a lot of money on a Saturday, if they know to listen out for news of weddings and manage to get to more than one.

Manuel tried to marry once. She was decent.

Watt titters again, his belly shaking on his thighs. He is now trying to revive the moment when they were both laughing, two minutes ago. The night is puttering to a stop like a car with no petrol.

Manuel takes another draw on his cigarette and gets back to his train of thought.

She was decent and clean. Manuel didn't know if he loved her but he felt something strong about her. She reminded him of his mother. Peter wrote anonymous poison pen letters to her, warning her off Peter Manuel. He is a beast and has a dark past. You can do better. Peter still doesn't know why he did that. It bothers him.

'We going in for a cup of tea?'

Watt turns to Manuel, smiling drunkenly. He is drawling badly and his blinking is uncoordinated. Manuel imagines his mother's face if she saw Watt. He imagines her heavy silence hanging in the house over the next few days. He imagines her, bowed in the dark at the kitchen table, reciting her rosary for him when he happens in for a drink of water. He imagines her naked and raped and stabbed and lying in the neat front garden.

'No.'

Watt doesn't know what to say about that. He shuts his eyes and shakes his head.

'Wee cup of tea?'

Manuel looks across the garden to the window into his parents' front room.

It's dark behind the glass but light glimmers from the kitchen. On the inside sill of the front room is a small plaster statue of St Anthony. A beacon. A priest gave it to his mother.

Watt slurs, 'I'm too tired to drive back without a cuppa. Come on, let's just go in.'

'No.'

'Come on, Peter, I *need* a cup of tea.'

'Wish we'd got in the cellar.'

Watt follows the misdirect, laughs and nods and gives a low whoop, a half-laugh, and looks away. They are both glad they didn't get through the door. The erotic frisson of that part of the night is distant and confusing now.

'You been in there?'

'No,' said Watt, 'but I'd certainly like to!'

Manuel breathes an affirmative 'Ha!'

'Ha! Come on.' Watt has the car door open, leans back in the seat to lever himself out.

'No!' Manuel grabs his arm. 'No!'

Their eyes meet. They are both surprised that Manuel expressed an emotion. He is breaking character.

'No,' Manuel corrects his tone. 'I'll bring tea out here.'

Watt looks sad. 'You won't have me in your home.'

Manuel glances at the dark front-room window. His mother's face bobs to the surface. Brigit steps back, swallowed by the shadows again, but she has seen the car and knows he is there.

'I can't bring you in.'

Watt is looking at the window too and saw Brigit's face.

'Was that your mother?'

Manuel stubs his cigarette out in the car's brimming ashtray.

'Why can't I come in?'

'She's seen you in the papers . . .'

Watt looks at the window, as if all of the rejection he has been subjected to is there, behind the glass, denying him tea.

Manuel rubs the salt in gently. 'I hardly can, Bill. It's my family.'

Watt is drunk. His moods slide across the surface of his face, water on oilcloth. 'I know, I know . . . It's your family.'

Manuel opens the car door.

'Wait here.'

As he slams the car door, he savours the pleasure of manipulating Watt into doing something else, of being in control of another person. He slams it loud, hoping the neighbours will look out and see him getting out of a car. He walks along the fence to the gate and jumps it with one hand on the post. Around the back his mother has already hung out a smalls wash.

The front door is unlocked. He steps into the hall and finds her in the kitchen. She is standing facing the door, waiting for him. Stern, hands clasped in front of her, the thin gold crucifix around her neck catching the light from the door. She looks as if she knows where he has been.

'Mum.' He sees her soften. She loves him. She is glad he is back. He goes into the kitchen. 'Say, where's the cups?'

She glides across the kitchen to the cupboard and takes out two cups, puts them on the table and pours well-brewed tea from the pot. As she is adding a sugar to each she asks who the man in the car is.

'Just a guy, Mum.'

He has said Mum twice, which means he has done something. He sees her face twitch.

'Does the "guy" have a name?'

She adds the milk. Manuel is tempted to tell her the name, to shock her. His mother is horrified by William Watt, a man who would kill his own family. She's talked about it a lot.

'John Patterson.'

A Protestant name. She doesn't approve but understands now why the man was not invited in.

'What happened to your face, son?'

Manuel steps over to the small mirror hanging over the sink. It's not as bad as he thought. He was worried his eye might swell up but it is just a cut on his lip and bruises on his jaw and forehead. He looks at his mother.

'Scrapping,' he explains, as if he was a naughty boy.

Brigit's mouth tightens but her eyes twinkle. She so wants to love him, for him not to be lost. Peter can feel the heat of her longing. But it isn't a choice. He hasn't chosen to be lost.

'There's your tea, son.'

Manuel takes the cups. He wants to thank her but thinks it will make her more suspicious. He goes back out to the car.

Watt takes the small brown cup from Manuel and slams the door as if he longs to be alone with the tea. As Manuel walks around to the passenger door he can see Watt drinking as if it is whisky, glug-glugging it.

By the time he gets in the car Watt has finished. He looks at Manuel's cup avariciously. Manuel laughs. He doesn't even want the tea that much but he drinks it, holding Watt's eye over the rim of the cup. As he drinks they both start smiling, Manuel with his eyes, Watt wide-mouthed, hoping still that he will get more tea. But Manuel drinks it all down.

He pulls the empty cup from his face and Ha! laughs.

Watt pretends he doesn't care. He opens the glovebox in the middle of the dashboard and takes out a hip flask, keeping it out of grabbing distance. Ha! he retorts and unscrews the lid, keeping his eyes on Peter.

This is a leather hip flask, not an overpriced bottle bought from behind a bar. This is good stuff. The smell of peat fills the car.

Watt drinks from the flask, smiling, then not smiling, remembering what Manuel has done for him, taken for him, what happened at the Gordon. He stops drinking. He swallows. He looks away as he hands the flask to Manuel. It is a peace pipe.

Manuel sucks a tut between his teeth and snatches the flask, drinking it all for spite.

It wasn't piss-whisky in the hip flask, it was an old blend, unexpectedly strong. The vapours are rolling around the back of his nose. Now Manuel feels sick but he can't complain of nausea because hard men don't feel a wee bit sick. He lights another cigarette and hopes he won't spew.

'Peter?'

Manuel looks at Watt's saying-sorry-eyes. He tuts and looks away.

'It wasn't my decision,' pleads Watt, 'I didn't even know you then.'

Manuel cannot talk about this any more.

He gets out of the car, chucking his burning cigarette away and swaggering around the back of the car. He's sure he's going to be sick. As he passes he slaps the flat of his hand down on the roof and the loud bang makes Watt jump in his seat. Manuel can't bring himself to smile. It would make him sick. He can't jump the fence either, it would come flying out of him if he did that. He opens the gate like a housewife and shuffles through. It takes so many tippy-tappy wee steps to get through, he hates that. Hates to be seen to do that. He doesn't look up for a last sighting of Watt but steps in through the front door with one stride, knowing Watt is watching him.

He stands in the dark hallway of his house, his back to the cool plaster wall. He hears his mother at work in the kitchen. He hears creaks from upstairs as his brother swings his feet over the edge of the bed, as his sister steps across the room upstairs and he's glad he didn't let Watt come in here, to his family.

17

Monday 26 May 1958

PETER MANUEL HAS CALLED his mother as a witness. Brigit Manuel is a small woman with salt-and-pepper hair pulled back and tied at the nape of her neck. She wears a two-piece suit and a plain blouse. She has tucked her crucifix inside her blouse because she knows most of the people here are Protestants. She doesn't want to offend anyone.

She looks tired. She is. She has been awake all night praying for the strength to do the right thing. She stands now in the cavernous courtroom and says a final *thy will be done* as the Bible comes towards her hand. When she swears by Almighty God to tell the truth, the whole truth and nothing but the truth, she means every word. She means it unconditionally.

Laurence Dowdall is in among the lawyers watching on the lower gallery. She can't see him but she knows he is there. He said he would be. It gives her strength. Mr Dowdall is a good Catholic gentleman. He represented her husband: when the police came for Peter they also arrested her husband, Samuel, for having a pair of gloves in his dresser that had been stolen from one of the houses. Peter gave them to his father as a Christmas present. Samuel said he didn't know where they came from, maybe a cousin in America? They arrested him. Mr Dowdall said they were just trying to put pressure on Peter.

They know how attached he is to his family. Brigit cherishes that statement.

Mr Dowdall refused to take Peter on as a client but he did take Samuel on. He explained that he couldn't take Peter and his reasons were legal. Brigit doesn't understand why. She would have liked a Catholic lawyer for her son.

By and by, she and Mr Dowdall have become friends. They have been saying a novena to St Anthony together. St Anthony, patron saint of lost people.

As the Bible withdraws she glances up at the public gallery, sees the faces of the watching women. Brigit recognises the expression. She is used to being pitied. She has thought and prayed about it a lot. She thinks pity isn't really about the recipient, the only thing it is eloquent about is the giver, but it still stings.

Both of Brigit's sons have been in prison. Her husband was expelled in disgrace from the local council when the police caught him watching women through bathroom windows. Now her son may hang for murdering women and girls and children. If God is testing her this must be her Gethsemane. But God has not called her here. Her son has called her here. She flinches from the realisation, looks up again at the pitying faces and thinks: they're all Protestants and bound for hell anyway, so who are they to pity her?

No. Dear Lord. The sin of pride. She thinks truncated, familiar prayers asking God to grant her the grace of humility, grant forgiveness, grant acceptance. Thy will be done.

Peter is standing in the court, looking up at her. He looks well and healthy and confident. His hair is immaculately swept back covering the tiny bald spot on his crown he worries about so much. His sports jackets and shirt and tie and slacks are nicely pressed. His face is clean-shaven. Very formally, and in just the right sort of language, he asks his mother to identify herself by name and address and she does.

'I believe,' he says, 'you are also my mother?' He flashes her a wry smile. It is about nothing and for nothing and asking nothing. A fond, wry smile.

Brigit smiles back. 'I am,' she says softly.

Peter and Brigit look at each other, both think of St Peter denying Christ three times. Or rather Brigit thinks of that and Peter knows she is thinking of it. He always knows what she is thinking of. It's one of the things he loves about his mother, her predictability, the signs and signifiers, her clarity.

Taking the confessions from the productions table, Peter shows her the signature on each of them and asks his mother to compare them. 'Do these look like my signature?'

No, she says, they don't look like his signature.

Peter tries to make her say that he couldn't have signed them but she can't lie. She's under oath. She frowns at the papers. She says his writing is usually very neat and in this particular one the signature goes over the line. That's unusual for him. He stays inside the lines.

He smiles at her. His writing is very neat, he likes his writing.

'Does anything strike you about the variations in the form of the signature? "P.T. Manuel", "Peter Anthony Manuel" and so on? Would you say they are the signature of the same man?'

She knows what he is trying to make her say but she can't. She holds his eye and tilts her head softly and says she has no way of knowing that.

'*Could* a policeman have signed these instead of me?'

Brigit wants to say the police are to blame but that isn't true.

'I don't believe they could have,' she says quietly, 'I'm not sure they'd know your confirmation name is Anthony.'

Manuel flinches and changes the subject. He asks her about times of alibis and she remembers nothing. He goes into a lot of detail and she says over and over that she doesn't remember what happened on the evening of Monday the 2nd of January two years ago.

He is deflecting. He doesn't want to discuss his fraught relationship with the Church but knows that his mother does. He certainly doesn't want his confirmation name discussed in court. Confirmation is a sacrament for Catholic children. No one in the Lanarkshire Police is Catholic, they're unfamiliar with the naming convention. Catholic children choose a saint's name for themselves, a saint they hope to emulate, or for whom they feel a special devotion. Peter Manuel was ten when he chose St Anthony, the patron saint of lost people. Two years later he was convicted of stealing a collection box from a Catholic chapel, a crime against the Church. The court sent him away to a Catholic approved school run by the De La Salle order. Manuel went in a petty thief who committed troubling offences against the Church and came out a rapist. He was so disruptive there that he was transferred to Hollesley Bay Borstal. Throughout his life Manuel's relationship with the Church is intense and defiant. He will not talk to priests or go to confession. He commits many of his worst offences after attending mass.

On the stand Brigit does remember one particular detail though and swells with pride at the telling: Peter attended midnight Mass last New Year's Eve with her and his father. They came back to the house and had a sing-song. Then everyone fell asleep and the Smart murders happened.

Peter doesn't want to discuss his confirmation name in court, or his relationship with the Catholic Church.

He moves on to asking his mother about the morning he was arrested. She says that when the policemen, 'gentlemen' she calls them, arrived at the house with the warrant, Peter was asleep in the bed chair in the living room. They arrested him. The next time she saw him was two nights later, when she was called into Hamilton Police Station to see him. Peter asks if she could tell them about that night?

Brigit says that Detective Superintendent Brown and another policeman arrived at her house at two thirty in the morning.

No, she wasn't in bed. She was awake. She couldn't sleep. She was drinking tea and trying to say the novena to St Anthony. Day two of the novena: *O holy St Anthony, gentlest of saints, the answer to my prayer may require a miracle.*

Mr Brown asked her to come with them to the police station and see her son; Peter had something to tell her. When she got into the police car her husband, Samuel, had already been picked up from Barlinnie where he was being held for the night on the charge of having the gloves from the housebreaking. He was handcuffed and surprised to see her. He looked exhausted. He asked if they had arrested her too? No, she said, no, Samuel, we're going to see Peter, he has asked to speak to us together.

Brigit and Samuel are driven to Hamilton Police Station. Outside, a mob has formed despite the hour. Mostly the public, coats over nighties and warm boots, but also journalists, eager for scraps of information to call in for the second or third edition. The car is driven round the back and they are taken through the back door to the station lobby.

The hallway stills as they walk in. Everyone has stopped moving. They are ushered to the bottom of a big staircase and Brigit looks up. Uniformed police officers line the stairs, two or three on each step. They are all staring at Brigit and Samuel. They've gathered here to look at them.

Samuel shouts up at the police officers on the stairs: this is mistreatment. He will write to his MP about this, make no mistake. Brigit can hardly look at him. He's making things worse.

But she stands by her husband at the bottom of the stairs lined with angry policemen. She puts her foot on the first step and thinks of the Via Crucis. She takes a second step and berates herself for the arrogance of supposing this an emulation. She takes a third and tries to offer up whatever is about to happen. She tries to pray but feels herself beset by enemies, forgotten by God, in the valley of death.

The policemen on the stairs shrink away from Brigit and Samuel as they pass. She sees their eyes widen, drinking in the sight but somehow vacant, as if they are already remembering this, telling someone else the story of seeing this: that couple, with a son like that. She has been laughed at and insulted and shunned. Once, down in Coventry, spat at by a policeman because of her son. But it has never been as hostile as this. Brigit knows, then. *The answer to my prayers may require a miracle.*

They are led down a passageway to a grey metal door. DS Brown says that they are about to meet Peter, that he has something important to tell them.

Brown knocks carefully and identifies himself. The door opens and they walk into a green-tiled room with a sharp overhanging light.

There are ten or fifteen policemen inside, standing around the walls, staring solemnly at Brigit and Samuel as they shuffle in. William Muncie is there. He has searched Brigit's house many times over the past twelve years. He takes milk and three sugars. He drops his eyes at the sight of her. She always feels that Mr Muncie wants to cry when she catches his eye.

The door is shut behind them.

Peter is sitting in the middle of the room on a low chair. His feet are planted firmly on the floor, as if to resist more shoves. His hands are behind the chair, cuffed, she thinks. Usually immaculate, Peter's hair is messy and he has no jacket or tie on. His neck is bruised, the shirt undone at the neck. It looks as if someone has yanked him by the shoulder. It looks as if they have been hitting him. Not on the face but on the body. He is the only person in the room who is sweating.

He looks up, sees her and sighs. His head flops on his chest. She can see a bruise creeping up from under his collar.

DI Robert McNeill steps out of the mob of cops. She nods a hello.

'Come on now, Peter,' says McNeill, 'you asked to see your parents. Don't you have something to tell them?'

Peter keeps his eyes down and shakes his head like a drunk.

McNeill is exasperated. 'You said you wanted to talk to your parents. We've gone to a lot of trouble to bring them here.'

Brigit steps forward like St Veronica. 'Son? Are you all right, son?'

Peter flinches from her. His jaw is tight.

NcNeill is annoyed. 'For goodness' sake – look, it's the middle of the night. We've got them both up out of their beds because you asked to see them.'

Peter lifts a hand and runs his fingers through his hair. She sees now that he isn't handcuffed to the chair. He was assuming a pose, like in a film. Brigit steps back into the crowd. She isn't St Veronica. She is a fool who falls for his lies every time.

'Let my father go,' says Peter, full of grand biblical touches.

McNeill is livid. He has realised it was all a trick too. He says, 'Peter, we've been through this already. I've told you it's the Fiscal who decides that. Your daddy will have to appear before the court in the morning.'

But Peter doesn't even listen to the explanation. He blinks and nods, wiping the setback from his mind. Brigit has seen him do that before, many times. Then Peter looks at his father and nods beneficently, as if they have agreed to let him go on Peter's say-so. But they haven't agreed to let him go.

She says, 'Look, Peter, what is it you want to talk to us about?'

But Brigit knows what it is. He looks at her and sees that she knows. Silently, Brigit starts to cry.

He slumps, puts his elbows on his knees and mutters at the floor, 'I've never found it easy to talk to you . . .'

Brigit falls to her knees in front of him. She holds his hand to her forehead. 'I know. I know there are things you find hard to say to us.'

Her tears drop onto the back of his hand.

Peter whispers, 'I don't know why I do these terrible things.'

'Oh, Peter.'

She holds his hands and kisses them. She kisses them so that she doesn't have to look up at him. Then she does. He is looking at her and then at his father. His eyes are dry but his face is the mask of a man who is crying. But his eyes are dry.

'I'm going to help the police solve some mysteries that have been happening in Lanarkshire recently.'

He directs everything else he says to his father but she doesn't hear it because she knows. Her son is not coming back. He's never coming home again. She's grateful and ashamed of her gratitude in equal measure. *The answer to my prayers may require a miracle.* A miracle has been granted but not for Peter. She realises that Peter wasn't the lost person. He's not coming home ever again.

The next day the newspapers report that a man and a woman were driven away from Hamilton Police Station at three thirty in the morning in the back of a police car. The woman held her face in her hands and seemed to be crying uncontrollably.

Standing in the dock now, with all the eyes of the world boring into her, Brigit relates the cold facts of who was where and when. She only adds one bit of illuminating dialogue:

'You said that you didn't know what made you do these terrible things.'

Peter freezes, one hand on his notes. 'Are you sure?'

Yes, she says, she is.

He nods as if he understands and forgives her mistake. 'Is it possible that you *misheard* me say that?'

No, she doesn't think so.

He half smiles. 'Yes, I see. But the room was full of policeman, was it not?'

She agrees it was.

He sighs indulgently, giving her an out. 'It was the middle of the night, you were in a room full of policemen: is it not possible that you heard me say something *like* that, or were told I'd said that or that Brown told you I'd said it before you arrived or something?'

'No, Peter,' she says, her voice unwavering, 'I heard you say that.'

No one else ever mentions this comment. Is Brigit misremembering? Is she more honest than anyone else or more emotionally engaged with the comment? Or is she lying, breaking her sworn oath to God to tell the truth, committing a terrible sin that may hang her son and save the world from more carnage?

Later, M.G. Gillies gets up to cross-examine her. He knows what the jury are thinking about.

'Just to be clear, Mrs Manuel: earlier you said you heard Peter say he didn't know why he did these terrible things?'

'Yes. I did say that.' Brigit is very sure. 'Peter told me he didn't know what made him do these terrible things. That's what he said.'

'Did you hear him talk about the charges against him? The charges on the warrant?'

'No. But at some point he said, "There is no hope for me".'

Gillies is very uncomfortable about having to cross-examine Mrs Manuel. She was called to the witness stand by her son but it doesn't make her presence here any less soiling. He can see why she was called: she is a decent woman, Manuel is showing the jury that he comes from good people, but it doesn't mitigate Gillies' feeling that she is being publicly identified to no real purpose. Gillies bows slightly and thanks Mrs Manuel very much. He hasn't thanked any of the witnesses very much.

Peter gets back up. He is very obviously annoyed and Brigit cowers. They are all afraid of Peter's temper. A domestic terrorist, he controls the house with his moods. They can all gauge his humour from the sound of his footsteps, from the way he turns a door handle or pours himself a drink from the tap in the kitchen.

He can't let it go. 'Why do you think I said "I don't know why I do these things"?'

Brigit is confused by the question and hesitates. 'Um, do you mean what do I suppose was in your mind when you said it?'

'No, I don't mean that. I mean "why do you think I said it".'

The question is no clearer but Brigit knows better than to ask him twice when his eyes are narrow like that and his jaw is set. She answers simply, 'I heard you say it.'

He pauses. He nods at his papers. He gives a bitter little smile. If they were in the house Brigit would be looking for the doors out of the room. They are not in the house and she needn't be afraid but she is. Her stomach is churning. She feels beads of sweat ping in her underarms. She wants to run away so much her knees are tingling.

'Did you hear me say it' – his voice is very loud now – '*plainly* and *clearly*, or is it just an instance where you *think* you heard me saying it?'

Her voice is quiet. 'I heard it, Peter.'

My prayers may require a miracle.

He nods heavily. 'You *heard* it?'

'Yes.'

His raises a threatening eyebrow. He huffs a bitter laugh. He shakes his head. She has a desperate need to calm him down, offer tea, give him money to go out, put the wireless on to distract him, but they're in court. It occurs to her that maybe she doesn't need to calm him down any more. He isn't coming home. As if he can feel her slipping the leash, he raises his voice and tries again.

'Then can I put it like this: did you *definitely* and *plainly* hear me saying "I don't know what makes me do these things"?'

Brigit's panic rises to a pitch. She is lost in a sea of pitying Protestants and her son is shouting at her to recant. And still she says, 'I did.'

Peter glares at her. Brigit sees the darkness there, worse than ever. If he gets out he will kill her.

They've all finished with her.

Brigit gets down, stiff-kneed with tension. She tiptoes across the wooden floor, keeping her eyes down as she passes her son. He doesn't glance at her. He picks up a sheet of paper to examine it and the tip of the page trembles, amplifying his fury. Brigit drops her head and hurries out.

Samuel is standing inside the door of the witness hall and the Macer calls him to give evidence before they can speak to each other. She passes him and Samuel sees her sorry face. He knows the look. It hasn't gone well. He bristles a reproach.

Samuel takes the stand and denies everything. Those confessions are definitely forged by Muncie, who hates Peter and drags him in for questioning every time a pin is dropped in South Lanarkshire. Peter never left the house when any of the crimes were committed, he remembers perfectly. Muncie has been harassing Peter non-stop. Peter was at home on the night when Anne Kneilands was murdered and on the night of the Watts' deaths. The police have been trying to arrest him for ages. DI Goodall from the city is a nutcase. After each of those murders William Muncie came to the house and searched it incompetently. South Lanarkshire cops routinely confide in Samuel: they know Peter is innocent. They're only here to please their boss. Old man Muncie has a thing about Peter because he's so clever.

He says one of the search warrants specified the Watt murders. Lord Cameron interjects to ask: did that particular warrant, the one concerning the Watt murders, not also mention the murder of Anne Kneilands?

Samuel cannot remember.

Lord Cameron doesn't believe him. 'I should have thought it would rather stick in your mind if you had police coming along with warrants for murders.'

Well, Samuel just can't quite recall. Prompted by Peter, he remembers that he didn't have his glasses on when the warrant was shown to him and he 'read it kind of hastily'.

Lord Cameron asks him why he claimed the sheepskin gloves came from a cousin in America when they actually came from Peter? Samuel says he was excited and doesn't know why he lied. Lord Cameron points out that he isn't excited now, is he? No, I'm not excited now. Well, says Cameron, perhaps Samuel could now furnish the court with his reasons? Samuel still doesn't know. He just doesn't know.

He is asked if he has ever been arrested and again he lies: no, he has not.

Asked about the statement 'I don't know what makes me do these terrible things', Samuel tells Peter: 'You NEVER made any such statement.'

But everyone knows Samuel is a liar now. No one is really listening, except Peter who is hearing what he wants. He nods and smiles and nods and smiles and thanks his father very much.

18

Tuesday 14 January 1958

IT IS A MONTH and a half since Watt and Manuel spent the night carousing together. It's eight days since the Smarts' bodies were discovered. Peter Manuel has been in Hamilton Police Station for fourteen hours. No one is allowed to speak to him. He knows they are following orders because he has asked for tea, for smokes, for a lawyer, he has goaded and teased and threatened and he is not getting back as much as a muttered curse. It is torturous for him. They know it is.

At nine in the evening he is taken from his cell in complete silence, led downstairs to a long basement room lined with raw concrete. It is damp and cold. Manuel is made to stand in an identity parade of five men. The room is so cold that their breath hangs in front of them, moist and dense. It's unfriendly as line-ups go. No one looks at each other which means at least one of them is a cop or working for the cops. The five men wait, ignoring each other, huffing cloudy puffs, shuffling from foot to foot to keep warm.

A door opens at the far end of the room. A wee guy of about eighteen, in a drape jacket with a velvet collar and wide-neck shirt comes in. He's a Teddy boy. His hair is slicked back. Manuel knows him from somewhere. The guy keeps giggling but his eyes look frightened.

Prompted by the cops he walks along the line of men, looking at them and then giggles over to the cops: hee tee hee.

DI Goodall speaks and it sounds like a bark because of the reverberation from the concrete: does he see the man who was spending the sequentially numbered notes in the Oak Hotel lounge bar on New Year's Day?

Tee hee: the man touches Peter on the arm and then jerks his hand away as if he has been burnt.

'Him?' asks Goodall.

Hee tee hee, yes. It's him.

Manuel recognises the guy now. He works behind the bar at the Oak Hotel. He was working the bar on the New Year's Day after the Smart murders. Peter was in there but the guy doesn't dress as a Teddy when he's working. He just looks normal then. Manuel remembers being very drunk that day. He remembers reading out the numbers to the barman. He was showing off, showing that he had money but pretending that he was just noticing the notes because the numbers followed on from each other and that was unusual. He tipped the boy five bob.

As if acknowledging this, the barman mutters a sorry as he is taken back out of the door.

Manuel steps out of the identity parade but Goodall tells him to stay where he is. All of you just stay where you are.

Another witness comes in. This one is a small angry man. He's been wound up by the buzzies and storms straight over to Peter.

'*This one*,' he shouts, staring in Peter's face. 'It's this one.'

'This is one of the men you saw driving down from Sheepburn Road on New Year's Eve?'

'Yes!' shouts the angry man. 'This is one of the two men.'

One of two men. Peter hears that. He's taken back to the cell. Again, no one will speak to him. Finally, after another two hours alone, in silence, he is taken to an interview room.

DI Goodall and William Muncie come in.

They sit down opposite him. Goodall is CID: a city cop. Muncie is country, local to Lanarkshire. They are having to work together and neither one is pleased about it. Goodall and his bosses think the Lanarkshire cops are a bit Home Guard, basically a Masonic Lodge with truncheons.

DI Goodall acts calm and neutral. He is a watcher. He is tall and sallow-skinned.

Chief Inspector Muncie is a beefy, square-jawed man. He has a military bearing and speaks like an angry sergeant major. He hates chaos and disorder and things not going the way he wants. But most of all he hates Manuel. His men call it 'Manuelitis'. He tries to arrest Manuel for every major crime that happens on his patch. In fairness he hates all the little scrotal criminals of South Lanarkshire, but Manuel is a special obsession of his. Muncie first arrested Manuel on a domestic burglary charge when Manuel was just nineteen. Muncie hates Manuel because he stubs cigarettes out on the arms of chairs, he eats his victims' food and grinds it into the carpet, he climbs into clean linen beds wearing muddy boots. He desecrates the houses he has broken into.

Muncie is here as a courtesy but he is not in charge. Goodall is calling the shots here. Muncie is made to sit and listen.

Peter asks after his father. Samuel was taken away by the cops this morning during the search of the house. He kept threatening the cops with his MP, with the papers, disrupting the search until they found the gloves and used it as a pretext to huckle him out to the car. Manuel doesn't know what happened then. They ignore his questions and confront him with the eyewitness statements.

You were seen driving away from the home.

Mr Smart was paid his wages on New Year's Eve. He was paid in sequentially numbered notes. We have a list of the numbers. You spent those very notes in the Oak. We have a witness.

Peter says nothing to that. He asks after his family.

Peter, says Goodall, we've arrested your father for going housebreaking with you. He's in Barlinnie. Imagine how your poor mother feels about that? She's in the house there, without your daddy.

Muncie smiles. Goodall smiles. They love the effect that has on Peter.

'Poor lady,' smirks Muncie, relishing being in charge.

Goodall says, 'You were seen driving away from Sheepburn Road on New Year's morning by an eyewitness.'

'I wasn't alone.'

Goodall sits up. Muncie clears his throat. His cheek twitches, as if he wasn't supposed to speak but he has swallowed the bait and can't stop himself. 'Who was with you?'

Now Peter is in charge and they are listening to him.

'I was with someone. He asked me to help him scout the area for houses to break into. I live there. I know the area. He was with me in the car. On New Year's Day he paid me those sequential notes for doing that.'

'Who is this man?'

'Someone you know,' he tells them and Goodall and Muncie look at each other. Muncie is excited. Goodall's top lip is beaded with sweat. They drop their voices confidentially.

Goodall asks, 'Peter, d'you think you could pick him out of a line-up?'

It is ten thirty at night. Peter Manuel is behind the door, having the identification process explained to him. You have to touch his arm, do you understand? He understands perfectly well. It's almost a joke, them explaining it to him. Muncie is breathing funny, as if he's going to laugh any minute. Goodall is smirking and even DS Brown, the CID high heidyin, has come down to watch from the corridor. Manuel doesn't understand why they think his accusation is funny. The door opens and Peter walks into the concrete basement.

Five men standing in a row, a drunk, a cop and three other people. Manuel walks sombrely along the line and stops at the flurry of colour and patterns. He puts his hand on Dandy McKay's shoulder.

Muncie, eyes shining, barks: 'Are you alleging that *this* man asked you to show him the bungalow in Sheepburn Road for the purposes of housebreaking?'

'I am,' says Manuel.

Muncie steps away, giving off a little nervous gasping titter. It's as if he's tricked a naive classmate into swearing in front of a teacher.

Dandy is angry. 'YOU SPASTIC BASTARD SON OF A CUNT. WHO THE BUGGERING SHITE ARE YOU TO FINGER ME?'

Dandy's shouting is painfully loud in the small concrete room. It booms so loud it doesn't just hurt the ears but the eyes. The cop and the drunk in the identity parade scurry out of the open door, their shoulders at their ears. Outside the door DS Brown leaves, laughing. A press of uniforms gather around the door to watch. The two spare men in the line-up linger for a moment, neither police officer nor habitual drunk, unsure whether they can leave. Goodall nods them out.

Muncie tries to disguise his glee by speaking with excessive formality. 'Mr McKay, Mr Manuel is alleging that he drove you around Uddingston scoping for houses to rob on Ne'erday last.'

'THE FUCK I DID. I'm Dandy McFuckingKay. The fuck am I doing stealing jewellery from fucking bungalows?'

'Do you own a gun, Mr McKay? Say, for example a Beretta automatic?'

It's an incendiary question. A Beretta has been mentioned in the papers with regard to the Smart murders. Dandy understands the implication.

'ME?' His voice rises to a roar. '*ME* OWN A BERETTA?'

Muncie smiles at Manuel, his voice calm and creamy. 'Is that a "no" from yourself, Mr McKay?'

'COURSE IT'S A FUCKING "NO". What is this? I was never in Uddingston.'

'Would you know anyone who does own a Beretta?'

Dandy reads Muncie's expression. It takes a minute for him to get the prompt but then – 'Aye. I do. *This* cunt owns a fucking Beretta.'

'Are you indicating Mr Manuel?'

'Aye, *he* owns a fucking Beretta.'

Goodall is smirking at Manuel. 'Do you have any idea where Mr Manuel might have got that gun from?'

Dandy looks Manuel in the eye and shouts, 'FROM ME. HE'S BOUGHT A BERETTA FROM ME.'

Muncie is loving this. He has been after Manuel for twelve years and only ever gets him for minor offences. He doesn't care what the charge is, he just wants Manuel in jail for a good, long time.

'Would you be willing to testify to that fact, Mr McKay?'

Dandy leans into Manuel as if he's going to nut him.

'AYE, I fucking would. And anything else you're worried about, Muncie, *any* evidence yees are needing, let me know. I'll get it sorted.'

Muncie looks Manuel in the eye and sneers, 'Legally we can't do that, Mr McKay, but I greatly appreciate the spirit in which that offer is made.'

Goodall is worried by the public nature of this conversation. There are witnesses in the room. He frowns at smirking Muncie and offers McKay the exit door.

But Dandy is fixed on Manuel. He's muttering swear words, a jumble of cut-up curses – youfuckcuntfuckingbastcunt. Dandy goes for Manuel. With animal annoyance the back of his hand swats Manuel on the ear. The other hand comes up and a fist hits

Manuel's throat. Dandy turns to Manuel, widening his legs into a boxing stance.

Goodall shouts 'NO!' and lunges in to stop it. But then he pulls back. He's a Glasgow cop, he can't touch Dandy McKay. He shouts, 'NOT THE FACE, MR McKAY!'

The cops who were leaving come back to watch Dandy punch Manuel's side, his chest, his side, his throat, cursing all the time.

Goodall is holding his hands out like a referee, watching nothing happens to the face. They can't appear in court with an accused with a sore face, not on a case this big. SMACK to the side and Manuel's lungs empty. SMACK in the gut. Manuel is bent double, struggling to get air back into his chest, drawing shallow, squeaky little breaths. Dandy stands tall. This is the beating he meant to give him at the Gordon Club.

Suddenly, Dandy straightens his jacket and spits on the floor. He tips his chin at Manuel who is bent double, huffing. Dandy is scared. Manuel will do anything. He'll finger-point and make up lies and tell stories until one sticks. Dandy shoulders his way out through the throng of open-mouthed cops at the door. Muncie follows him to take his statement about the Beretta.

Goodall and four uniformed cops take Peter back to the cell. He is left alone in the cold stone.

No one will speak to him. He can hear other prisoners, sounds echoing, but no one will answer him or speak. He tries goading the officers outside the door but gets nothing back.

Finally at midnight he says he wants to confess. He wants to talk to McNeill. Someone goes away but he doesn't know if they are going to get McNeill because they won't speak to him.

They leave him waiting, in this hellish silence, until 2.15 a.m.

The door opens abruptly. He is taken to a bleak interview room. The walls are grey. He is shoved into a lone chair in the middle of the room. Five uniformed cops line the wall. Peter speaks to them. I know you, don't I? Nothing. Or is it your sister I know? Not a flicker. It's as if he isn't there. They don't even look at him. Two stand by the door. One sits against the wall reading the *Daily Record*. Two more stand guard by the window. Manuel sits there for an hour, thinking.

DI Goodall and DI Robert McNeill come in.

'Hello again, Peter,' says McNeill. 'Would you like some tea?'

They give him tea. They give him cigarettes.

'What did you want to see us about, then, Peter?'

He knows before he says it that this will get a reaction: 'I want to see my parents. I want you to let my father go.'

'Hm,' says Goodall. 'Why would we do that?'

'I'll confess.'

'To what?'

'To certain matters.'

They all look at each other, mapping the cracks in one another's psyche. They appreciate that, together, this group of three very different men are going to try and navigate these rapids, come to a negotiated settlement. Goodall breaks the gorgeous, promising pause. 'Be specific.'

'Certain mysteries,' says Manuel carefully, 'that have been happening in Lanarkshire recently.'

They all smirk. They all know it isn't enough.

'Namely . . .?'

'Let my dad go.'

'We can't let your dad go. The sheriff will have to decide that in the morning. However, obviously, if you confess and take responsibility for the charges brought against him –'

'Which is it?'

'Smarts.'

Manuel reels at this. 'You're charging my *dad* with the Smart murders?'

'Well, Peter, he had gloves from their house in his dresser. He can't explain how they got there.'

In fact, Peter gave them to his father as a present. They were sheepskin and still had the label on them. Samuel can't bring himself to tell the cops something so damning about his son and they know that.

'So, it all depends on what you confess to.'

It's a clever manoeuvre. Manuel is a famous talker. Silence is intensely uncomfortable for him, he can't sit in silence for another moment.

The three men look at each other. Manuel wants something, a concession of some kind, a win. He doesn't really care what it is.

'I'll confess to everything if you bring my parents here.'

Everyone is slightly stunned.

' "Everything"?'

Manuel lists them quietly: Smarts. Watts. Isabelle Cooke. Anne Kneilands.

'What about Moira Anderson?'

She is an eleven-year-old girl who has gone missing.

'No.'

Even Manuel draws the line at little girls.

'Not Moira?'

'Not her. But I'll need to see my mother and father.'

'Are you *sure* not Moira?' The girl went missing in Coatbridge, not too far from Manuel's home. It would be good to get a proper mop-up.

'Not her, not the kiddie.'

'OK. The rest though?'

'Yeah, but I want to see my parents now.'

'Now?' asks Goodall. 'It's the middle of the night.'

'Now,' says Manuel, pleased with the effect of his request.

Before they arrive Manuel gives a vague confession, referring to certain matters. He signs it. It's not detailed enough to be of any legal use. It mentions no names or places or times. Goodall points this out so Manuel gives a second confession, addressed to McNeill, numbering the crimes he will solve:

1. Anne Kneilands
2. The Watt murders
3. Isabelle Cooke
4. The Smart murders

He signs it and McNeill reads it. No. They need details, for God's sake, Manuel, a general statement simply won't do. Manuel talks to Muncie and then signs a detailed narrative confession. They bring his father from Barlinnie. They get his mother from the family home in Birkenshaw. He sees them in the company of a room full of policemen.

Afterwards his mother cannot stop crying. She has to be helped down the stairs but resents being touched, even by her own husband.

Left alone with the cops, in penitent mood, Manuel is taken to Barlinnie and checked in.

Goodall, Muncie and McNeill are there with him at the reception bar. It is five thirty in the morning and they can almost smell their pillows.

They stand in a companionable silence. Manuel is handing over the contents of his pockets. Loose change. A handkerchief. The Sirs will be pleased. There has been criticism of the force in the newspapers – angry demands for them to catch the killers. It is personal: Muncie and Goodall are named and pictured in the papers as the men who have failed to stop this.

They're too tired to talk and too afraid to go home.

Goodall has been investigating this Smart case for eight solid days with little sleep. He notes his exhaustion in every limb, his shallowness of breath, his laboured heartbeat. He looks across the room and sees a prison guard sitting at a desk, reading the *Daily Record*.

'Jesus Christ!' he exclaims.

The front page of the paper has every murder Manuel confessed to. Every detail on the front page is mentioned in his confession. The handbag full of stones. The barbed wire. The tin of salmon.

It would produce a reasonable doubt in anyone's mind if the newspaper is produced in court.

Has Manuel pulled off a stroke of genius? Have those Masonic idiots in South Lanarkshire used Manuel's confession to mop up every single unsolved case on their books?

He confronts Muncie – are you jeopardising this collar for your own career advancement? Certainly not, smirks Muncie. You have a very suspicious mind there, Goodall, my man.

Goodall doesn't give a flying fuck for these games. We need more against the man, he says and Muncie sees that he is serious. Muncie makes them give Manuel his shoes back, his jacket back.

'Put them on,' Muncie tells him. 'There's one thing left to do. Tell us where Isabelle Cooke is buried.'

Manuel says, 'I can't. I don't know where it is.'

The room holds its breath as Goodall asks, 'Why not?'

Manuel smiles up at them. 'I am tired and I am cold,' he says.

'Cuff the bastard,' barks Muncie. 'Get the cars. We're going out to Burntbroom. He'll walk us to her.'

Chill January wind rages across flat black fields. Spiteful rain stings their faces. A ring of eight officers stand around them in case Manuel tries to run.

'Where now?' shouts Muncie.

By Muncie's account Manuel takes them straight to a hole and says he nearly buried Isabelle here but a man came along on a bike and interrupted them.

The group walk together for half a mile and Manuel stops. He bends down and moves a brick out of the way and one of her dancing shoes is exposed.

They walk on. They stop. Manuel says, 'I think I'm standing on her.'

Goodall and Muncie take him back to Barlinnie with an escort of four officers. They leave the other four at the site and send out a team of diggers. By the time they get back to the station the diggers have sent word: Isabelle Cooke has been found. Manuel had been standing on her.

They lock him in a cell and he falls asleep immediately.

19

Tuesday 27 May 1958

WILLIAM WATT IS IN the witness hall, waiting to be called back into
court. It is morning. He hasn't been able to eat since he heard he
would have to appear again and be questioned by Manuel. He
smokes a couple of the courtesy cigarettes provided by the court
but they're not his brand and they make him feel sick. He drinks
a lot of water to wash the taste away. Then he just sits, slumped,
in the painful, muffled silence and wishes he was dead. Dowdall
hasn't even briefed him for this court appearance. There is no
point. Anything could happen. Dowdall has reassured him: the
jury can't bring themselves to look straight at Manuel, Dowdall
thinks that means Peter will hang. It's a sure sign. The verdict is
the least of William's worries. Dowdall doesn't know that.

It has been a week and a half since the car crash and Watt's
last appearance. He is on a single crutch now. At Dowdall's
insistence, for the benefit of the drink-driving charge, he hasn't
had a drink since. Watt cannot believe how joyless his life is
without drink. Everything is grey and frightening and awful.
And now this.

Manuel can ask Watt about anything. Any single thing about
Watt's entire life. Watt's mind flips through a Wheeldex of
secret, awful shames spanning his life from early childhood to
the present. These are memories of falling, spilling, dropping,

losing, failing, failing, foolish. It is not a good way to prepare for an interview of any kind. He draws back and balances those recollections: winning, winning, bettering others, having, winning, getting.

The door opens and the Macer's face appears. 'Mr Watt?'

William stands up and promises himself drink tonight. Whisky. Amber glinting, good and plentiful, imbibed alone, until he passes out. This gives him the luxury of distance, he is removed, just enough, from this humiliation. It is half bearable. He could walk through fire and walls to get past this to a night on the drink. He takes the steps down into the court one at a time, using his crutch expertly.

Watt can see women looking down from the public gallery. They're not watching Watt hobble in on his crutch, though. They are watching Peter Manuel. He is sitting at the solicitors' table, absent-mindedly playing with a pen. Watt takes another step and glances over to the jury. They are looking at Manuel too. Dowdall said they weren't looking at him but they are looking at him. In the lower stalls, among the journalists and lawyers, Dandy McKay and Maurice Dickov sit in the front row. They deliberately catch his eye as he passes. Careful, their faces warn.

Nothing is going to be all right. Nothing is going to be all right. Dickov will get angry. Mrs Manuel will die and then Watt will be the only loose thread left.

As William Watt gets sworn in again his hands and feet are cold. He feels faint, doesn't even trust the walls of the room to do what they're supposed to. He imagines the balcony sliding forward and guillotining everyone.

Manuel is standing at Harald Leslie's place, at a table in the well of the court. He has stacks of papers in front of him. He looks smart and able and plausible and the jury are looking at him.

Lord Cameron clears his throat and speaks directly to Peter.

'Now, Manuel,' he booms in his sonorous voice, 'you wanted to ask questions as to certain matters which, according to you, passed at the meeting which you had with Mr Watt but were not put in court by your counsel?'

'Yes, My Lord.'

This is the first time Watt has heard Manuel speak in court. His voice is clear and confident.

'All right, now,' continues Cameron sternly, '*that* is the limit of the questioning.'

Cameron has limited the questioning to their night together. That's the worst thing he could have done. It's the one thing Watt doesn't want to answer questions about.

Watt can't bring himself to look up at Manuel but the jury are looking straight at Manuel. They shouldn't be. Watt thinks he will set an example by refusing to look straight at him. He stares at the jury, moving his gaze along the two rows. He can see the shape of Manuel in the corner of his eye, he's the only person moving in the court. Everyone else is completely still, mesmerised by him.

He sees the shape of Manuel come around the table, undo the buttons on his jacket, pull it back to rest his hand on his hip, look at papers. He's Clarence Darrow to the very life. He seems to be smiling at the jury.

As Watt watches, one of the women jury members presses her lips together in a non-committal reciprocative smile. The rest of the jury glance away as if they don't trust themselves not to submit to his charm. They don't meet Watt's eye though.

'Mr Watt,' Manuel begins, 'do you recall the first occasion upon which you and I met?'

He sounds so normal. Watt is aware that he can't keep staring at the jury, it looks very odd, almost threatening, so he shifts his eye to Lord Cameron.

'*I do*,' he says soberly.

It sounds as if he is agreeing to marry Lord Cameron.

An abrupt laugh explodes from a woman up in the public gallery. She stops herself, afraid of being thrown out, but the reverb hangs in the air long after it can be heard, a tuning-fork hum. Watt doesn't mean to be funny but he is. Journalists are smirking. The jury are screwing their faces up. Even Lord Cameron frowns deep at his papers. People have always found Watt ridiculous, he knows that, but this is not the time.

Manuel continues. 'It was a meeting, I believe, which you said transpired between you and I with no one else present, other than Mr Laurence Dowdall and he departed our company after ten minutes or so. Is that your recollection?'

Watt has never heard Peter Manuel talk like that. Even his accent sounds different.

'That assertion is correct,' Watt tells the side of Lord Cameron's face.

'Do you remember meeting me in a restaurant in Renfield Street? "Whitehall's", I believe, is the name of that establishment?'

Watt says yes to the side of Lord Cameron's face.

'Do you remember going over Crown Street to a public house, "Jackson's Bar" in the Gorbals. Is that your recollection?'

'Yes.'

Whitehall's. Jackson's. Manuel is working through the night, through the venues. Watt is suddenly back in Jackson's, remembering the smell and the noise and the ambience. It is a whisky-smelling, happy memory of being best and winning. The room is glowing orange and they have the corner and he is warm and drunk.

But Jackson's is rough. Everyone knows what Jackson's Bar is like, the sorts of people who go there. Still, it's not the roughest bar he was ever in. Thinking that brings the Moulin Rouge to Watt's undisciplined mind. The Moulin is the roughest bar he was ever in.

The Moulin was a dive, a crumbling basement in the Gorbals, rats under tables, sawdust on the floor, warm cloudy beer and whisky best-drunk-not-smelt. Watt was a half-partner in the Moulin just after the war, a time when everything was up in the air and a man could make his way.

The Moulin Rouge. Watt stands in the pristine High Court, every eye on him and the worst, the very worst, of his youthful late nights at the Moulin invade his thoughts in bright snapping images. Big Mamie doing her act in a back room. That guy Hector doing the elephant trouser gag. Moroculous Martin being sick into his pint glass and then trying to drink it because he thinks it is still beer.

The disembodied voice of Manuel continues, asking if Watt recalls being in Jackson's from seven o'clock until about a quarter past nine?

Watt feels caught out. He can still see Big Mamie's open-mouthed grin and tiny teeth. Well, he tells Lord Cameron, the timing was not something he was keeping a record of, but his throat is closing up. His fingertips are tingling. Talking to Cameron is like talking to a wall with eyebrows.

Manuel asks if he remembers the conversation which, at that time, took place between Mr Watt and himself?

Watt blusters, 'There was a *very* great deal of conversation during the time we were there.'

Cameron ignores him again, but his eyes slide over to him as if he is building up to telling Watt to leave him alone.

'Do you or don't you remember our conversation?'

'I do.'

Manuel can't take it any more and raises his voice. 'The question has been asked by me, *not* by His Lordship.'

Watt has been shocked into looking straight at Manuel. And it certainly is Manuel.

It's Peter Manuel and he's looking back at him. Peter Manuel has his back to the rest of the court, trespassers on their conversation. He gives Watt a tiny encouraging smile. We're still us, Billy, he seems to be saying. We're still pals. The two guys in the car, in those bars, at the Gordon.

Reflexively, Watt's eyes smile back. Now they're locked together, looking at each other.

Watt attempts a smile at the rest of court, feels his lips and cheeks sliding around in smile-suggesting ways. He knows he hasn't pulled it off. The press look back at him, blank. The women on the balcony are staring at him, mouths agape. He looks at the clerk, the stenographer, other officials. Everyone here hates him.

But then Marion's voice comes into his head so strongly and clearly that it makes him want to cry: don't be silly, Bill. This isn't about being liked, it's business. You're just being silly, aren't you?

'You remember our conversation, I take it?'

'Yes,' Watt tells his dead wife, Marion.

'Do you recall, in particular, part of the conversation in which you professed yourself agreeably surprised?'

It's such a wordy sentence that it throws Watt. He's angry that Manuel is using words like 'profess' and 'agreeably'.

But he must answer. He begs pardon and asks what he was supposed to be 'agreeably surprised' by?

Manuel purrs, 'Why, by meeting me.'

Watt tuts, 'I do not remember saying anything of the kind.'

'Do you remember telling me that you could "drive a car better than Stirling Moss any day of the week"?'

'That is a lie. You are lying.'

As Manuel fiddles with his notes Watt realises he's alluding to the driving back overnight from Cairnbaan allegation. Manuel isn't bringing up Dickov or the Gordon Club. He catches sight of Dandy in the public benches, sitting back, happy.

'In the course of that evening,' says disembodied Manuel, 'do you recall raising the matter wherein you alleged you had been selected, or nominated, as President of the Merchants' Guild of Glasgow?'

In among the lawyers in the well of the court, one or two faces rise slowly to look at William Watt. Lips tighten, glances are exchanged among the professionals. President? Of the *Merchants' Guild*? Did they hear right? How has Peter Manuel come to be discussing the Merchants' Guild?

Watt is embarrassed and assures Lord Cameron, 'Most certainly *not*.'

'You do not recall discussion of the Merchants' Guild?'

'No.'

'Really?'

'I have no recollection of that aspect of our conversement *at all*. No.'

Manuel takes a gentle breath and asks, 'Six and a half months before we met in Whitehall's did you take Scout O'Neil to the police?'

Right over Manuel's shoulder Watt can see Dandy sitting forward, lips tight. Manuel half smiles innocently. Watt clutches the rail. There is no point in denying it. It has already been raised in court. Scout talked about this. Watt has already been asked about it on the stand.

'I did.'

'And –' Manuel flicks through his notes – 'that would be on or around the 26th of May 1957?'

'Would it?' This isn't about their night together. Lord Cameron should be stopping this line of questioning. 'Hmm, I don't know . . . dates and so on.'

Manuel nods slowly, smiles quickly. 'I believe you met Mr O'Neil at the Gordon Club that night, did you not?'

Dickov sits forward too now.

'And I took him to the police,' says Watt, getting them out of the Gordon Club as fast as possible, 'to tell them that he had sold you the gun used in the Burnside Affair.'

'You met him in the Gordon Club, though?'

Lord Cameron interjects, 'These questions are not within the parameters laid out in my original direction, Mr Manuel.'

But they are. Four people in the court know they are. Manuel looks at William Watt and raises his eyebrows. He huffs a little laugh – hah – and looks down at his papers again.

Watt saw a picture of Mrs Manuel in the newspaper this morning. She is just a little woman. Ordinary.

'When you met Scout O'Neil that time, did you give him money to tell the police this story?'

'Certainly not.' Manuel is trying to discredit Scout, which is fine by Watt, he is happier with this line.

'Did you give him money?'

'No. That is a lie.'

'Yes, you did,' says Manuel confidently. 'You gave him money. When you dropped him home after, you gave him money.'

This doesn't matter really, this isn't the big lie, so Watt explains to Cameron: 'The man was in rags. His clothes were in tatters. I only gave him a pound to get a drink.'

Manuel lets that sink in and says, as an aside, 'After you met him at the Gordon Club . . . what did the police do with Mr O'Neil's information?'

'Nothing.'

'Nothing?'

'Nothing. They did nothing at all. They wouldn't listen to me.'

'Why?'

Watt drops his chin to his chest. He doesn't need to answer. Everyone knows. The press benches know. Everyone in the city knows. Watt isn't credible.

Manuel says suddenly, 'Do you recall describing to me the manner in which you killed your wife?'

Watt is winded. He struggles to draw breath and when he does his voice is faint. 'I never did anything of the kind.'

Manuel looks disappointed at the answer.

'Do you remember telling me that it was never your intention to kill your daughter?'

'I did not say that.'

'Do you remember telling me that after you had shot your little girl, Vivienne, it would have taken very little effort to turn the gun on yourself?'

'No, I don't, because I never said it.'

Manuel nods, as if this is just as he suspected. He turns a page in the notes, denoting a change of pace. 'Mr Watt, in the course of the night, after we left your brother's house, do you remember offering to give me the biggest boost I had ever had if I pulled up my socks and played the game your way?'

'That, also, is a lie.'

'You don't remember saying that?'

'I didn't say it.'

'You must have been very keen to clear your name?'

'Yes.'

'I expect you would have been desperate, Mr Watt?'

'I was very keen to clear my name.'

'Do you remember a conversation whereby you put to me this scheme: I was to find someone to take the blame for these crimes, a "joe" I think you called it, with the intention of clearing your name?'

'Nonsense.'

'Did you not tell me that your only mistake was taking the Renfrew Ferry to get to your house that night and being seen?'

'I did *not* cross on the Renfrew Ferry. I can prove that now.'

Watt means that the ferryman did badly in court but it isn't clear and he sees Manuel's neck twitch. Peter thinks something new has come up. Something that discredits the whole story of Watt killing his family.

'You have already appeared here before the court, Mr Watt, and you alleged that I described certain articles of furniture in the interior of your house to you?'

'You knew every stick of furniture in the place. It was uncanny.'

Manuel smirks at his hand. 'When you last gave evidence you made a statement on oath that I told you there was no safe in your house. Yet is it *feasible* that if I killed your wife, and was indeed in your house, that I would make detailed notes about the furniture and furnishings, but fail to note that there was a safe in the kitchen?'

Watt shrugs. It wasn't a question.

Manuel thinks he is being clever. 'Does it not in fact *prove* that I was never in your house, Mr Watt?'

'No, it doesn't.' Watt is right. 'Not noticing a safe doesn't mean you haven't been in someone's house.'

Manuel looks thrown by that. He doesn't really understand the art of adversarial legal questioning. He's watched it often enough and knows it looks like a fight without shouting or hitting, but it is infinitely more complex. It isn't just point scoring. Manuel is getting it wrong. He's angry about that and his voice changes. 'Mr Watt, you killed your family, didn't you?'

'No –' Watt is comfortable – 'I did not. I did not kill my family.'

'Well,' says Manuel, a nasty edge to his voice, 'did you ask someone else to kill your family?'

Dickov and Dandy sit forward in tandem and William Watt thinks of Mrs Manuel's picture in the papers. He's not surprised at Manuel doing this to his mother but he's sad, for her.

'No –' Watt's voice falters – 'I did not.'

'Did you pay someone to kill your family for you?'

Watt looks at Peter, trying to read him. 'No,' he says heavily, 'I did not.'

'That's what you're saying, is it?'

Watt nods softly at him. 'That's what I'm saying.'

Manuel holds his eye and takes a deep breath. Watt thinks he is going to shout. He's going to betray his mother. He's going to get her raped and killed. Watt braces himself. 'That will be all, Mr Watt. You can get down.'

Manuel and Watt look at each other. He hasn't. He won't. This is the last time they will ever meet. For a moment they're back in the car outside Manuel's house in Birkenshaw, giggling on a dark winter morning. Watt feels the warmth of a cup of tea against his cold fingertips. Manuel feels his gorge rise as if he's going to be sick. Watt sees Brigit Manuel fleetingly rise from the deep shadow of the Manuels' living room and drop back again, swallowed by the dark.

Dickov and McKay sit back in their chairs.

Manuel has saved his mother's life.

Peter and William both feel sad that it had to be him. It was always going to end here.

20

Tuesday 27 May 1958

IT'S THE FINALE. Peter Manuel is going to give evidence on his own behalf. He gets up, unbuttons his jacket and almost runs up to the witness box. He turns to face the court. The balcony, the lawyers, the journalists are mesmerised. Unlike most of the witnesses, he doesn't avert his eyes but has a good look at everyone. He's excited. He has been waiting to do this for a long time.

Now they will get to know the real him.

John Wayne Gacy wanted to write his own story. Ted Bundy wanted to be a writer and represented himself in court. Carl Panzram wrote his autobiography and represented himself at trial. Panzram had sailed the world raping and killing men and boys, he sailed full crew up the Congo from Lobito Bay and returned alone, yet satiated. When Panzram didn't like a witness's evidence in court he stared hard at them and drew a finger along his throat. Peter Manuel wrote fiction. All his life people commented on how much he liked to tell stories. Even early borstal assessments noted how much he liked to tell stories.

This is it. He'll never have a bigger audience, and they're discerning. They're actual writers: journalists, newsmen, novelists. Compton Mackenzie is here. He's been reading Lombroso. He notes the likelihood of Manuel having a 'Spain or Sicilian strain in his blood'. These people will see what the magazines couldn't. They will see Other Possible Peter.

Manuel speaks so fast at the beginning that Lord Cameron asks him to have mercy on the stenographer. Manuel smiles kindly down at the expressionless man who is tip-tapping out his every word for the record. He slows down.

Then he talks for six hours, largely without notes.

He tells all the stories of each of the murders individually. As he does this he recalls witness statements, word for word, stages small vignettes, recounts dialogue. Sometimes, to establish a new chapter, he reads the details of a particular charge before addressing the case against him.

In the defence's favour is his confident delivery, the fact that he is charged with horrific crimes but is just standing there, with legs and hair and a jacket on, speaking, doing normal human things. He couldn't have done those awful things, could he? But then, who could? Well, somebody did.

Against his defence is just about everything Manuel says, how he behaves and what he means. Ten minutes into the six-hour monologue everyone in the courtroom knows that Manuel has made a catastrophic mistake. He should not be speaking.

Peter Manuel does not know how other people feel. He has never known that. He can guess. He can read a face and see signs that tell him if someone is frightened or laughing. But there is no reciprocation. He feels no small echo of what his listener is feeling.

Anne Kneilands: it wasn't him. Sure, he was working nearby at the time, for the Gas Board. The only reason the cops liked him for it was the foreman on that job phoned them and telt them Peter appeared for work the day after the murder with scratches on his cheek and blood on his boots.

Now, Peter is a straightforward kind of person. He will not be spoken about behind his back. So he went to see the foreman and had a few words with him. Everyone knows what he means by 'a few words'. The guy, he says, walked off the job and went away to work somewhere else. Somewhere quieter. He snickers.

To Manuel this is how real men resolve disputes. He thinks he is telling them that Peter Manuel is a man in charge of situations, that other men respect him. Other men don't respect him. They are afraid of him because he is nuts.

Sure, he says, a witness claims to have seen him in East Kilbride that night, but they couldn't have seen him because he wasn't there.

The police were all over him at the time, searching his house, confiscating his clothes, bothering him, bothering his mother. His voice breaks when he says 'mother'. Jury members look up, hopeful. They want to find humanity in the man. But Manuel has moved on. He wasn't going to be harassed by the police. He decided to take action. He told a journalist to take his picture and to publish a story about the murder on the front page of the local paper with the picture. He holds up the page for them to see. Under the headline, LOCAL MAN QUESTIONED, is a photo of Peter standing in front of a car in his workman's clothing. He is smiling for the camera. This was published but did anyone come forward and identify him after that? No. Why? Because he wasn't there.

He moves on to the Isabelle Cooke murder and reads out the charge. He reads this out in a low, slow voice, hoping perhaps to sound sombre. He doesn't sound sombre, he sounds mocking.

"'On 28 December 1957, on the footpath between Mount Vernon Avenue and Kenmuir Avenue, Mount Vernon, you did assault Isabelle Wallace Cooke (17), 5 Carrick Drive, Mount Vernon, and did seize her, struggle with her, drag her into a field, tear off her clothing, tie a brassiere around her neck and a head square around her face and mouth, rob her of a pair of shoes, a brush, a fan, a stole, a pouchette of cosmetics and a handbag, and you did murder her, and such is a capital murder within the meaning of the Homicide Act 1957, Section 5 (1) (a).'"

The jury have already heard poor Mr Cooke talking about his daughter's disappearance and the discovery of her body. They've been moved by his quiet dignity. Now Manuel is doing silly voices.

Well, Manuel didn't do that murder. He wasn't there. He didn't know where the body was. Goodall and Muncie knew where it was buried all along and they just took him there in the middle of the night and said he'd told them where it was. 'I am standing on her.' Who actually says that? One might say 'I am standing on it', or 'I am standing on the grave', but 'I am standing on *her*'? No one would say that.

He doesn't say anything compassionate about Isabelle or Anne, two dead seventeen-year-old girls. To him they are no more than skin-covered stage flats in a play about him.

One of the jury men at the back yawns but sees Peter's eye on him and falters. He shuts his mouth and looks embarrassed. Peter wonders why he's embarrassed about yawning.

Next, he talks about the Watt murders. He tells the court he met Watt in Whitehall's and Watt was so impressed by Peter that he invited him drinking. Watt admitted everything to him. He told Peter that he drove back from Cairnbaan overnight and killed his own family. He didn't know his wife's sister would be there, but she was, so he shot her too. He meant to tie up his daughter, not kill her. Watt just meant to tie her up and then she would get free the next morning by which time Watt would be back at the Cairnbaan Hotel and have an alibi. It doesn't occur to Manuel that Vivienne Watt would recognise her own father while he tied her up. He says Watt told him that 'things got out of hand' and he killed her too. It took all of his strength not to turn the gun on himself after that. He does Watt that courtesy.

Later in their evening together, in the Gleniffer, Watt admitted that before he killed his family he had paid Charles Tallis five thousand pounds as part of an elaborate plan. Tallis was to break into the Watt house after the murders and ransack it, to make it look like a burglary, make it look as if the killer was in there for a long time to give Watt an alibi. Tallis was also supposed to take the gun Watt had left in the house and hide it. It doesn't occur to Manuel that Watt could save five thousand pounds by messing his own house up and hiding his own gun. Manuel doesn't address the fact that Charles Tallis had a cast-iron alibi, attested to by many witnesses. He just ignores that.

Jury members look at each other and shrug. They wonder why Lord Cameron is letting him say this stuff but Lord Cameron's job is to ensure that Peter Manuel is heard fairly and thoroughly, not that he is dissuaded from talking utter shite.

Manuel continues: why did he know where the gun was? Well, the day after the murders Tallis came to Manuel's house. He confided in Manuel and told him many details about the house, described the events and then, when Manuel was out of the room, planted the Webley in a dresser drawer. Manuel found the Webley later, while he was looking for string to wrap a parcel 'for a girl who was in hospital'. He immediately knew Tallis had planted it and knew what the gun had been used for. So Manuel wrapped it in one of his sister's gloves and threw it into the Clyde.

Laurence Dowdall approached Manuel and said he needed Manuel's help to clear his guilty client, William Watt, and frame Charles Tallis for the murders. Even Manuel knows this needs explanation because Dowdall is a famously smart lawyer and unlikely to go about sharing incendiary information relating to a client with someone like Manuel. Dowdall was desperate though because, with Watt as his client, Dowdall would be in for a share of Watt's wrongful imprisonment compensation payment, but they won't get anything unless someone else is convicted of the Burnside murders. When Manuel refused to be involved Dowdall threatened him: if you don't help us frame Tallis, then we will frame you.

Moving on to the Smart murders: Manuel tells everyone that he had been a friend of Mr Smart's for a long time. Mr Smart had both respect and deference for Peter Manuel, because Peter helped him when he was building his house. Peter knows about gas piping.

Just before New Year Mr Smart asked Peter to help him buy an illegal gun. Prowlers had been seen in the area and he wanted to protect his family. The two men met in the Royal Oak on New Year's Eve. When Manuel handed over the Beretta Mr Smart was so pleased that he gave Manuel fifteen pounds in brand-new, sequentially numbered notes. Then – oh! – Mr Smart remembered that a business associate, 'Mr Brown', was coming to call while the Smarts were away for New Year. Could Peter take this key to the family home and meet Mr Brown there and explain: Mr Smart isn't here. Mr Smart will leave out a bottle of whisky for Peter to give to Mr Brown.

He skips the part of the story where he goes to midnight Mass with his mother on New Year's Eve but suddenly, at half four in the morning, Peter Manuel is seeing 'a girl home safely from a dance'. On the way home Peter remembered that he had a key to the Smarts' house, that there was a bottle of whisky in there, so he just went in for another drink instead of going on to his own house. Jovially, he tells the jury that, although it was New Year, he was 'not moroculous drunk', just very drunk.

In the still bungalow, he found three bottles of whisky on the sideboard and a bottle of sherry. He had never seen that brand of sherry before: Romano Cabana. While drinking whisky he noticed that the house was in some disarray and it occurred to him that maybe the Smarts had not gone on holiday after all.

He went down the hall. He opened Michael Smart's bedroom door and saw 'someone in the bed'. He went to Mr and Mrs Smart's bedroom and saw that they were asleep in bed. So he put on the lights. It was then that he saw blood everywhere. They were both dead and Mr Smart had the Beretta in his hand.

Manuel went and looked at the boy. He was dead too. Mr Smart had killed his son and his wife and then turned the gun on himself. Manuel describes the scene: 'When you got to the bed and leaned over you could see blood on the wallpaper just on the far side of him and there was blood on the pillow.'

Realising that the gun was traceable to him, and not wanting to be implicated, Manuel got a pair of gloves and went around wiping his prints from anything he might have touched inside the house. He picked the gun up and wiped that too.

He looked at the dead couple. 'Normally, you would just leave them there, but they looked so bare.'

So he tucked the covers up around their chins.

Then he made to leave but a 'tiger' cat was in the house and wouldn't leave him alone. There was no milk in the house so he found a tin of Kitekat in the cupboard. Then he spotted the tin of salmon and thought, well, no one else here is going to eat that now. So he gave the cat the salmon. Then he took the Smarts' car and drove off and dropped the Beretta in the Clyde, by the suspension bridge, in the same place he hid the Webley for Tallis. That's why he was able to tell the cops where the guns were.

DI Goodall and DI McNeill are sitting in the court, waiting for the front page of the *Daily Record* to feature, but it never comes up. Manuel lies like a child, adding bits on, making narrative addendums when he realises that his story makes no sense – and then – and then – and then. He is spinning lies and then abandoning them. He's halfway through a lie when he switches back, or forgets.

He doesn't shape the story, seed the characters earlier and bring them on to behave consistently. New people who have never been mentioned before appear, cause life-changing events and then evaporate. Some characters even have placeholder names: 'Mr Brown', 'a girl in hospital'.

In Manuel's stories everyone is acting out of character.

The police are dumb.

Everyone confides in Peter.

He gives himself all the good lines and even stops to chortle at his own quips.

The jury hate him.

He sees them listening, puzzled by his lumpy edits, his grandiosity, his circular arguments.

The jury hate him, not just because he has killed lots of people, but for telling them such a stupid story. A bad story is annoying but a very bad story is insulting. Does he think they are stupid? Is he stupid? He clearly isn't stupid. He is very *something* but they don't know what it is. There's something really wrong with him.

Manuel feels none of this. He is Other Possible Peter and thinks the jury are as entranced by him as he is by himself. Other Peter is having a lovely time, talking, talking, talking. For the first time in his life he feels heard.

He doesn't feel what other people are feeling.

Other people are feeling insulted and bored and revolted. Other people are wishing he would stop talking about those poor girls that way. Other people are wishing they hadn't come here today. Half of the public leave during the break. They expected a dazzling monster, a Dracula, a shaman beast. This man is vulgar and commonplace and making mistakes all day. This man is ordinary. He doesn't know anything they don't know.

After six hours of Other Possible Peter everyone in the court wants him dead.

The jury have no qualms.

The lawyers feel he has tried himself.

This is his first capital case but Lord Cameron knows that if it comes to donning the black tricorn, it will cause him no sleepless nights.

Peter Manuel doesn't feel what they feel. Manuel thinks that went quite well.

21

Thursday 29 May 1958

'WHO SPEAKS FOR YOU?' asks the clerk of the judiciary.

The foreman of the jury stands up.

'Have you reached your verdict?'

He nods, takes out his glasses, curling the wire frames around his ears. He reads out the verdict.

Guilty.

Guilty.

Guilty.

Not guilty.

This is a shortened version. The actual verdict is very long; there are fifteen separate charges. It will be published in full in all of tomorrow's papers, reported verbatim in special pullout sections.

The foreman reads out the full verdict with details: this decision was unanimous, this one by majority. The murder of Anne Kneilands we found not proven, the murders of the Watts, the Smarts and Isabelle Cooke we found pursuant to theft.

The clerk writes in a large book, jotting it down in shorthand as the verdict is read out. When it is finished the clerk sits down at his desk and rewrites the verdict in longhand, leaving the foreman on his feet, clutching the rail in front of him. Transcription takes a full four minutes. While he writes no one in the room speaks.

The rustle and snap of the clerk's silk gown is heard clearly.

Up in the public gallery a woman struggles to muffle her cough. The panes of glass in the high windows buzz as a bus rumbles past in the street.

The city outside freezes. No one is waiting for the verdict, they're waiting for the sentence.

The audience in court is reverent but discipline breaks down in the street.

The mob heckle the building, chat cheerfully among themselves, laugh. Someone sings a baritone line of a song. The police are already annoyed at the crowd for blocking the road. Worried they'll be dispersed, the mob start to police themselves. Inside the frozen court they can hear the high hiss of distant hushing.

William Watt and Peter Manuel sit there awaiting their fate. Both stare straight ahead, aware of being watched.

As they await the sentence of the court Watt's beige suit darkens under the arms. Sweat drips down his back. He is trembling and cannot draw more than a shallow breath. He wants to loosen his tie but knows how guilty the cartoonish gesture would seem. He is not entirely without insight.

Manuel is calm. His heart rate is a lazy bump at his temple. It's easier for him: he has done this many times before.

They wait.

The clerk is finished transcribing the verdict. He rises to his feet, holds up the sheet he has been writing on and reads it back to the foreman of the jury. Is this record of your verdict correct?

The foreman says it is.

The clerk nods his permission to the foreman to sit. At the sudden release from duty the foreman's knee buckles and he drops awkwardly onto the oak bench. The loud crack clatters around the still room.

The clerk hands the longhand verdict up to Lord Cameron and turns back to face the public as he heads for his desk. When he is seated Lord Cameron whispers down to him. The clerk whispers back and Cameron, his patrician eyebrows unmoving, nods at Mr Gillies.

M.G. Gillies stands up and asks the court to pass sentence on charges four, six and seven. The murder verdicts.

Lord Cameron nods. Then he speaks to the room but his eyes are on Manuel, standing in the dock.

'It is the sentence of this court that you be taken from this place to the prison of Barlinnie, Glasgow, there to be detained until the 19th of June next and upon that day, within the said prison of Barlinnie, Glasgow, between the hours of eight and ten o'clock, you suffer death by hanging.'

The room is ready to spring but Lord Cameron was a commando in the war. He knows that swiftness is essential in the execution of brutal tasks. He reaches down to a special shelf below his desk, smoothly lifts a black tricorn hat with two hands, holds it over his head and recites the legal formulation that makes the sentence binding:

'This is pronounced for doom.'

He lifts the hat away from his head, a coronation in reverse. As he does there is a scurry in the dock. The manoeuvre is so nimble that the public, puzzled by the donning of the strange hat and the archaic grammar, don't look down until it is almost too late.

As if a plug has been pulled, the dock empties down the spiral staircase that leads to the cells below. The public leap to their feet and look down. All they see is an empty dock and the last police officer vanishing underground. All they hear is feet running on stone stairs.

It is a klaxon.

Suddenly everyone is moving, shouting, leaning over one another. William Watt covers his face to hide his shame. He is crying. In the shadow of the public gallery, standing flat to the wall, Laurence Dowdall sees his big, bald, bowed head nodding. Dowdall rolls his eyes up, turns his face into the shadows and says a silent prayer of thanks. The press benches empty round the two men. Above, the public bray with fury at the empty dock, robbed of their chance to heckle. From the balcony the women's voices are high and the resonance instantly unbearable.

The Macer leaps to his feet. 'SIT DOWN AND BE QUIET.'

They freeze. The rankling silence is cut through with a sharp metal click that ricochets from wall to wall. It is the sound of the door closing at the back of the lower tier. Journalists have gone to call in the news for the late editions. In the sudden silence called by the Macer the court can hear a stampede in the stone hall outside, thunder echoing in a high stone cupola as fifty journalists race for the four public phones by the door.

The story rolls out to the street.

The thousand people who are waiting to hear have been standing in smears of blustery May rain, waiting, staring at the Doric portico and waiting.

The cops have herded most of them across the street to Glasgow Green on the other side, but time and again they ooze over the kerb, spilling into the road, in the way of cars and carts and buses. It's nearly five o'clock, nearly teatime. Many of them have been waiting all day, some since the jury went out two hours ago. They've all been waiting, watching for movement in the court windows.

Now the doors to the court fly open and the journalists who lost the sprint to the phone boxes race down to the street, yanking their coats on. The mob surge across the Saltmarket to them, blocking the road, threatening to trap the journalists before they get their copy in. The journalists shout the verdict to fend them off: Guilty. Guilty. Guilty. Not Guilty. He'll hang in a month.

The triumphant roar can be heard over a mile away.

A green-and-gold double-decker bus is marooned in the flash flood of people. Excited passengers abandon their journey, spill out of the door to join the mob, amazed at their luck in washing up right here, right now.

Alone on the bottom deck of the bus, a behatted woman stares straight ahead. Her handbag is on her knee. She is stubbornly refusing to be interested in *that*. It is none of her concern. She does not wish to be involved. A man on the top deck calls out of a window for the score. The lady hears it hollered up from the street *guilty guilty guilty not guilty for Anne. Hanging.*

He shouts back, 'How come "no" for Anne?'

'Cameron's told the jury not to. Circumstantial. Auch, he'll hang anyway.'

'Good! *Good!*'

She looks in her handbag and finds a paper poke of peppermints, twisted at the neck. She takes one out, puts it in her mouth, sucking it sourly and staring straight ahead. She does not wish to be involved. But she is. The happy mob swirl and eddy around her bus, ribald, shameless.

High overhead a black rain cloud races across the sky, a tricorn hat darkening the city. It starts to spit.

In her empty bus the reluctant witness to history sucks her peppermint and stares forward to the driver's cabin. She is so distracted by the sharp mint oil on her tongue and the frenzy all around her that she is almost functionally blind.

Some have forgone the festival atmosphere in front of the court and are gathered around at the back. They know a van is waiting to spirit Manuel away to Barlinnie. This mob is not nearly-all-women but exclusively women. One hundred women stand and stare, headscarfed against the May rain, fingering stones and rocks they have gathered and put in their pockets. They would wait until the end of the world for this.

The police are ready though. The entrance to the cells is narrow and blocked off by mounted policemen in formation, holding the road open so that the prison van doesn't get stuck. From the moment the sentence was passed the prime objective of all the organs of justice is to ensure that he doesn't die until they kill him. Guards will sit with him, sleep with him, they'll be in his company every moment from now until the hanging so that he can't cheat justice.

After a few minutes a small black prison van races out from the enclosed yard, black smoke belching from the unwarmed engine. The horses bridle, the women shout. They throw their stones and scream words women shouldn't know. They chase the van down the street to a corner and watch it tilt on the bend. It gets away. Then they stop, open-mouthed, panting. They thought they would feel less angry but they don't. Their venom is enflamed but now it is aimless. Still panting, they head back for the heart of the mob at the front of the court, knowing they're not fit for any other company, not for a while anyway.

That van was a decoy. In an hour's time the actual van will leave and some of those who lingered will get a second chance to chase.

Back on the pavement, journalists are asking people for their impressions. Press photographers are snapping bulbs at the triumphant crowd. A television camera the size of a ray gun is mounted on a trailer in front of the court. The director is telling a man with a mic to go back, further back, Bill, we can still only see your shoulder. It is the first criminal case ever reported on Scottish television.

The mob disperse around the stranded Corporation bus. With a ting-ting from the bell, it jump-starts and rumbles slowly away. The peppermint sucker decides that she will not even mention being here when it happened. She smooths the hem on her coat. She is not interested in that sort of thing. Not that sort of person.

She will simply not say. Although, her sister-in-law is that sort of person. She might tell her. She rehearses her impressions as the bus rumbles across the Albert Bridge: the stillness, the howling roar, the chasing of the van, how the bus emptied but she stayed on because she is simply not interested in that sort of thing.

The edge of the mob thins and news sweeps up the smoke-choked valley of the Saltmarket, on up the High Street to the cathedral grounds and the Necropolis. It billows into shops and stations, around the looming black buildings of the begrimed city.

Strangers stop each other to ask, join conversations without invitation. Passed from mouth to mouth, the news crosses the river. It surges down through the black glowering valleys of Gorbals tenements and on to leafy Southside suburbs.

Swarming westward, the news reaches the shipyards and the dry docks. Crane drivers come down from their high cabs to hear. Welders stop in the middle of a line.

Along the river and up Gilmorehill, the news arrives at the ears of the students and matron aunts and academics. Translated into Polish, Gaelic, Italian and French, it blows east along the train tracks, through the gated community and crumbling tenements of Dennistoun, an area that has been rumoured to be coming up since Buffalo Bill's Circus performed on the waste ground there.

The news bursts open the door of the Saracen Head public house, announces itself to the smoke-yellow air. Two men, sitting in the very seats where Adam Smith and Dr Johnston had a drunken swearing match, chink their greasy glasses and cheer.

The news sweeps into pubs with facades that advertise a loathing of Catholics, a horror of Protestants, sores picked at and festering since the Reformation. It floods the dark satanic Parkhead Forge, manned by Irish Catholic immigrants because no one with a choice would do that work.

Far out on the Argyll coast the news reaches Brigit Manuel, sitting on a bed in a dark hotel room paid for by the *Empire News*. She cradles a small plaster statue of St Anthony that she brought with her from the house and weeps as her husband hangs up the phone.

News travels north, fast along the tram and train lines, hitting the solid cliff of black basalt that is the Campsie Fault and rolling back, reverberating over the city.

One hour before late-edition newspapers are dry from the presses everyone in Glasgow already knows they'll hang him in a month and they celebrate, because then their troubles will be over.

22

Friday 30 May 1958

THE DAY AFTER HE is found guilty his father and mother are allowed to visit Peter in the deputy governor's office at Barlinnie.

Brigit Manuel sits rigid. Samuel stands behind her, clutching the back of her chair. A scurry outside the door tells them their condemned son is approaching. The door opens and Peter is brought in by three officers. Both Brigit and Samuel expect him to be angry but he isn't. Peter is excited. His mood is up. He wants to talk about the trial.

Brigit is pleased initially, feels the relief of her husband at her shoulder. Samuel expected him to be angry as well, she realises now, though he never said so.

Peter sits down in the chair set out for him. He wants to talk about what happened, who said what and how he feels about it. He knows the *Empire News* has bought his mother's story for a lot of money. He encouraged his parents to do the deal. He thinks he is talking directly to the press through his parents. He doesn't know that Brigit has infuriated the *Empire News* with all of her conditions: she will not talk about the trial or the crimes or speak about any of those poor people. She will not describe the night of the confession or this meeting now. She will talk only about what sort of boy Peter was when he was growing up, how much she loved him and prays for his soul.

But Peter thinks he is holding a vicarious press conference. He grandstands about Lord Cameron's conduct of the case. Peter wanted to give a speech at the end of the trial, after the verdict. He wanted to address the room, he'd been thinking of things to say, about his treatment in the press and Harald Leslie's conduct, but Cameron said no.

'Maybe he thought you'd said enough,' says Brigit.

Peter nods towards her, not really hearing her but acknowledging that she has spoken. And then he's off again, rambling about his lawyer and the possibility of his appeal and how the van from the court wasn't very safe and he should have had a seat belt if they were going to drive at that sort of speed.

As he talks Brigit looks at her son's hands. They are in front of him, hanging between his knees, palm to palm. He is chopping them for emphasis as he would have in court.

Brigit imagines enfolding her son's hands with hers, transferring the warmth from her skin to his skin. The hands are not a big man's hands, not raping or strangling hands, but small chubby boy hands, swallowed by her mother-hands. She imagines wilting over his hands and washing them with her tears, drying them with her hair. She should tell him that she loves him and that God loves him, that Jesus loves him and forgives him, but sitting in the governor's chair, listening to her raping, murdering son ramble on about the injustices done to him, Brigit is too sad to speak.

Cameron should have let him talk, he says, he had things he wanted to say, to the public, to the journalists. He stops for breath. He looks at his parents, waiting for them to react. Samuel can't think what to say.

Brigit tries to reimagine cupping his hands again but she remembers him now. She looks at his fine, square face, an echo of his father as a younger man. Peter won't be home tonight. She asks God to forgive her for feeling so glad.

He talks about his appeal. He is hopeful.

The visit finishes. Brigit touches his sleeve and asks him to speak to Father Smith. Samuel shakes his son's hand. They take Peter away, back to the cell.

They meet their son three more times before he dies.

The second and third visits are uneventful. Normal prison visits. Brigit saves up news from the family and the papers, impressions from her day so that she will have something to say. She waits for the right moment and asks Peter if he has been to confession? Attended the blessed sacrament? Peter has done neither. It's a difficult subject for her to bring up but she knows that she'll regret it for eternity if she doesn't try. She values her redemption above her comfort.

The last time they meet is different. It becomes violent and Brigit leaves sobbing. She cries all the way home on the bus.

The last visit is two days before the execution date. They wait in the governor's office and Peter comes shuffling in, dried white saliva crusted at the side of his mouth. Two officers lead him in, one holding each arm. They guide him to his chair. They sit him down.

Peter's eyes are unfocused. His hands are trembling on his knees. The drool from his mouth begins to foam, small white bubbles gathering at the side of his lips. He is acting.

Brigit is instantly furious with him. She says his name. He doesn't react. She says it again. Nothing. She reminds him that this may well be the last time they ever see each other in this life.

Peter? Peter? Peter!

Nothing. His hands tremble and he lifts them slightly as if he is showing them to her.

In her head Brigit thinks: I am your mother. I have cried for you since the day and hour of your birth. I have tried to love you. And now I am nothing but an object in your play. I am a tablecloth. I am a cup. My feelings mean nothing to you. You don't care.

Brigit stands so suddenly that the chair topples behind her and she shouts his name. She shouts that he can't fool her. She's here to say goodbye.

Nothing. Not a spark of recognition, but even a madman can hear shouting.

Brigit does what she would never dare to do if they weren't in a prison. She slaps him. His face falls to the side under her hand. His head comes back to true. Still nothing.

She grabs his hair and tugs it hard. This is something Peter cannot stand because the bald spot on his crown is a weakness to him. Messing his hair, tugging his hair, is the one thing that will always send him into a rage. Nothing. The prison officers are not stepping in either. They want her to hit him.

Peter stares forward but she can see he is angry from the hooding of his eyes.

She sits down and, weeping, speaks to him in a monotone:

'I have never found it easy to talk to you. My knees are broken with praying for you. I fed and clothed you and you did nothing but hurt me. And still you hurt me. You asked me to choose between my God and my son. I prayed and I wept for you. I chose you. You made me choose and I chose you, always. I kept you in my heart. When I saw you go out of that door I never knew what harm you would do. And still I kept you in my heart and my home. I loved you and you never gave me a spark of love back. You did nothing but shame me and mock me. You have broken my heart you vicious, godless man.'

She waits for him to say something. She waits but he does nothing. She stands up without permission from her husband or the officers or her son. She stands and says, 'So, goodbye.'

She doesn't try to touch him any more.

She is glad to get out to the open air.

Samuel comes hurrying after her. Perhaps the boy, he calls him the boy all the time now so he doesn't have to say 'Peter', perhaps the boy is really ill? Brigit just looks at him. She looks at Samuel through her tears and thinks he is an eejit. He's a lying, f.ing eejit and he is kinky in the s.e.x. department. But she is married to him. So be it.

Samuel burned the boy's clothes in the garden after Anne Kneilands' disappearance. He lied under an oath from God. He gave the boy alibis for crucial times. He stood by him and lied to let the boy go free to kill those poor people, those poor girls, because Samuel was afraid of his son. So be it.

She stares at him. He reaches for her hand and she barks, 'Don't you touch me.'

The bus approaches them. They don't put out their hands. In the gritty back draught of the bus passing she says, 'Don't you touch me ever again.'

23

Friday 11 July 1958

THIS CELL IN BARLINNIE is specially adapted. A hook hangs from the ceiling. A trap door opens down into the cell below. Simple engineering principles have finessed the process of hanging. The lever is pulled, the trap drops open and catches on a swing latch. In the old days, the rough days, if a gibbet trap was heavy it could bounce back and snap a man's thigh bone. Sometimes it would shear a limb clean off. This happened on gibbets all over the world. But the swing latch has solved that problem. Swing, click, still.

Capital punishment will soon be abolished. Peter Manuel will be the third-to-last person ever hanged in Scotland. In the meantime, as a compassionate compromise, attempts are made to meet the complaints of abolitionists and the practice has changed. Chief among the changes is the hanging rehearsal. Rehearsal is essential to perfect the hangmen's timing, to ensure the mechanism is oiled and working. Fast is best. Gibbets are always near the condemned cell to avoid long journeys, but prisoners shouldn't be tortured by having to watch or hear the incessant rehearsal of their own death. Legislation has just been passed: the hanging rehearsal must be completely silent and out of sight. Rubber stoppers have been fitted to the levers and the trap to silence them completely.

The public are no longer allowed to witness hangings. Death has moved indoors. Far from an enlightened sense of propriety or a shift in social mores, public executions became impossible to police. The mobs were strange and massively overexcited. Public indecency and drunkenness and missile attacks on the condemned were common.

Scotland uses the 'long drop' method. It is as clean as hanging gets and resolves the two main pitfalls: the head being pinched from the body like a grape from the stalk, or slow strangulation.

If the drop is steep and the body too heavy the head will be ripped from the body, in whole or in part. If the drop is too gentle and the weight too slight, the condemned person will choke to death. It can take up to fifteen minutes. During this time the eyes and tongue swell to grotesque proportions, the body twitches and jerks, the condemned scratch at their neck. It is distressing to witness. None of this happens with the long drop method. Still, a hood is fitted over the person's face, in case something goes wrong.

The long drop method snaps the neck between the second and third vertebrae. Done properly, death is instantaneous. It is a careful calculation of weight, height and muscle tone.

Manuel was weighed and measured when he first came to Barlinnie. His food intake and physical size is monitored so that they don't have to weigh him again. Thirty-one-year-old men don't lose a lot of muscle in six weeks and it would be obvious what they were weighing him for. That would be inhumane.

Across the corridor from the hanging cell is the condemned cell where Manuel is living now. It is more of a suite, three cells knocked together. The bare brick walls are painted green and it is furnished with a table and bed, three chairs, a wireless, a set of drawers for clothes, a commode and a washstand.

It has to be three cells big because officers are in there with him at all times, working eight-hour shifts. After every shift the departing officers fill out the Deathwatch Journal, a notebook bound in navy-blue leather. In it they note Manuel's moods, his behaviour and what he has eaten, then the date and time of the shift, when it started, when it ended.

The officers play cards with Manuel and dominoes, they listen to popular music on Radio Luxembourg with him. It is the job of the prison service to keep Manuel calm by pretending that the hanging is not happening. Dominoes is happening. Cards and dinner and books is happening. But death is not happening. In this respect it is just like normal life.

These men are the most experienced officers in the Scottish Prison Service, all ex-army. Manuel already knows some of them from his long-ago rape sentence in Peterhead Prison.

None of these officers are bleeding hearts but they know Manuel will die soon. At the beginning of the Deathwatch Journal their notes are dispassionate but tinged with tenderness.

Prisoner had a nice night's sleep.

Ate well at breakfast.

Prisoner seemed in good spirits.

But Peter Manuel is not a man whose company fosters affection. The lingering kindness soon evaporates.

Prisoner boasted about his heroism during the war.

Prisoner smoking and talking incessantly.

Prisoner apparently listening to Radio Luxembourg but talked over all the music, seems to think he knows a lot about it.

Prisoner told us his adventures as a spy in the Soviet Union.

The cover of the Deathwatch Journal is marked 'Do Not Destroy – Ever'. It is essential that judicial killing is provably fair, measured and decent.

The Deathwatch Journal details Manuel's urination and bowel movements. It notes what time he fell asleep and when he woke up. It says what he eats and how much of it he had – *today he left all of his bread but ate the fish and chips.* It also documents what he says. Peter Manuel is all stories.

I was a spy for the Soviet Union. I was flown to Moscow and met a handler in an aircraft hangar. The Soviets had heard of my reputation as a housebreaker and wanted me to do a job for them, a specialist job, like Gentleman Johnny Ramensky. When they realised I was an American citizen they just flew me home.

Is that right, Peter?

During the war, when I lived in Coventry, a German pilot came down in the fields outside my reform school and I strangled him with my bare hands.

Did you really?

I was on a plane and the pilot fainted and I took the controls and I landed it. They couldn't believe I'd done it. No experience, nothing. And I never even broke a sweat.

Is that so?

Manuel only ever tells the same story about himself: Manuel is doing clever things and other people are amazed by him. Manuel is always winning. He is never attacking women in the dark. He is never hiding in dusty attics, waiting for people to leave their homes so he can steal their mother's engagement ring. He is never lying on pristine linen bedclothes with dirty boots on or dropping food on precious rugs and grinding it in with the heel of his shoe, spoiling a modest home for spite.

He is never dragging women down embankments, scattering their shopping in puddles, telling their three-year-old son to shut the fuck up or he'll kill their mum.

Women are never screaming and running away in the stories he tells. Women are never weeping in dark fields, gathering their broken dentures or clasping ripped and bloody underwear to their chests. Women are never kneeling, heads bowed, hoping that if they are very, very quiet he will not kill them.

In his stories women are not sitting in court being stared at by the hard, accusing eyes of the jury as the foreman tells the judge that the rape charge against Peter Manuel is Not Proven by a unanimous decision.

Women are never being spat at by Samuel Manuel at the bus stop for going to the police about his son after swearing that she wouldn't if he let her go, so she's a liar. They're never sitting on the bus with Samuel's voice ringing in their ears, *you dirty fucking lying cow*, watching out of the window through a blur of tears and wondering: is breaking a promise not-to-tell worse than what he did to her?

Peter is never standing over dead families, eating a sandwich in the roaring silence. He is never looking at a dead girl's tits and rubbing himself through his trousers. He is never hiding behind a tree, letting Anne Kneilands think herself saved before jumping out at her.

These are not the stories Manuel tells, but the POs know them. They have access to his records. Everyone knows everything he has ever done now, because he's famous.

As he talks Peter sees them glancing at each other, like POs do. The thrill of all that attention dissipates and Manuel starts to realise that they're laughing at him. This and their tepid, sceptical reception of his best stories make him angry. They don't fucking know him. They don't know anything about him. This is the mood in the condemned suite and why it goes so sour.

It becomes very acrimonious.

The trouble starts the day before his appeal against the death sentence. Peter begins frothing at the mouth and fitting. He is rushed to the infirmary and his stomach is pumped. They find nothing. For a week he twitches and is mute, froths and stares. He still eats though. He still smokes.

The Deathwatch Journal notes *Prisoner doing his usual act.*

Prisoner still away with the bees.

Despite mental condition, prisoner mysteriously managed to tune the wireless to Radio Luxembourg when I couldn't find the station. Smoking incessantly.

Prisoner said nothing but the word 'chips' five times. Prisoner maintained act all through parents' visit.

The day before his execution he stops the act.

That morning he wakes up. I feel better, he says. He has no memory of the past two weeks but remembers that the appeal was due to happen then. Did it happen? Yes, Peter, it did. You were at the court. In a side room. What happened? You lost by unanimous, son. It's happening tomorrow.

No, see what happened was PO Sullivan hit me on the head a week ago. I've had a massive head injury. We'll need to have the appeal reheard because I wasn't fit to plead. We need a second appeal.

Manuel shows them a chip off the side of the chest of drawers. That is where PO Sullivan attacked him. He remembers listening to the radio and the attack and then nothing for two weeks. Unspoken in this is the fact that Sullivan had a similar accusation levelled against him ten years ago. He hit a prisoner with a nightstick during a riot in Peterhead. The man was in a coma for two months. He came out of it just before Sullivan was charged with assault. Peter Manuel was in Peterhead at the time.

Manuel is examined by two prison doctors. They find a mark on his scalp, but it's healed. It looks as if he scratched it there himself.

This is the day before the execution date. Brigit Manuel has submitted a petition to the court to delay her son's hanging. Peter never hears about this. Abolitionist groups have petitioned for a delay too. A group of teachers have formed a committee and made a submission to the court: they have analysed Manuel's behaviour from the court case and reports in the papers and believe they have diagnosed a 'mental illness'.

Peter Manuel should be shown compassion because he is not one bit well.

But there will be no second appeal because the two Harrys are already in the prison.

Harry Allen and his assistant, Harry Smith. Professional hangmen, long-drop-method men.

That night Manuel doesn't sleep. He stays awake all night, listening to the radio and smoking, chatting.

At 5 a.m. he eats chips and drinks a pint of strong tea. At 7.20 a.m. Father Smith comes in and asks to take his confession. Manuel says no but lets Father Smith pray for him.

The governor and two other officials join them in the cell, checking all is well.

At three seconds to eight the two Harrys come into his cell. In complete but companionable silence, they bind his wrists behind his back and lead him across the corridor. Harry Allen fits the noose and the hood while Harry Smith ensures the witnesses are standing clear. Smith pulls the lever.

The trap door swings and catches on the latch.

Second and third vertebrae are separated.

From the moment the Harrys walked into the condemned cell, it takes eight seconds.

Peter Manuel is dead.

Normally during a hanging in Barlinnie the prisoners down tools until it is over. There is a moment's reverence, a comradely silence. Not prayers exactly, but an acknowledgement that it could be any one of them up there. A knife in the wrong place, a punch and a bad fall, it's part of the life. But when Peter Manuel is hanged the prisoners pointedly carry on eating breakfast. Some slam cups down on tables or rattle their trays against walls. Even other criminals want to distance themselves from him.

Father Smith and the medical examiner, Dr D.A.R. Anderson, leave the other witnesses in the hanging cell and go downstairs.

They take their time, dawdling down the corridor, lingering on the stairs. They pause behind the door to the corridor below. A lot can happen to a body after hanging. Twitching, effluvia, noises. Best to wait. Then they walk along the silent corridor to the cell below the trap. They listen at the door. They hear the occasional creak of the swinging rope and nothing else. They open the door and go in.

Dr Anderson feels the wrist for a pulse. Manuel is dead. As he fills out the certificate – 'Cause of death: judicial hanging' – Father Smith performs the last rites.

At the moment of Manuel's death, groups of people gather all around the city. They stand in silence and watch the sky. They gather in streets, outside his parents' house. They stand at bus stops, on train platforms, looking up at the sky waiting for something to lift. The moment passes. It starts to rain. Trains move off. Buses arrive. Crowds disperse.

Immediately, the children begin to tell each other that Peter Manuel could see in the dark.

Three hours after his death Manuel is buried in an unmarked grave within the prison grounds. His family are not permitted to attend. Father Smith performs the ceremony.

Three weeks later a muted paragraph in the *Daily Record* reports that a woman has been found murdered near Burntbroom Farm, strangled and beaten, her clothing left in disarray. No mention is made of Manuel or Isabelle Cooke or the other women who were murdered and left there before her. Muncie finds and charges someone within twenty-four hours.

Three months later William Watt gives an interview to the press. For the first time he is pictured at home, smiling. He invites the city to celebrate with him on the occasion of his engagement to his young fiancée, Phamie. He expects people will be pleased for him, after all his troubles.

Three years later the value of commercial property is re-assessed by Glasgow Corporation surveyors. They find it has tripled in value, and blame changing conditions and the commercial boom. Strangely, landowners do not protest the rate rises that follow from this. The land is quietly bought at these heightened valuations by the Corporation and then levelled for redevelopment.

The Gorbals is flattened.

Cowcaddens is flattened.

The city is reborn so completely that it becomes a memory of a memory of a place.

The people are bonded by loathing for Manuel. The children are bonded by fear. The women are afraid enough to stay in their homes and do their work and be glad of the menfolk who protect them.

Everything goes back to normal. Peter Manuel becomes a scary story people tell each other. Just a story. Just a creepy story about a serial killer.

Acknowledgments

More thanks are due for this book than I can possibly recall because of its unusually long gestation.

David MacLennan, Graham Eatough, Alison Hennessey, John Wood, Jemima Forrester, Peter Robinson, Ford Keirnan have all contributed. Some added significant ideas on this story, some gave me a simple shove on the back. To the National Archive of Scotland for their help accessing materials and court records. Thank you to the ladies of the Girl Guides main office in Elmbank Street for giving me access to blueprints of their office floor plan from 1957 and then pointing out that I was in the wrong street. The office moved from Gordon Street in the 1960s. To Steve, Fergus and Ownie for patiently stepping around huge maps, photos of Berettas and creepy site photos for two years.

More especially Hector and Malcolm MacLeod for their excellent book *Peter Manuel, Serial Killer* (Penguin, 2010), which inspired the night portions of this book, and Allan Nicol's book *Manuel: Scotland's First Serial Killer* (Abe Books, 2008) for an astute legal breakdown of the case.

At its most joyous, writing a book is living a parallel life, part-time. There were times when I could stand and feel the blackened old city growing up around me. Thank you to every-one who shared in this obsession, generously sharing glimpses of the dead and bringing the dirty old town to life.